RISING FROM THE ASHES

GUARDIANS OF THE HIDDEN LAIR

GREGORY M. JUZWICK

outskirtspress
DENVER, COLORADO

Rising from the Ashes
Guardians of the Hidden Lair

v2.0

Outskirts Press, Inc.
http://www.outskirtspress.com

ISBN: 978-1-4327-8972-5

PRINTED IN THE UNITED STATES OF AMERICA

This book is dedicated to my mother. Dolly B. Juzwick, who devoted her life to her family and gave her all for her children, her love will live on in all of our hearts. I thank you for supporting me in my writing and everything I have done in life. It is also dedicated to my dearly departed wife of twelve years who gave her support and pushed me to get my series started. Thank you, Pamela for your love.

Author Biography

Born in 1964 Gregory Mark Juzwick in Tampa Florida, Gregory was raised with his three brothers and sister by very caring and understanding parents. They moved to the Pittsburgh Pa. area where he grew up most of his childhood. While going to Moon Senior high school he dabbled with his writing ability creating poems, short stories and a novel called, " Phoenix 5", around the age of fifteen. After graduating from school, Gregory entered the United States Army for three years serving in Fort Benning Georgia. Returning to Pittsburgh in 1986, he began his retail career in the Jewelry industry. In 1988, his family moved to Hendersonville North Carolina to assist his parents with their Jewelry store. In 2004 he moved back up to Pittsburgh Pa. where he continued his sales career as well as continued working on his books.

After years of writing, rewrites and editing this book Rising from the Ashes has been completed.

Book Description

By the end of the twentieth century the world as we knew it had become worse than anyone could have ever thought. Crime was rampant, war was breaking out all over and terrorist acts around the world were growing more numerous as each year passed. As the twenty first century came and went it kept getting worst. In the United States crime was out of control and terrorist began striking within this once great country. Everyone prayed for a savior to come. Years went by before a ray of hope shined through. A new President came into power named Jonathan T. Matthews. With harsh laws and the use of martial law, he was able to get crime under control within two years. The American people were pleased with his work and his abilities. Unknown to them President Matthews had a hidden agenda he had been working on for years. Matthews set into motion the events that would lead up to nuclear war making it easy for him to take over the world. The nuclear missiles fly and three fourths of the world's population is lost. With his military, he begins to capture and kill those who have survived. His dream of world domination was nearly accomplished.

Luckily, all men dream. One in particular dreams of protecting his family and friends from the now hostile world they now live in. Greygor Josephs rises from the ashes to find a safe haven for his family called the Hidden Lair. After settling his family in, he sets off to find his other surviving family members before the military finds them. Along the way from North Carolina up into Pennsylvania, he finds other survivors who assist him in staying one-step ahead of Matthews. As he finds more and more survivors he begins, creating fighting groups to help get them all back to the Hidden Lair. Friends and family unite in an action packed adventure from start to finish! A legend is born and from the ashes of devastation, The Guardians of the Hidden Lair came forth!

Characters in order of Appearance

North Carolina
Greygor Josephs- Journeyman, warrior
Pat Josephs- Greygor's wife
Jacob Josephs- Greygor and Pat's older son
Austin Josephs- Greygor and Pat's younger son
Daniel Cause- Pat's father, carpenter, Creator of the Trapster group
Paula Cause- Daniels wife
Jessica Swan- Pat's sister
Tony Swan- Jessica's husband
Shaun Cause- Daniels younger brother, Trapster group member
Tom Cause- Shaun's son, Trapster group member
Bert Mellows- horse farmer old friend of Daniels
Uncle Mike- Paula's brother, Trapster group member
Uncle Mark- Paula's brother, Trapster group member

Tennessee
Captain Frank- Leader of tank squad
Phillip- first of three survivors rescued by Greygor
Anna- Phillips daughter
Kent- Ex-soldier Rapid Rider group leader

Kentucky
Arthur Josephs- Greygor's younger brother, Sharp Shooter group leader

Kay - Arthur's older daughter
Candice- Arthur's younger daughter
Eric- Arthur's son
Robert Josephs- Greygor's father
Darla Josephs- Greygor's mother
Jake Trotter- Darla's brother
Ann Trotter- Jake's wife
Donny Trotter- Jakes son, Barbarian group member
Danny Trotter- Jake's oldest son, Barbarian group member
Rich Trotter- Jake's youngest son, thief group member
Beth- Jakes daughter
Dutch- Beth's husband, Thief group member
General Snorpaly- Matthew's second in command
Jonathan Tobias Matthews- Leader of the military

Ohio
Cole Cramer- Greygor's best friend from high school, Thief group leader
Lori Cramer- Cole's wife
Mandy - Cole's older daughter
Jess- Cole's younger daughter

Pennsylvania
Chad- Greygor's high school friend
Rider Randolph- High school friend of Greygor's, Warrior group leader
Hogan Randolph- Rider's brother, Warrior group member
Will- Arthur's old high school friend, Sharpshooter group member
Marie Josephs- Greygor's older sister
Gary - Marie's fiancé
May- Marie's older daughter
Janice- Marie's younger daughter

Lou- May's husband, Warrior group member
Carl- Maries ex husband, Warrior group member
Charles Josephs- twin brother of Marie, Guard group leader
Angel- Charles' wife
Jack -Charles's son, Warrior group member
Mrs. Cramer (Mrs. C) - Cole's mother
Toni- Cole's sister, Warrior group member
Dale- Wayne Joseph's best friend from high school, Barbarian group member
Peter- Dale's brother, Barbarian group member
Wayne Josephs- Greygor's youngest brother, Barbarian group leader
Jan Josephs- Wayne's wife
Dorina- Wayne's oldest daughter
Ashley- Wayne's second daughter
Torina- Wayne's youngest daughter
Ray- old high school enemy of Greygor's
Matt- Ray's younger brother
Landon Yonder- Greygor's friend from adulthood, Thief group member
Mick- Landon's older brother, warrior group member

Prologue

Another beautiful morning here in our home, I rise from my bed and walk out to my balcony here on the second floor of my home. For years, I have stood here gazing out on my surroundings and everyday it still amazes me. I look up at the sky, I can remember when there was a time when the sun could shine down on our face from the blue sky as white billowy clouds floated by. That was many years ago though. Now I look up at the reddish gray clouds that stretch from horizon to horizon never disappearing from sight and always swirling around high above. Tornado like funnel clouds dip down towards the earth but quickly collapse back up into itself as streaks of lightning cross the sky repeatedly with no sound of thunder. It's an eerie feeling looking up at this and after all these years it is still hard to get use too. The nuclear war did cause many changes to our world. I look out at the mountains that surround our whole valley, like great barriers they reach up to the sky protecting us from the dangerous world outside of our home. The trees that cover the mountains display their red, yellow and brown leaves so vividly; it is strange to see this in the middle of summer. Since the sunlight cannot reach them directly, green leaves are also outdated. Even still, it is a breath taking sight. These mountains have been our protection from many evils. Only three roads lead in or out of the valley, each are watched and protected at all times.

Yes, the nuclear war took a lot from us, from a highly advanced civilization scientifically and in technology, we now live in a medieval type state. No longer, do we see fuel driven vehicles of the past that filled our streets and sky, Horses, wagons and an occasional bike now takes us from place to place if we do not walk. Television and radio no longer entertains us, we must rely on books, art and good conversation now to spark our imagination. Weapons of high destruction are gone also; we use blades, bows and an occasional pistol or rifle to protect ourselves. The greatest loss we endured was the deaths of three fourths of the world's population when the Missiles started flying.

Many battles have been fought outside of our Hidden Lair, many of the Guardians gave their lives to protect this place, I knew most of them and together we fought side by side for our family and friends whom we swore to protect. I look over to the large stone centered by the lake in the valley that has inscribed on it the names of the many Guardians who we have lost over the years.

They say, "Power corrupts and absolute power corrupts absolutely." That was just part of how it all started, one man dreamed of being ruler of the world. He plotted and planned and waited for the right opportunity and when it arrived, he pushed all the right buttons. He came close to realizing his dream. What he didn't count on was another man's dream to always keep those around him safe from evil, to protect them at all cost and to stare into the eyes of evil and confront it and destroy it if need be. It began even before this though, years before the battles and even before the nuclear war. There is no exact date or year that anyone can pinpoint, over time, it was inevitable. I think back now and I see the signs of the coming storm and wish something could have been done.

I remember back to the last few decades of the twentieth century, though we were making great strides in technology, medicine and science there seemed to be underlying problems throughout the world. Corruption in most of the governments and religious orders throughout the world was growing worse. Wars and terrorist were headline news every time you turned around. Nuclear capabilities even in third world nations were causing concerns of the inevitable nuclear war of the future. For years, the United States main threat was that of Russia and the communist party, by the end of the nineties and into the year 2000, we were more concerned with the Middle East and the Asian nations. Every nation was in debt and slowly our fuel resources were depleting. Drug and alcohol abuse among the young and adults as well was out of control and crime was elevating horribly. Looking out for number one and the total disregard for life seemed to be rampant in our society. Even children were committing violent crimes in schools and in our own backyards. Every day the newspapers and the television news were filled with horrible stories on all subjects. Unfortunately even our journalist started being more preoccupied with the dirt of all the stories instead on normal reporting. Our judicial system also was going downhill as well; criminals were getting away with murder literally. I can remember our nation sitting in front of the television for days watching court events as if it was entertainment instead of serious crimes.

This all over flowed into the twenty first century and as the years went by it got even worst. Even natural disasters such as earthquakes, major storms and the like seemed to be worsening every year. Of course, with the bad, some good did shine through, or so we thought.

In the Middle East, countries that had been enemies for years came together and merged into one whole nation called the Arabic National Alliance, (the A.N.A. for short) after years of hostilities amongst themselves they formed a new super power. The world felt this new alliance would slow terrorist acts and create peace around the world. Guess again. The ANA decided to declare the rest of the world their enemy and began halting all shipments of fuel, mineral and other essentials throughout the world. Terrorist attacks around the world escalated, all were blamed on the ANA.

As the ANA began to rise up the United States was having problems. Crime had hit an all time high, and it was getting more and more difficult to live a safe and normal life in America. Everyone hoped for a savior of some type but it did not look good. Finally, from the Western states of this country a presidential candidate entered the race unlike any other ever seen. His past seemed spotless, and his political career untarnished. His slogan of "Zero crime in two years time!" was simple but what America wanted to hear. For months, his loud baritone voice rang over the radio, television and in every city, he campaigned in. I have to say he knew how to talk the talk. Even his features were appealing to the public eye. With jet black hair he stood a good six foot, he seemed rugged but to look into his deep dark eyes you could see he was a compassionate man. He always was seen in public with his suit and tie always perfect. His strong words made his audience feel safe and secure. The election came and went and our new president was sworn in, Jonathan Tobias Matthews took office and proceeded to keep his promise of "Zero crime in two years time!" Congress was ready to back him on all aspects of his vision thinking his ideas were short term. His first law he put into effect was the Matthews doctrine. This made the right to own weapons of any kind illegal in the United States. All civilians had thirty days to turn in their weapons or face fines and prison time. Though he met with objections from the National Rifle Association and other organizations, he was able to get it passed. His law, "Peace within." disbanded all organizations of a disruptive nature throughout the country. The JTM Proclamation went into effect next. This merged the Military of America and all law enforcement agencies creating what was now called, "Matthews Military!" Martial Law was established throughout the country. The Tobias Act was the next law passed, this allows for house to house searches for illegal weapons and drugs, anyone caught with any illegal items were arrested on the spot. Anyone opposing Matthews or talking out against him seemed to disappear or met with a quick death. Within two years crime seemed to diminish and by his second year it was about to zero. With his military behind him he used his "Peace within Law" to overthrow the senate and congress and proclaimed himself sole leader of the United States. America was no longer a democracy, it was a dictatorship!

Terrorist acts around the world were growing at an alarming rate, fuel prices skyrocketed, all being blamed on the ANA! War was declared on the ANA by the rest of the world. The ANA was joined by the Asian countries and battles raged all across the world. As fuel depleted in the next two years it was declared that all fuel would only be used by the military and civilian vehicles slowly used up what they had left to use. As the battles raged, the allied forces began hitting the ANA hard and slowly closed in on the total defeat of the ANA. During the battle of the Mediterranean Sea that which should have been the final blow, the Asian countries attacked and with everything, they had to assist the ANA and turned the tide of war. Together they drove back the Allied military and eventually took over parts of Europe and Africa along the way.

President Matthews in a last ditch effort declared that if the ANA and the Asian countries did not surrender Nuclear weapons would be used to stop this war. Within hours of his broadcast, the ANA with a stealth bomber slammed three nuclear missiles into Washington D.C. and started launching missiles in an all out attack. Nuclear war had begun. Every country began to launch what they had. You can call it what you like, Armageddon, Genesis, Revelations or World War 3, I like to keep it simple, the world went to hell in a hand basket! Jonathan Matthews's dream of possible world domination was now in motion as the world laid in the ashes of this horrendous event.

Luckily, another man who also had a dream rose up out of the ashes of the war and set out to protect and save those he cared for. He set out to rescue a few and found many whom he put together to form a fighting group unlike any that had ever been seen. It is said that all men dream, and dreams have a way of becoming reality, and reality can lay the foundation of a person's destiny. Though the world was knocked back into a medieval type state with the losses of three fourths of the world's population, from the ashes of war came the legends of The Guardians of the Hidden Lair.

Chapter 1

Upon his patio, he sat in his favorite chair looking out at the beautiful Blue Ridge Mountains of North Carolina. He had moved from the north many years ago and loved living here deep in the mountains. Greygor at thirty five now still had deep dark brown hair cut short for his work, he stood only five feet five and kept his body in very good shape. It helped that he had to ride a bike ten miles to work and back home each day. He loved to work but enjoyed his days off spending time with his family, especially now that his boys were out of school for the summer. His dark brown eyes gazed out at a squirrel dashing across his yard trying to make it up a tree before being spotted by one of the families dogs; he smiled as it disappeared into the tree. He was always happy and not often seen frowning, he always tried to make the best out of any situation no matter how tough things got. He had been raised by very loving parents alongside his older twin brother and sister and two younger brothers. Love, respect, good morals and working hard were instilled in him as he grew up. Though his family had spread out across the eastern U.S. they kept in contact on a daily basis by phone, computer and mail.

He could hear his wife Pat singing from inside the house, he smiled as he listened. She had a beautiful voice that went along with her angelic face and body. Her smile radiated happiness and love, her personality was best described as pure country girl. She was sweet and soft spoken most the time but you could tell if need be she could be very stern and outspoken. Greygor and Patricia loved each other deeply; over their eight years of marriage, they had overcome many obstacles that made their love stronger as time went by. She walked out the front door carrying two glasses of ice tea; they smiled at each other as if they were seeing each other for the first time. Her long blonde hair shined as the bright sun touched it as she made her way over to her husband. He loved looking into her dark brown eyes from a distance and even more when they were face to face. Pat as she like to be called leaned down and kissed his cheek as she handed him his tea and sat down by his side. He put his arm around her shoulder hugging her to his side.

"Hi baby." She said sweetly enjoying being held by his strong arm. "You okay?"

"Yea, I was just sitting here thinking of you." He smiled.

"So why is your brow wrinkled?" She asked, knowing that he had more than that on his mind. "You're worried about the military showing up again aren't you?"

"Not really, "He fidgeted. "The ones who come around here are normally very friendly so far and I am always nice to them."

"True, but I can tell they annoy you when they do come up and inspect our home." Pat replied, "You're nice but I can tell that if one of them did something you didn't like you would be on them like a rooster in a cock fight."

"Now honey," He smiled, "It's just I have heard some horror stories at work about how some of the military are taking advantage of innocent people. I just don't want the boys or you getting hurt."

"I don't want you to get hurt either dear." Pat said sternly. "You hide your strength and abilities well but I want you to promise me that you won't do anything to cause you to get hurt."

"If one of them ever tries to lay a hand on you or the boys I don't know if I can promise you that."

"Let's cross that bridge then when we have to ok?" She laid her hand on his thigh gently caressing him.

She knew that he was overly protective of his children and her and nothing she could say could stop him from destroying anyone who caused his family any harm though she stilled hoped it would never come to that. The military did not come out this far in the mountains too often and the one's who inspected homes out here seemed okay so far.

Patricia had lived in this mountain area all of her life growing up with her parents who now lived right down the road and her sister who lived right next door to. This was her families land and she loved it with a passion. She had climbed most of the trees around her home when she was a child as well as enjoyed running through the woods and fields that made up this area. After marrying Greygor she loved taking him for long walks in the woods and telling him the stories of her childhood. She did that for the first two years of their life together, unfortunately, she became ill. She remembered the months before her diagnosis, dizzy spells, loss of balance and loss of feeling in her arms and legs. She tried to hide it from him but he caught it quickly and took her to the hospital. The tests were long and some were painful, brain scans of different types all showed the young couple what was happening to Patricia. She had developed Multiple Sclerosis after her pregnancy. Though she started taking medicines to slow the diseases progression over the next three years and exercised daily the MS slowly disabled her. By the end of the third year, she was bed ridden. He would hold her close everyday praying for a miracle to save his precious wife. Finally, a serum had been developed that could possibly save her, a young doctor from South America made headline news with his cure for different nervous system diseases. He pulled a few strings and was able to get the serum to Patricia, it took a few weeks but as the nurses administered the drug, Pat began respond! A whole year went by and she began physical therapy that which strengthened her muscles as the serum repaired her nerves and brain. Together they worked out daily as the years went by this not only built up both their bodies but also built their faith in each other and in life as well as making their faith in God stronger than it ever had been.

She placed her head against his shoulder and thanked God for giving her a man that stood by her through some very rough times.

"I love you baby." She smiled up at him

"I love you more than you'll ever know" He brushed his hand gently across her cheek.

They both looked up quickly as the sounds of laughter came from behind the house. Down pass, the patio two young men ran down into the front yard followed by a yellow lab mix and a black Labrador who did their best to trip up the boys.

They laughed as they watched their sons run around and wrestle each other to the ground as the two dogs leaped around them and on top of them. Jacob the older of the two at fifteen was tall but sturdy, his muscles were tight and close to the bone. He kept his blonde dishwater hair short and had a very handsome face. Both the boys looked like their parents. Austin at the age of thirteen was a bit shorter than his brother but his muscles were bulkier, he also had blonde hair but his was longer than his brothers was. They were good boys most of the times but were typical teenagers who got into trouble when the chance came.

The yellow lab that he named Luck did his best to get between the two boys; though he was a medium size dog, he was very strong and agile. They laughed as the black lab circled the fiasco at top speed looking for the opportunity to jump into the fray. Pepsi finally tired himself out and laid down a few yards away to watch the wrestling antics of the rest. Pepsi heard him laughing and leaped up and ran up towards the patio, he jumped up over four of the five steps landing directly next to him. He reached down to scratch the dogs head.

"What's wrong pup, too much action for you?" He smiled down at his dog.

"He is a few years older than Luck, dear." Pat replied.

"He still is a rough and tough one though!" He said in a deeper than normal voices as he rubbed the dogs head a bit harder.

"I couldn't believe the news this morning Matthews sounded like a fool this morning," Greygor said. "He ranted and raved and threatened the ANA with nuclear retaliation if they didn't give up."

"Do you think he really meant it?" Pat asked.

"I think it was more of a bluff than a promise," He stated. "But who is to say what the ANA will decide to do."

"Aren't you scared honey?" She asked.

"To a certain extent but I hope the government is smart enough not to use nuclear weapons." He replied. "We will just have to hope and pray nothing horrible comes of it."

"I heard on the news that the new nuclear weapons don't leave a lot of radiation but are still devastating." Pat remembered.

"You're talking about the STOR-COM missiles." He replied, "They create a nuclear hurricane of some sort over land as well as the ocean destroying everything in its path. Even if the older nuclear missiles are used the nuclear storm is so fierce that the older nuclear blast will just add to its fury."

"In other words we all die?" Pat asked.

"Many people could dear," he answered. "I think these mountains around could give us some protection."

He looked back out towards the yard where the boys now were sitting in the grass talking and laughing as Luck sat between them ever watchful of them. He glanced down the road spotting a man walking at a rather quick pace.

The man was wearing baggy overalls and work boots; He was a skinny man with large brown-rimmed glasses. As he got closer to the yard though winded, he shouted to Jacob and Austin who quickly got up and ran to him. He placed his hands on both their shoulders, he began saying something to them and they both began running down the road towards his house. Greygor stood up as he began walking up through the yard towards the house. Daniel Cause, Pat's father reached the patio and stopped to catch his breath.

"Dad, what's wrong?" Pat asked.

"Patricia you need to come with me!" Daniel said, "Greygor I need you to gather as much food, blankets and clothing as you can and bring it down to my house. The ANA has just bombed Washington and now every country is launching their missiles at each other!"

As Pat started towards the steps he reached over and kissed her on the cheek, "You get going baby I will be right there."

Daniel took her hand and began walking quickly down the yard as he bolted inside. He began bagging food in the kitchen and carrying it out to the patio. He noticed his dogs were gone and thought they must have headed down to Daniel's house with everyone else. He ran down the patio steps and over to his barn grabbing his large handcart that he usually used to pull wood to the house and pulled it over to the steps. He loaded with the food he had bagged. Running inside he froze in front of the television hearing what was going on that had Daniel so scared.

"Again, I repeat!"The Newsman stated. "Take shelter immediately! Nuclear Missiles have struck Washington D.C. and more have been launched towards the United States! A full-scale nuclear war has begun around the world! Our government has also begun to launch our missiles in response to this attack!

I repeat! Take shelter immediately!"

A radar screen on the television showed missiles being launched from different countries heading over the Pacific and the Atlantic Ocean towards every continent.

He turned and ran back to the bedrooms grabbing blankets and clothing and took them out to the cart. He looked down towards the road and saw Pat's sister and her husband Tony rushing down towards Daniels house as well with everything they could carry. He made one more trip inside quickly grabbing anything he thought could be useful in this situation. He ran it out to the cart and started pulling the cart down through the yard. Dark clouds began to form above faster than normal, the sunlight that had made it such a beautiful day was slowly disappearing as he reached the road and bolted towards his father in laws house. He reached Daniel's long driveway and ran hard up to the two-story house. He went around the side of the house and reached the cellar door as Daniel was coming up the cellar steps. Without a word they both began unloading the cart and carrying it down into the cellar. He followed Daniel down the steps into the small cellar wondering how they all were going to fit in this small space. He was surprised as they moved through the small dank space and went through another door and down a flight of steps that he had never seen before. He stopped in amazement at the sight of an underground room that he knew was not there months back.

"You've been busy!' He said as he put down his bags.

"I actually started it a year ago," He smiled. "I figured it might come in handy for something."

The room was at least forty foot square, the walls were lined with stone and large timbers crisscrossed the ceiling adding extra support. Daniel was a carpenter by trade and knew how to build things. He had built shelves around the room and had even built an air filtration system as well. There was no telling what else he had created in this room. Greygor felt that they might just make it. Pat was over by the shelves helping her mother Paula and her sister Jessica load them up. Paula looked over at him and smiled; he smiled back and nodded a hello to her. She was a short medium built woman with a sweet demeanor; He always enjoyed visiting with her and talking for hours. Jessica was the total opposite of Pat; she was a few years older and a businessperson. Where Patricia was passionate about her family Jessica was passionate about her work and her family. Pat was built very physically Jessica was built like their mother. Both sisters were very strong willed and spoke their mind and as country as country could be. Jessica had gotten married to Tony just a year ago. He was tall and had a slight belly on him, with brown hair he sporting a beard and moustache making him looks a bit like a mountain man. The two of them had started their own computer business from their home that had been really going well.

Greygor and Daniel headed back up the steps to finished getting the supplies, they emptied the cart in two trips as Tony and the boys finished grabbing things from Daniels house. Once finished, He helped Daniel barricade the first door by nailing strong boards across it. The wind outside began to pick up as a rumbling sound could be heard miles away. They finished their work and headed for the second door. Both of them strained to pull the huge wooden door shut as they entered the shelter. Once the work was completed, they all sat down on the cots that were set up in the room. They could hear the winds outside picking up even more and could feel the earth beneath them begin to tremble. He held Pat close to him as their two boys sat on either side of them. He put his other arm over Jacob's shoulder as Pat put hers around Austin's. Jessica and Tony sat next to Daniel and Paula holding each other. Everyone sat quietly waiting for what was to come. He held his family tight as he began praying to himself that his family that was far off had found shelter somewhere. He knew that his brothers and sister close to Pittsburgh Pennsylvania were in the most danger but was worried as well for his parents and brother in Kentucky though they were deep in the forest there. He knew that everyone in the shelter had people they loved and cared about on their mind and each was praying for them. He began thinking about his loved ones around him now and prayed that this shelter was enough to protect all of them. He glanced around at each of their faces and smiled as memories of many good times with them flooded his mind. Outside the wind roared louder and the ground began trembling harder as dust began filling the room. He kissed Pat on the head as noise outside got louder. They all could hear distant explosions going off as the winds outside grew louder. They knew that hell had been unleashed on to the world and it was coming their way.

The ground began to vibrate violently as dust and dirt was shaken from the rafters above, making it very hard to breathe in just a short time. Daniel got up and ran to one of the shelves and grabbed dust mask for everyone and quickly handed them out. The winds outside howled even louder and the sound of shattering glass and cracking beams could be heard by all. The temperature in the room rose, as did the humidity. Up above Daniels Garage and workshop collapsed from the force of the nuclear winds, it was not long after that the house above the shelter also fell.

Debris of all kinds flew through the air being picked up and propelled by the winds, boulders, trees, cars as well as parts of buildings and bridges were thrown for miles. Cities and towns that were not vaporized by nuclear explosions were smashed to the ground, Highways and bridges were destroyed and overpasses and tunnels collapsed. Anything living that was not able to find shelter died in the destruction within the first few hours.

Inside the shelter a beam began to crack above, Daniel motioned for Greygor to follow him. They lifted a long metal pipe from the corner of the room and carried over to the trouble spot. They crammed it under the beam and lodged it tight. They listened as other beams creaked but held up to the pressure that was above them. The hours went by until it was finally night, everyone tried to sleep but the noise outside kept up loud and steady. They stayed awake throughout the night watching the ceiling for any possible problems. Morning arrived slowly with still no changes outside, the howling nuclear winds were just as strong as they were the day before and every so often, a distant explosion could be heard. They could only speculate on how bad it really was outside so far. Paula got up and began passing out breakfast as best she could, dry cereal seemed to be the most realistic thing to eat right now with so much dust in the air. Jacob and Austin actually had the best idea for eating by covering up their heads with blankets as they ate, after a little laughter about it, everyone did the same. Talking was practically impossible due to the loud noise outside. Throughout the second day, everyone sat looking up at the ceiling deep in thought and frightened. Greygor kept thinking of his family far away, still praying that they were all right. Deep down he knew there would be only one way that he could ever know; he also knew that his wife would not like it a bit. He stayed on the bed with her that night and held her close; he placed his hand over her ear so that perhaps she could fall asleep. After a couple hours, her eyes closed and she sweetly breathed as he watched her finally get some rest. Greygor smiled at his sleeping love and gently kissed her on the forehead before he finally fell into a deep sleep. He began to dream.

From high above he looks out on an expansion of land surrounded huge wall like barriers, as his eyes focus he can see that they are mountains reaching high into the grayish red sky above, flashes of light and what look like tornados fill the sky. Light seems to be minimal where he was. However, beyond the mountains it seems to be pitched black. He stared into the blackness trying to focus wondering what was out there. The darkness for some strange reason seems to be trying to overpower the mountains but something seemed to be helping keep it out. Cold chills run down his back as the thought of the darkness getting in worried him deeply. He begins looking down the side of the mountains looking at what looks like forest. Down below he can see a huge lake as well as three roads that seem to be the only way in and out of this area. His eyes begin to focus on the huge valley below; he can now see houses and even people. It makes him smile to see how peaceful it seems within this place, he feels a warm feeling within his heart as if he may have helped make such a peaceful place. He feels a familiar hand gently touch his shoulder; Greygor turns his head to see Pat standing behind him smiling at him.

"You should be happy and proud baby," She whispers to him, "you made this all happen."

He begins to smile but from the corner of his eye, he watches as a sword slices through the air towards Pat and him!

"No!" He shouted over the noise outside and sat straight up in the bed.

"Baby, what's wrong?" Pat yelled placing her hand against his chest feeling his heartbeat thump hard in his chest.

He could feel the sweat pouring down his face; he knew it was just a dream. Pat held him close to help calm him down.

"It was just a bad dream honey." He whispered in her ear, "I'm ok now."

Lying back down they held each other tight Greygor closed his eyes but could not fall back to sleep, he kept thinking about that dream.

The third day came and seemed to go fast, the winds outside stilled howled loudly. Every one tried to stay busy and ignore the noise outside. Paula, Pat and Jessica checked over the supplies as Daniel and Greygor checked and fixed the beams above. Tony worked on the water and air filtration systems with Jacob and Austin; they changed the filters and cleaned the dust and dirt away as best they could. By evening everyone was tired, they washed up and had a quick meal of canned pasta and bread. By bedtime it was easy to fall asleep after all the work they all had done. He held Pat tight as he listened to the sounds from outside the shelter; his thoughts were with those he loved up north. He finally fell asleep as he prayed for them to all be all right.

He was the first to wake up in the morning; he sat up in bed looking up at the darkened ceiling. He raised his hand to his ear and snapped his fingers to assure he had not lost his hearing over the last few days. Daniel must have heard him and uncovered his head and looked over at him with a smile on his face.

"Am I dreaming?" He whispered. "Or have the winds stopped?"

"I am as awake as you are Greygor," Daniel replied, "I think it's over."

Daniel motioned for him to get up. He did so quietly as to not wake Pat up. They stood close so that they could talk without anybody else hearing them.

"Is there something wrong dad?" He asked.

"I just wanted to talk to you about what we need to do next." Daniel said. "The nuclear storm has stopped but there is still a chance of fallout and radiation up above us. Another thing that we have to worry about is our family's safety once we get out of here."

"How long do you think we need to stay in the shelter?" He asked.

"Well, we have enough food and water to last us at least four months if necessary that will get us into September, the filtration systems and the generators should hold up even longer if need be. The shelter roof seems to be holding up well after all it has been through so I don't think we have to worry about that much anymore now that the storms are over."

"So what are your main concerns then Dad?" He asked.

"Being stuck down here for that many days could really be hard on everyone. We have to also take in account that something that we didn't think of could happen."

"Like illness or a part of the roof caving amongst other things." Greygor thought aloud as Daniel shook his head in agreement, "what we need to do is try and be ready for anything."

"Exactly," Daniel said, "we need to have a talk with everyone and discuss all of this after we have breakfast."

"I know we have enough food to last into September, but do you think we should wait that long dad?" He asked, "What if it's hard to find food up there we may need the extra time to search some out, water is another thing I know is going to be hard to find."

"That's true." Daniel said. "Let's get everyone up and eat and then we can all talk about all of this."

After a good breakfast everyone gathered around to talk about what their next step would be they talked about what the two men had already discussed letting everybody to give their input on each concern as well as ask questions. They agreed that they did have to wait a few months before going outside to allow the radiation to subside. They all agreed that waiting until September may be a problem, food and water would be very low by then and attempting to find food after all of the destruction above may be close to impossible right away, July instead was agreed on. Everyone agreed that to keep any type of cabin fever from happening they would all have to stay busy with work, exercise, talking and letting each other know if shelter life was pushing them too far. Paula brought Daniel a calendar so that he could mark on it the exit day and he hung it up on the door. He appointed Jacob and Austin in charge of marking the days off as each one went by. After the discussion, they all began working on what needed to be done.

Greygor kept thinking about his family so far away, he knew that eventually he would have to know if they somehow survived. What he might have to do after they get out of the shelter and are safe may not go over well with Pat or anyone else. Deep down he knew that not knowing what had become of them would drive him crazy. He knew though that he had to follow his own rule of thumb that was to take it all one-step at a time.

Most of the time the days seemed to fly by quick but once July finally arrived; they seemed to slow to a snails crawl. Supplies were holding up well and there had been no problems with the filtration systems or generators. The walls and ceiling were checked daily for any weaknesses, anything found was repaired quickly. No noise could be heard outside, except for an occasional rainstorm throughout the months that had gone by. There had been a time or two that the shelter life was getting to someone but with the support of the others, they would get through it. Everyone looked forward to the day they could get outside and see daylight once more.

Chapter 2

The thought of finally going outside had kept Greygor up most of the night, fear of what it may be like out there filled his mind. It had been decided that Daniel and Greygor would be the first to go out and then if everything seemed all right after a few hours the rest would join them. So much could happen though, rapid radiation sickness, attacks from animals or desperate men could attack out of nowhere or fallout could still be happening. Questions of what it would be like outside after the nuclear storms were also within his mind, though an optimist he knew it could not be too good. Pat kept waking up throughout the night asking him if he was all right, he would act as if he had been asleep and shake his head yes. She held him tight and nuzzled his neck after each time then whisper I love you.

Morning finally arrived and they all ate breakfast together, the concern everyone had about this day showed on each face around the room. After a prayer, together they walked to the door after hugging everyone. The two men unsealed the door and undid the lock, Daniel pushed the door hard but something must have fallen against it because it would not budge at first. Greygor placed his shoulder hard against it and pushed with all his strength, slowly the door started to move as his muscles bulged and his face reddened from the strain. Tony and the boys came over to help and the door finally opened wide. They quickly went out into the cellar and closed the door behind them. Each smiled at each other as they rested for a minute or so.

"You ready?" Daniel asked as he walked up the steps to the outside door.

"Yes, let's get out of here." He said following.

They unsealed the second door, unlocked it and pushed it open as they both walked out to see the world for the first time in months. They were shocked and bewildered at what they each saw. The sky above was filled with reddish gray clouds stretching from horizon to horizon; the clouds were very thick and low in the sky and did not allow much sunlight to get through. Lightning flashed continuously across the sky but no thunder was heard. Tornado like funnel clouds dipped down towards the ground all over but collapsed back up into the clouds above. Lightening swirled around the funnel clouds as they dipped down and then would follow back up into the sky. The mountains were scorched and the forest had been stripped from them. What trees that were left had taken a lot of damage. Around the area not a single building stood, each had been blown over or had collapsed in on itself. They walked around looking at the damage and deep in thought. Huge slabs of metal and cars blown from miles away laid everywhere. They walked out to the road and looked up to where their houses had been for years, both had been blown apart and scattered up and down the hill. The road was filled with sand and dirt as well as other debris. They listened for any sounds, no birds singed and they heard no signs of life around them. They walked back up into the yard; they sat down on a small brick wall that had been left of what once was Daniels house.

"This isn't good." Daniel said wiping sweat from his forehead.

"You feel alright?" Greygor asked, "You're not feeling sick are you?"

"No, I'm just shocked at all of this." He said. "We have to figure out what we are going to do; I don't think we can even rebuild anything. Only thing we can do is go through all the rubble and find things we can use."

"What are we going to do for shelter?" Greygor asked, "We can't stay down in that hole forever and we don't know what kind of danger we might be in if we stay out in the open here."

"Your right about that anyone or anything that may have survived will be desperate for food and water and might decide to take it from us even if they have to kill for it."

"What if we find someplace that can give us security as well as shelter, somewhere far off of main roads with a source of water?"

"Do you have a place in mind already? Daniel asked.

"We will have to check it out first but I think it could be a possibility and it really isn't that far from here, only problem we have is moving all we have there."

"There might actually be a way." Daniel said, "First we need to salvage whatever we can from all the wreckage."

"Hope we can move some of this rubble, it will take a lot of muscle."

"Believe me Greygor; what I just thought about will help with that too!" Daniel smiled and patted his shoulder.

"Sounds good dad, guess we should get everyone out of the shelter now so we can get our plans in action."

"Hold up a minute son," Daniel said seriously. "Let's talk about something else.

"What's that dad?"

"Now Greygor, I've got to know you pretty good over the years and I can tell when something is weighing heavy on your mind. I know you're worried about your parents and relatives up north, and the need that you have to go find out if they are alright or not and your need to keep us here all safe is tearing you apart inside."

"I'll be alright dad, Pat and the boys need me here."

"No you won't," Daniel said firmly. "If everything goes well with supplies and the move to the safe place, I will help you figure out a way to go and find your other family members. Tony, your sons and I can keep things safe till you return."

"Traveling that far may take a long time on foot though." Greygor said.

"Well that may also be taken care of also with the plan I have." Daniel smiled, "Let's keep this part of our conversation to ourselves though for now."

Daniel patted him on the shoulder as they walked back to the shelter; it was time to bring everyone out.

Pat stood against her husband with her head on his shoulder, she wept as she looked up at what once was their home. Jacob and Austin walked around the yard looking through the debris that littered the hill. Jessica and Tony had already walked back to Daniels yard after looking over what had once been their home. He placed his arm around Pat's shoulder comforting her as best he could.

"Don't worry baby," He whispered. "Things will be alright."

"I know honey," Pat replied. "But we worked hard for all we had in that house now everything is gone."

"I don't see it like that dear." He smiled. "I still have the boys and you that is all I need."

She smiled as she hugged him feeling a little bit better with what he had just said, she knew he meant it and loved him so much. They kissed very deeply and held each other tight out on the road, the boys walked up to them unnoticed.

"This is unbelievable!" Austin said to Jacob. "Our house gets blown to bits and our mom and dad can stand here kissing like nothing happened."

"I've always told you we have the weirdest parents on this earth!" Jacob replied shaking his head.

He stopped kissing Pat and winked at her, she knew what was going to happen as she smiled at him.

Jacob and Austin also knew what their father was about to do and both of them took off running for their grandfather's yard. He took off after them, he stayed right on their heels waiting for them to make it to the yard, they turned into the yard and Greygor made his move! He leaped forward as hard as he could and dived into the back of their legs with his arms outstretched tackling both of them to the ground. Both of his sons twisted out of his grasp he tried to stand up fast, Austin jumped on top of him knocking him back to the ground. Jacob jumped on top of him too, all three wrestled to gain the upper hand but Jacob and Austin got him pinned to the ground. Laughter came from all three of them as everyone up near the house watched with smiles on their faces and shaking their heads. The boys had their father trapped and were tickling his sides as he tried to squirm out of their grasp. Suddenly the boys froze as twisting pain hit both their ears; they released their father and stood up quickly. Pat had hold of both their ears and pulled them up off their father and started walking them up towards everyone whom now were laughing loudly.

"Now, I have told both you boys not to pick on your poor old father!" Pat said as she walked them up the yard.

"Wait a minute! He shouted as he got up on his knees. "Who are you calling old?"

Pat looked back at him and winked as she giggled at him. She let the boys go who rubbed their ears and watched as their father walked up towards them. He walked pass Pat slapping her on the behind and then stood next to her as everyone began discussing what their next step should be.

Within the hour everyone began rummaging through the buildings in Daniel's yard, the men first went into the debris of Daniel's tool shed finding shovels, rakes and tools that might come in handy. He also had an ample supply of work gloves that would protect hands from glass, metal and brick. The women found a number of tarps in the shelter and spread them out in the yard for anything found that could be useful. By evening, the tool shed and the garage had been rummaged thoroughly through. Greygor built a fire pit with what stone and bricks that he found scattered around the yard, Jacob and Austin gathered firewood. After Paula cooked dinner on the fire, they all sat around the fire watching the clouds and lightening up in the sky. Daniel began telling everyone about the next steps in their survival.

"Tomorrow morning while everyone continues rummaging through the buildings, Greygor and I need to go for a little walk."

Daniel said, "I really don't want to say anything in depth about it but if we find what we are looking for the work and the move may go a lot easier."

"Where are you thinking of moving too dad?" Jessica asked.

"I'll let Greygor tell you." Daniel nodded to him.

"Well, we were talking about how we are out in the open and it might be dangerous to stay here," He replied as he stood. "We need a place far from any main roads but easy to get supplies to, it has to be safe and secure with buildings that we can use as houses. The only place close enough that is surrounded by mountains and may have been protected from the nuclear storm might be the lake area a few miles from here. It has only three roads that run in and out as well as a lake that could supply us with fresh water and maybe even some fish if they survived."

"I use to walk the trails and rock climb all around that area," Tony added, "Those Mountains are treacherous to try to get over either way, the roads are small two lanes so we could probably figure a way to keep trouble out."

"I believe I can figure out and set up some security traps along the roads. Daniel replied.

"Another good thing," Paula said. "The valley inside this area is huge and if we do find any family and friends alive we can move them into it."

"Do you think anyone may still be alive there?" Pat asked.

"Everyone pretty much left out of there once they closed down the lake and it became a ghost town." Jessica reminded her.

"We have to check it out first before we start making any major plans." Greygor said. "Let's get tomorrow done with first then we will go from there."

The snapping branch coming from the road made Greygor leap up from his seat, he grabbed the machete that was next to him and stood ready for whatever may be out there, Jacob and Austin had grabbed long heavy sticks and stood beside their father ready to help. He squinted trying to see anything in the darkness. Someone was out there. He could feel it.

"Hello?" Someone said from the darkness, "Daniel, you there?"

Daniel got up and walked down the driveway, "Sean, is that you?"

From the darkness walked a younger version of Daniel as well as his son Tom with his wife, his daughter Karen and her husband Jeff. The groups greeted each other with hugs and handshakes. Just as Sean and Daniel shared looks, they also shared the ability to build things. Sean explained that he had also built a shelter beneath his house and had been there for about as long as Daniels group had been. When he heard noise up in Daniels yard, he had decided to check it out. Thank goodness he did. They all gathered back around the fire and began talking about the shelter life as well as the plans that had already been discussed. Tom and Tony volunteered to go with Greygor to explore Lake Lair in the days to come. It had gotten to be very late and everyone grew tired, Sean and his group headed back down to their shelter after wishing everyone a good night. Greygor stayed up as everyone went to bed stirring the fire, he was happy that Sean and his family was with them now.

He started thinking about his family knowing that he would have to go off and find them after they settled in the safer area. He also knew that Pat and the boys were not going to like the idea but it would have to be done. He looked up at the sky as the lightning flashed across it as the clouds swirled nonstop. He watched as clouds swirled down towards the earth and the lightening encircled it sending sparks into the air once the funnel cloud collapsed back up.

After breakfast, Sean and his family met up with Daniels and together everyone started rummaging through the buildings. Daniel and Greygor kissed their wives and began walking down the road, Daniel had still not told anyone where they were going and he trusted him enough not to ask. They reached the end of their road and made a right and kept on walking. Houses that had been on either side of the road were now rubble and they walked a good three miles and turned left on an old dirt road that had never been paved. Greygor started to realize where they were going and what Daniel had been talking about.

"I see it on your face that you finally figured this out." Daniel said smiling.

"You didn't want to say anything in case it fell through?"

"Exactly," Daniel said, "I know my friend Bert Mellows is a pretty smart man and he probably made sure his investments were taken care of."

He had met Bert Mellows a few times; he was a well-known horse farmer in this area. Bert had mainly Himalayan horses and a few Arabians as well. He used the bigger horses to pull wagons for parades in the area when they had them. Daniel called Bert's horses his investment but both of them knew that Bert loved his horses just like family.

They went another two miles before turning up on what was called Mellow Mountain road, they walked up a thin winding road for another mile before reaching the small house they had been looking for. Going down the driveway, they could see the windows of the house were all smashed out and the outside walls that had been a white ivory color were now black and gray. The inside of the house was dark and no sign of life could be seen or heard.

"Bert!" Daniel shouted, "You in there!"

From within the darkness of the house a shuffling sound started and seemed to be getting closer to the front door, both Greygor and Daniel quietly waited.

"Is that you, Daniel?" An old voice stammered.

"Yes sir," Daniel answered, "My son in law and I need to speak with you if you don't mind?"

"Good to have some visitors," Bert replied back. "Come on in and sit a spell."

The two men went to the door and cautiously went in as their eyes adjusted to the darkness; they heard Bert pull a chair out in the kitchen and seemed to fall into it. They followed him into the kitchen and both were shocked at the sight of him. Bert's left side of his face had been burned horribly by radiation; his right side seemed to be untouched. He used his right hand to lift his left arm up and onto the table. It also was horribly mangled. Though he must have been in a lot of pain, he did his best not to show it to his guest. Daniel sat next to Bert shaking his right hand gently; Greygor sat down on the other side of him and did the same.

"Sorry," Bert whispered, "but I have nothing other than water to offer you to drink."

"That's alright Bert," Greygor said with a smile. "Do you have a first aid kit anywhere maybe we can help your injuries first."

"You're a nice young man I thank you but there is nothing that can be done for me now," Bert said straining to breath. "We best figure out what I can do for you."

"Well my friend," Daniel said. "Our homes have been destroyed by the nuclear war and we are trying to rummage for supplies and get to a safer place, we wanted to borrow your wagons and horses and use them to get us there."

"I got most of them safely into the old mining tunnel down by the barn. My poor horse Sherlock, he was taken right before my eyes," Bert said sadly as a tear flowed from his eye, "I was pulling him into the tunnel when the first wave of winds hit, I saw him implode before my eyes as my left side was hit by the fire. I woke up a few days later; the tunnel entrance collapsed enough to protect the horses and myself."

"How many did you save?" Daniel asked.

"There are six of the big Himalayans' and three of my Arabians." Bert answered. "I believe we can work out a deal or something."

"We would appreciate it Bert." Greygor said, "You should come with us sir."

"Unfortunately, as I said before there isn't much that can be done for me now, Bert replied. "And the military your going be running from will be out and about faster than you realize."

"Oh no sir," Greygor said. "We aren't running from the military we just need to find a safer place till things get back to normal again."

"You don't know do you?" Bert looked at the both of them, "It's not your fault of course, and how could you know?"

"What are you talking about Bert?" Daniel asked.

"As you both know my son Ben has been in the military for a number of years," Bert said reaching out and pulling a large journal to him from the middle of the table. "He wrote about all the things that were going on inside of this book as well as the letters to me on a weekly basis. His last letter to me was about the coming nuclear war and how if I made it I should head for the deep forest to keep out of reach of the military. Seems our president has a special plan for the world after the war, seems he wants to take over what's left it."

"How can that be?" Daniel asked, "He can't!"

"Why can't he, Daniel? Bert replied, "There isn't anyone left to oppose him, he has power over the whole military, no civilians have any weapons, most of the world's population is gone and all he has to do is have his military capture or kill anyone gets in their way. You need to take this journal and read everything that is in it as well as the letters in the back of it. It tells about how Matthews set everything into motion as well as how the nuclear war was going to be started and it tells of the aftermath plans."

Bert started telling his two visitors a little about what his son had told him, the terrorist acts that were blamed on the ANA were actually done by the military in the past two years. He also explained how once the nuclear missiles started to fire that the Middle East would not be the only target. Greygor remembered on the television how the radar showed U.S. missiles heading towards Europe and other countries. Bert told how the military was to take shelter in secret shelters around the country until it was all clear. Their orders were given before entering the shelters. They were to meet at the rallying points. Along the way they were ordered to capture and detain any civilian survivors along the way, kill any that were of no use or dangerous to President Matthews plans.

"The journal goes into more detail on all that I have told you," Bert said.

"We don't have much of a chance now do we?" Greygor replied.

"Well you do have some advantages though," Bert, said. "For one thing most of their ammunition was used in the Mediterranean Sea war and what they didn't have on them was probably destroyed in the bunkers of the military bases around the country. So unless they can find a way to make ammunition they will have to resort to old style weapons like swords, bows and things like that. Of course whatever fuel they have won't last long so any military vehicles they still have won't last long, they will have to find horses or just walk."

"Greygor is pretty good with different weapons too." Daniel said.

"Yea, but a throwing knife against a rifle isn't much of a fair fight." He said.

"Daniel, hand me that long box up on that shelf up there." Bert said.

Daniel got up and grabbed the box, he handed it to Bert who opened it and pushed it around to Greygor.

"This will help you a bit." Bert said.

His eyes grew wide as he reached in and pulled out a long sword by its leather-twined handle. He knew good blade, it was sharp and well balanced able to take a strike from another sword and still hold its edge. The sword had to be from Scotland due to its Celtic engraving etched in the metal.

"Thank you Bert." He said as he placed the sword in its sheath.

"You're welcome young man," Bert said sadly. "It was to be a gift for my son when he got home; unfortunately he was killed after his last letter to me."

"We are so sorry to hear that Bert." Daniel said.

"They found out he was telling me things and they shot him for being a traitor." Bert said sadly, "Well now you need to go down and get the horses ready, there are three wagons in the barn you can use for your trip as well as food, tools and supplies for the horses. Before you take off stop back in and I will let you know what I want in return."

"Thank you Bert." Daniel said shaking his hand.

Greygor reached over and shook his hand. "Yes, thank you."

They left him in the house and started down towards the barn, once there they opened the doors to the harsh smell of horse manure and urine. They worked quickly hooking up the horses to the wagons, each horses name was on the stall. They hooked up Sampson and Mazda to the first wagon, Rascal and Damsel to the second and Leo and Delta to the third. All six Himalayans were chestnut brown with white down their faces; all six were larger and wider than regular horses built for the pulling wagons and working farm land. They tied the three Arabian horses to the back of the third wagon; they loaded six saddles and the supplies in the wagons. All the wagons were tied to each other so that Greygor and Daniel could drive the first one and the other horses would follow in the line. They got up on the bench of the first wagon and started up the hill towards Bert's home pulling up in front of the house. Daniel jumped down from the wagon and walked inside while Greygor got down and checked all of the riggings and ties. Daniel slowly walked out of the house and up to him.

"We have another job to do." Daniel said sadly handing Greygor a short letter.

He took it and slowly read it being a bit choked up.

Dear friends,

All I ask of you is to take good care of my horses; I am in no shape to do anymore for them. I want to wish you all good luck and may god bless your family. Be very careful on your travels. When you get the letter I will be on my way to heaven, please bury me in my family plot in my back yard.

I thank you, God speed, Bert

They wrapped Bert in a blanket from his bed and carried him out to the back yard, the grave was already dug and they gently lowered him into the ground. After burying him they prayed for him and then headed to the wagons. Both of them were quiet on the ride down from Bert's house. They made a right onto the dirt road and headed home.

"I know what you're thinking." Daniel said, "You're concerned about leaving us and searching for your family now that you heard about the military and Matthew's plans."

"I feel like I would be putting all of you in jeopardy," He answered "We have no way to defend ourselves if anything happens."

"Remember something." Daniel smiled, "Matthew's isn't the only one who can make plans and think ahead. Do you really think that the only thing I thought of was to build a shelter in case this happened?"

"Not that I underestimate you dad. But I don't know what else you could have done to prepare for this."

"Well son, I believe you will be pleasantly surprised when we get back to the yard."

They were greeted with smiles and hugs from everyone once they pulled into the yard; piles of supplies were sitting on tarps and covered so weather could not harm the salvaged items. Daniel led Greygor over to one of the bigger tarps behind the wrecked house. He pulled the top tarp away showing him the surprise. They had recovered a large supply of rifles, shotguns and pistols along with a huge supply of ammunition as well as bows and arrows.

"Where did all this come from?" He asked.

"Uncle Sean and I had it buried in his root cellar about a year ago right before the laws came out against ownership of weapons." Daniel answered, "We stocked up on it all paying with only cash and using false names so that it could not ever be traced."

"A couple of these as well as your own weapons I know you have hidden and that trip your planning will make it a lot better for you."

Daniel replied, "Once we get to the lake area I believe these will really keep the rest of us safe."

"I am impressed." Greygor said.

"I thought you might be son." He smiled. "Well let's get back to the others and help find more things."

By evening, the group was tired out and ready to rest, from the two yards many needed supplies were found so far. The horses were used to help pull heavy debris from different areas so that even more things could be found. Everyone worked well together and the work went faster than had been expected. After dinner, everyone relaxed around the fire and began talking about the days to come, and all the things they would have to do. It was decided that Greygor, Tom and Tony would ride out in two days to explore the travel route and the area, they were to spend three days checking out the terrain and making sure it was safe while everyone else finished salvaging around the yards.

The next morning Greygor woke Jacob and Austin up early and they walked up to their yard with shovels in hand. They began digging in front of the porch right next to the septic tank; the boys already knew what their father had hidden in this spot so long ago. The three of them dug five feet down until one of their shovels clanked on the metal top of the box; they chipped away at the dirt around the sides until they could actually feel it move.

They grabbed hold of the boxes handles and pulled the box from the hole and up into the yard. They wiped the dirt away from the top and sides and then Greygor pulled out a key from his pocket and looked at it sadly.

He had hoped never to have to open this box and that it would stay, buried deep in the earth along with the memories of his past. He had gone into the U.S. Army right out of high school; he loved the hard training and military life. He started out in artillery but then decided to volunteer for airborne ranger, the army offered him free martial arts training and that is where he met his teacher, Master Phillips. Along with learning the martial art called Shoatan, Phillips taught him about weapons and weapon making. Within a year, he had become a human weapon, with the ability to use any weapon he touched or made with deadly consequences. The army saw this and decided to use him as the deemed fit; they placed him in a special squad that the army used in secret. For two years his team was used for very special secret missions that no one would ever know about. He performed his duties very well but after two years of doing what he did best he finally was burned out on it. He was honorably discharged and decided to go back to civilian life, He married Pat and settled down with her in North Carolina with their two growing boys. He worked out with all of his weapons every morning before Matthews declared that civilians could not own a weapon that's when the boys and he buried them in the ground in case they were ever needed again.

He unlocked the box and opened the lid, Jacob and Austin stood back as they watched their father pull out the coverings that protected the weapons within. From the box he pulled out a large round, metal shield painted black, black fur cloth lined the inside of it with an arm and hand strap. Sheathed inside it was a black short sword, he pulled it out and looked it over before putting it back and handing it to Jacob who placed it in the wheel barrow. Next, he pulled out two long swords and a knife belt with different size throwing knives. He handed each item to one or the other boys. He opened a tin box that carried different stars and shurikens of different types and sizes, he handed Jason that and then handed Jacob his pistol crossbow with bolts. Nunchakus and a three sectional staff along with a five-foot staff came next, then a multitude of knives and chain weapons.

Last but not least he pulled out a weapon he had create unlike any other, it was a round metal disc made of steel with six blades flipped inward to the center. He stood up and held it in his hand smiling at his creation. Jacob and Austin backed up staring in amazement at the weapon. He looked out at a piece of wood sticking up out of the ground about twenty-five feet away; he swung his arm outwards rapidly letting the metal disc fly towards his target. They watched as it spun quickly through the air and as it did the six blades snapped out! It sliced right through the wood cleanly and went a few yards further before turning like a boomerang and headed back towards him as the blades snapped back in. He caught it in his hand right above his head, after looking it over for any damage, he handed it to Austin who placed it with the other weapons. It was called the flying guillotine by him, though only the size of a large Frisbee it was a dangerous weapon.

After they reburied the box the three of them walked up to the garage that now was collapsed in on itself, they pulled up the tin roof and used wood beams to prop it up so that they could reach the door to the root cellar where more of his weapons were hidden. The door was jammed shut; they all pushed hard feeling it give little by little.

They got it halfway open when something jumped out from the darkened cellar slamming into Greygor's stomach! The boys jumped back as he fell backwards feeling the wet slimy tongue slash across his face, He wrapped his arms around Luck and hollered happily as did the boys! The three of them petted him and cheerfully let their dog greet them with licks and nuzzles. He let the boys stay outside with Luck as he started down the stairs of the cellar; He shined his flashlight around the room and slowly figured out how Luck had made it. In the corner of the room sat a huge bag of dog food that had been stored here, in the other corner was a puddle of water that must have formed during the storms. He was saddened as he looked over into another corner to see his other dog, Pepsi lying dead on the ground. He walked over and laid his hand on his head.

"Well pup guess this whole thing that happened took its toll on you," he said silently. "You were a great friend."

He got up and walked over to the far wall that had been built many years ago, wallpaper had been placed on the wall by him about a year ago. He pulled the paper away. It gave way as he ripped it, exposing the hidden rack behind it. A large battle-axe hung in the center and beside it was a five-foot iron staff, along with an array of knives and other unique weapons that he had collected over the years. Finally yet importantly, he grabbed a hanging bag and carefully opened it, he pulled out a long black leather jacket that still looked brand new. The inside liner had pockets throughout it and places to put different weapons of choice. The bag also contains four pairs of black jeans and four black pull over shirts he had stored with the leather jacket.

The three of them loaded up the wheelbarrow and with Luck running around them they started down to Daniel's yard. Pat was the first to see Luck and let him jump up on her as she hugged him and laughed as the dog licked her face. She got up and hugged Greygor happy that he had found their dog. She pulled away from him and looked over at the wheelbarrow.

"I see you found your toys?" She said with a smile. "Do you remember how to use them?"

"I believe I can get the hang of them again."

"I know your good honey," she said, "but promise you'll keep a gun with you too."

"I promise." He said leaning over and kissing her cheek.

"Well I know you hate guns." She replied.

"Its not that I don't like them I am just better with my toys as you call them." He laughed.

"I know you're the type who could take a knife to a gun fight and actually win but having a gun will make me feel a bit better."

After placing the weapons on a tarp and covering them, they all walked up to the campfire to have breakfast with the rest; everyone seemed in good spirits and ready for another day of hard work. Luck enjoyed a bowl of left over scraps from breakfast that Paula had made for him while everyone else started working on the salvaging.

Chapter 3

He was starting to have second thoughts about picking Sampson to ride, his wide back and heavy steps were killing Greygor's backside. Tom and Tony had chosen two of the Arabians and had even tried to warn him about the consequences of his choice. They had started out at six and had made good time traveling down the curvy mountain road that would lead them away from the town and out towards the road that would lead them to the area they were to check out. They walked the horses cautiously listening and watching for any signs of danger. The light from the sun did its best to filter through the thick clouds above as they swirled and blanketed the sky. Lightning flashes across the sky stayed steady as the funnels clouds dipped and sucked themselves back up into the grayish red clouds that they had come from. The trees and plants that were left along the way were black and damaged everywhere they looked. It was cool for a summer day it could not have been higher than sixty degrees. Greygor wore his long leather jacket after filling it up with his special weapons, all three carried a pistol in their belts and a rifle tied to their saddles. He also wore his new sword across his back ready for a left hand draw if the need arose. They felt that the sight of weapons might discourage anyone dangerous from attacking them.

They reached the only main road that they would have to cross, a four-lane highway covered with thick sandy dirt and littered with crushed cars and other debris. They cautiously crossed it and could see that the overpasses in each directions had caved in and down onto the road. The wind covered their tracks almost immediately as they quickly got to the other side and went on. They found and followed the long narrow road that led to the Lake Lair; on each side of it were the large orchard fields that before the nuclear storm had grown apples of different kinds for many years. Very few trees had been left standing and they could see the broken stumps of those that were totally ripped apart. The road started to descend and curve as they traveled down into the mountains, over to the right they could see the side of a mountain that had been dug out at one time or another and made a mental note that it could be used as a lookout point.

"There's a trail that runs down from there straight into Lake Lair." Tom said to him pointing in the direction they both were looking at.

"That could be useful." Greygor replied.

They traveled further down the winding road as the mountains on their left seemed to grow higher but on the right the drop off seemed to get deeper, they could set up traps up on the mountain of boulders and logs that could be dropped on any dangerous elements that tried to enter this place. It took another two hours to reach the end of this road where they turned left onto the main road that would lead them through the center of the valley. The old buildings that lined each side of the road were not in to bad of shape and looked repairable. They stopped in front of the lake and looked out over the miles it went out before disappearing around the mountains. The road going to the left led to large fields all the way around as the road to the right led to more buildings and houses that seemed untouched by the nuclear storms. Behind them stood three large concrete buildings, one of which had been a lavish hotel at one time. A small road went between two of the buildings that they knew led back to the hot springs and to a few caves that had once been tourist attractions.

A few years before Matthews had taken power this whole area was a resort named Lake Lair, where millions of people use to come, the lake was used for swimming and boating and a golf course ran along the side of it. Grand summer homes ran along the other side, and the mountains and forest were visited by hikers and rock climbers. Unfortunately, the area went bankrupt due to poor tourism and everyone sold off their properties and the lake area government was disbanded, within three years it became a ghost town.

The three men set up camp in front of the lake and had a quick lunch; Tony wanted to check out the road that went to the left of the lake that would take him along the golf course and up into the trails where he had once hiked years ago. Tom would explore the buildings and cave areas around the front of the lake and keep an eye on the camp and Greygor would be riding up the road to the right of the lake checking out the houses and forest. Each of them walked their horses off in their separate directions to begin their exploration of the lake area, Tony headed towards the road that led through the golf course and up into the mountains. Tom went back up the road that they had come in on to check out the buildings that they had passed on the way in and work his way back down to camp.

He led Sampson up the winding road to the right of the lake where the beach had once been, he only had gone a half a mile before coming to the large municipal auditorium. He let Sampson's reins go and walked to the double wooden doors of the building, he pulled hard on the door and opened it slowly listening for any movement within. He slowly walked into the large auditorium on one side bleachers lined the wall and on the other side long wooden tables and desk had been moved against the wall. He figured this was where the government of this area had held public meetings years ago. He slowly looked around checking out every room and corner. He walked out to where Sampson was trying to graze, the horses ears perked up and he walked towards Greygor as he came out.

They walked up the road once more stopping at each building that they came to and checking them out. They stopped about three miles up the road at another large building that looked to have been a warehouse. Greygor went in and checked it out as well. It was close to six in the evening and he decided it was time to head back. He reached camp about the same time as the other two explorers did.

They checked over the horses and fed and watered them. They then built a fire and ate dinner of dried beef and canned goods and then sat back relaxing and making notes of what they had found.

"The buildings along the way seemed very livable as well as the old motel back here." Tom said as he wrote.

"I checked out the municipal building as well as the old shops and some of the houses up the road and they seem in pretty good shape too," Greygor replied "But I think once we get our families in here we need to stay as close as possible."

"I checked out the old motel back there and with a little work at least six to eight families could live in it together." Tom said.

"Could it be made for each family to have their privacy and not be too cramped up?" Tony asked.

"Easily, "Tom smiled. "With a little work it can."

"Did you find anything interesting down your road?" Greygor asked.

"Well the golf course has grown over a bit but the buildings along the way are in good shape and the road is pretty clear all the way up into the mountains." Tony said, "I didn't see any signs of life up there except for a bird or two."

"Tomorrow we can all explore some more but from what we have seen so far it is looking really well." Greygor replied as he put his notebook away.

He pulled out the journal that Bert Mellows had given him and started reading from where he had left off. He shook his head at different things as he read.

"Is there anything good in there?" Tony asked.

"Mostly bad," Greygor answered, "It says here that his brigade went to Alaska and were the ones who blew up the Alaskan pipeline not the terrorist groups of the ANA."

"That was one of the reasons the Mediterranean war got started." Tom said.

"It gets worst actually," Greygor, replied. "It also says that all soldiers of the military were pre-warned about the nuclear war months before and given orders to head to their bunkers in different areas of the country. Their orders also gave them specific dates that small squads were to leave their bunkers and head to a rallying point in different areas of the country."

"Why would they travel in small groups though? Tony asked. "Wouldn't it be better for them to move in large groups?"

"Says here that the reason for small squads leaving at different times would be to capture any survivors along the way at different points of time, knowing that people would come out of shelters at different times as the weeks and months went by. "All survivors were to be assessed at time of capture and those not useful to the military or those a threat to Matthews were to be eliminated."

"Why would the soldiers go along with such a thing?' Tom asked. "Their own families would be caught up in this."

"Seems like old Matthews has made some very big promises to all those who stay loyal to him." Tony replied.

"Well first and foremost the threat of execution seems to have worked pretty well from what I have read as well as a promise of all the gold that is kept in Fort Knox and the treasures of the world would be divided amongst all of those whom stay loyal in the years to come." Greygor said.

"Have you read anything about their ammunition, weapon and fuel supplies? Tom asked.

"Not much about that but the way I figure with the Mediterranean war that has gone on they are probably low and being cautious with what they have."

"That's true but they have ammo bunkers all over the country, they can resupply their selves rather quickly." Tom said.

"Not really though," Greygor said, "The ANA not only hit cities and industries with their attack but also every military base that they could. Not only would the initial strikes take out most of their ammo bunkers but also afterwards, the nuclear storms helped destroy a lot more as it went on. Also, if you remember on the news most of our military were out in the middle east when this all happened and were probably killed so he doesn't have that many troops here in America."

"That's why he merged the military with the law enforcement agencies." Tony replied.

"Right," Greygor said. "And from what I get from the journal only military troops were warned and moved into shelters. The way Matthews planned this all out he knew that survivors wouldn't have weapons so he could actually take over with a smaller military force with minimal weapons."

"And if he has very loyal people around him even if some soldiers decided to overthrow him it would be almost impossible." Tony said, "Sounds like he has been planning this for years."

"Well if you think about it, "Tom added. "He knew how to manipulate everyone and everything he ever came in contact with."

"It was handed to him on a silver platter by the voters of America." Tony laughed, "I even voted for the bum!"

"The good news is that he doesn't have the technology or anything to help him like he did before the nuclear war so we may have a chance to survive and stay out of his way." Greygor said.

"You know if he even gets wind of this place his military will come here to get us?" Tony replied.

"We will just have to do whatever we have to do to keep it very secret." Tom said.

"I believe that can be done." Greygor said. "We will keep it hidden from the world outside these mountains that surround it."

"Instead of Lake Lair we can name it the Hidden Lair." Tony joked.

"I think that's a great name for it." Greygor smiled.

The three men quieted down as the night went on and finally went to sleep after a few hours.

Morning came sooner than they really wanted it to, they ate and each of them began their rides to explore in different directions. They each went a little further than the day before still not seeing any signs of survivors around the area but finding the valley like area in good shape. Greygor started back towards camp a lot sooner than the others, he stopped about a half mile before camp and found a path that he had seen earlier. He left Sampson at the beginning of it and walked up the narrow path, it grew steeper as he went up. It leveled out as he came out on the flattened area high above; He walked to the edge of the large cliff and looked out at the huge valley below. It was a breathtaking sight to him to see the open land to the left of the lake and the small road that led up into the mountains, the lake glistened, and it seemed to stop at the foot of the mountains that rose high surrounding the whole valley. The road he had been on just hours ago snaked up into the mountains also disappearing into the forest as well. He again felt very peaceful looking down at the beauty, which soon would keep his family safe from the dangers of the world. He decided to lie down and relax a few minutes before starting back down. He placed his hands under his head and stared up at the sky above, though he wished for sunshine he was growing use to the sky above and rather enjoyed watching the swirling reddish gray clouds and lightening. Slowly he fell to sleep high above the valley he began to dream;

He stands here on lookout cliff observing the valley below, now though the streets are filled with people and they all seem so happy. He cannot see this from his vantage point but he feels it within him, they are happy and in a very safe place. He feels a hand on his shoulder and he turns to look into his beautiful wife's eyes. He wraps an arm around her shoulder as he looks out.

"You should be very proud baby," she smiles placing her head on his shoulder, "you made all this happen."

"No," he replied. "We all did."

He holds her close as a smile crosses his lips, from the other side of him he catches a flash of metal headed towards him! He moves Pat out of the way as he ducks and draws his sword bringing it up to block the attack! The swords clang loudly and he backs away waiting to block another attack! The shadowy figure swings again but this time Greygor feels pain as the blade slices across his arm. He twirls around and lunges his sword into the middle of the shadow feeling it sink into skin and muscle!

He jumped up looking around to see nothing around him, he looked at his arm but nothing was there and his sword was still lying next to him still in its sheath. He leaned down and picked up his sword and began walking towards the path that would lead him back down. The dream lingered in his mind as he walked down the path. He was now wondering whether this was just a dream or some sort of premonition. He reached his horse and walked him back to camp where he watered and fed Sampson before the others arrived back. Tony and Tom arrived at camp about an hour later with their tales of the areas they checked out. They all talked and decided that they would start back the next day due to everything looking so good so far. After a good meal they all relaxed around the fire a enjoying the peace and quiet.

The three of them rode slowly up the mountain road so not to tire out the horses to fast, all three of them were happy to be heading home. They stopped once they reached the top of the road and let the horses rest for about an hour. They watered the horses and let them relax as they grabbed a quick drink as well. They began riding once more going by the old orchards and heading towards the interstate only a few miles away, that they would have to cross. At the high way, Greygor stopped his horse abruptly as the other two did the same. He listened carefully as the wind blew in his face.

"Someone's moving this way." He whispered. "Let's take cover!"

They reined their horses back and headed up towards the debris that had once been a large discount carpet store where they could keep the horses quiet and look down at the highway without being seen. Tony took the horses by the reigns and walked them back into the woods as Tom and Greygor took their rifles and carefully hid behind large concrete slabs and watched the road below. The sound of a group of people walking up the highway came from the south as well as horses as they listened and carefully looked out. Finally, from around a curve in the highway came a small group of people, there were several soldiers riding horses and two driving a wagon as they slowly came up the dusty road. Three men and three women walked with them with their hands tied. Greygor slipped back behind the concrete and stared over at Tom who also was shocked at the sight.

"That's Uncle Mike and Uncle Mark with them Tom!" Greygor whispered at him, "Paula's brothers."

"I know," Tom, replied, "we have to do something."

"You want to go down there and ask the soldiers to let them go?" Greygor asked sarcastically.

"Maybe, if we say please?" Tom smiled. "What do you want to do?"

"Saving them does cross my mind." He said, "I don't want to be the one to tell our wives that we let loved ones go off to be killed."

"You have a point there!" Tom agreed.

The two men carefully headed down to where Tony stood with the horses, they quickly explained to him what they each saw as they mounted their horses.

"What's the plan? Tony asked.

"We ride hard down Highland Road, they won't see us or hear us and we set up down by the airport overpass and when they come into sight we take out all of the soldiers and rescue the people they have!" Greygor said.

"That sounds, a bit extreme!" Tony said as sweat beaded up on his forehead. "What if something goes wrong?"

"We do our best and make the best of whatever happens." Tom said checking his rifle to make sure it was fully loaded.

"Listen! You are hunters, you two can hide up under either side of the overpass and when the time is right you get them in crossfire."

"What are you going to do?" Tony asked.

"I am going to ride up behind them and take out any that you two happen to miss!" He answered. "So go for death shots don't just wing them!"

"Glad we have scopes on our rifles!" Tom said, "You better be careful!"

The three kicked the side of their horses into a run and took off down Highland Road. It was a seven-mile ride but they would take shortcuts through the woods along the way.

Tony and Tom had tied their horses back in the woods far enough out of sight but close enough that if they had to make a quick escape they could get to the horses within a minute. The both of them climbed up under the overpass where the bridge like structure met the road, the darkness and the fallen concrete would keep them safe if the soldiers got any shots off before going down, Tom had taken the left side closer to the airport and Tony took the other side. The concrete slabs they hid behind allowed for an easy visual of the whole road as well as gave them cover from any returning shots. Greygor waited a hundred yards away from them in a gully with Sampson; the soldiers would be only twenty yards away from him when they passed him. Tony and Tom knew to start firing once the group got by him. He checked his rifle and his weapons within his jacket making sure everything was ready for quick use. He could feel his heartbeat racing as time slowly went by, the sounds of a wagon and horses just coming around the bend in the highway made his heart beat even faster. He knew that it would start any second now, not the actual fight but what he knew as his warrior sense!

As expected he felt it begin, his senses began to heighten as his muscles tensed up and readied for what was to come. His focus was on the job at hand, as he heard the soldiers ride by above him; He closed his eyes visualizing how they were set up as they rode by. Tom took aim as the soldiers came into view, as did Tony, they both watched as the soldiers went by where Greygor was hiding. Two soldiers rode horses a few feet in front of the wagon as two drove the wagon with the survivors following behind it; another two soldiers rode their horses behind them. The captured survivors had their hands tied with a long rope that was attached to the back of the wagon that pulled them along the way.

Tom held the rifle tight against his shoulder as he aimed at the soldier riding behind the wagon on his side; Tony took aim at one of the soldiers in the front. Each of the soldiers had their rifles slung on their backs unaware of anything so far.

Tom pulled the trigger feeling it recoil against his shoulder! Hearing Tony's rifle fired right after his. The two soldiers they were aiming for were knocked from the back of their horses as the bullets slammed into their chest!

All of the horses were startled and began bucking as one soldier yelled, "Ambush!"

Tom again took aim as the soldiers tried to get the horses under control as well as move around to escape being shot. Tony took aim on one of the soldiers on the wagon and fired! The bullet hit the man in the forehead sending him rolling into the back of the wagon! The two soldiers on horses began firing back; Tom ducked behind a slab of concrete as a bullet ricochet right in front of him! Greygor reined Sampson up the small hill, the horse jumped the guardrail and his hooves thundered towards the soldiers ahead! He took aim and fired his rifle at the soldier to his left hitting him between his shoulder blades, he flew over the head of his horse and the animal ran right over his lifeless body! The captured people were all scrambling to the ground to avoid being shot or trampled. He rode hard as Tom and Tony kept firing out at the remaining soldiers. The last man on the wagon had jumped into the back and had began firing as the last one still on his horse fired tried to escape to the woods on the other side of the interstate! Tom fired his rifle at the one left in the wagon, the bullet slammed into the bench above his head! The soldier took this opportunity to fire back, as he raised up Tony fire his gun hitting the soldier in the neck knocking him back!

Greygor rode after the last man as he made it to the edge of the woods; he kicked Sampson and leaned forward as the horse quickened his run! The Soldier rode fast through the woods looking back every chance he got, his eyes widened in fear to see Greygor slowly catching up with him! The man attempted to fire back at him but his running of the horse hampered his aim immensely. He let his rifle slip back into its holster on the horse as he gripped the reins and followed the soldier through the woods!

The trees ended abruptly into an open field and the soldier thought it might give him a chance to escape as he slapped the horse's reins into a quicker run across the flat field! However, Sampson was a bigger horse than the stallion that the soldier rode; his huge leg muscles gave him an advantage! Sampson jumped out of the edge of the trees landing seven feet out into the field landing hard but taking off like a shot after the soldier sending up a cloud of dust. They gained on him as Greygor reached to the small of his back pulling out his flying G; he kept his arm back ready to throw it when the time was right! The soldier attempted another shot, and Greygor heard the bullet whiz by his ear as he let his arm spring forward taking aim. The weapon flew through the air as the blades sprang out and spun towards the soldier! It sliced into the back of the man making his body jump up into the air as the horse went forward and the soldier flew up and then tumbled across the ground! The horse stopped running after a few yards and finally came to a stop as he reined Sampson to a stop next to the man's lifeless body.

Drawing his pistol he jumped from the horses back and walked over to the body on the ground, he reached down placing his foot on the lower back of the man and pulled the flying G out! He wiped the blood off and made the blades spring back in before placing it back in its holder on his lower back. He rolled the man over looking at his wide-eyed expression that was still on his dead face. He felt remorse for the lives that he and the others had to take to save the survivors, he shook his head sadly, as he picked up the soldiers rifle and ammunition. He found a notepad in the man's pocket and pulled it out; he opened it and read what the soldier had written on the last page;

"*Found eight surviving civilians today pass the South Carolina border we are keeping three, 2 old ones eliminated! Still no sign of any other military traveling this way...*"

His blood began to boil as he looked back at the dead man on the ground. He still felt remorse for taking life but felt anger welling up at the military! He got back up on Sampson and rode over to the tired horse, he grabbed the horses reins and tied him to his saddle horn and headed back towards the interstate.

Tom and Tony had already released the prisoners when he arrived back and were hiding the dead bodies with help from the men. The women were helping gather what supplies they got off the soldiers and placing it on the wagon. He hopped down off Sampson and greeted Uncle Mike and Uncle Mark who were very glad to see him. They were invited to travel with them up to Daniel's home and to join them when they went to the Lair. Uncle Mike told them that a group of relatives and friends were still hidden up close to their homes in shelters; Greygor promised them that once they were settled into the valley they would go find them and bring them to the safe place that had been found. The small group quickly finished and started their ride up the highway and towards home.

Greygor rode ahead of everyone deep in thought but still keeping his eyes and ears open for any problems ahead. They reached the place where the three men had spotted the soldiers and prisoners and made a right heading towards the town and mountains behind it. The buildings that had once stood very close next to each other were now lying on the ground like dominoes on top of each other. Again, there were no signs of life anywhere. They got out of town fast and headed up the mountain road towards home he stayed ahead thinking. Tom reared his horse to catch up to him and came up on the right side of him.

"Are you alright?" Tom asked, "Your awful quiet."

"Just thinking about getting everyone moved and settled in the Lair." He answered quietly.

"You have a bit more than that on your mind from what I can tell."

"It just bugs me to have to take a life even if it is to save people in danger and then to read how those soldiers killed two people for just being old, it gives me mixed feelings."

"Do you think we were in the wrong for saving these people's lives?" Tom asked looking back towards the people,

"Of course not," he said. "Just wish we didn't have to kill anyone to do it."

"I know you feel remorse for the lives we took today and that is good, just make sure you don't lose that because once you do your soul is lost."

"I realize that my friend and trust me there won't ever be a time I enjoy killing." He said shaking his head, "Now let's get home!"

The day went by quickly once they were back at their homes; the three men recounted their stories of how they rescued Uncle Mike and Mark from the soldiers along with the other four people, before telling about the lair area. The three women and the other man were a neighbor of the Uncle Marks. They were all greeted warmly and invited to join everyone for dinner. Pat held him tight after hearing the story of the rescue thankful that he was safe. He could feel there was something more on her mind but did not want to get her more upset, so he left it alone for now. They all sat around the fire planning the move to the safer area, after hearing that it had turned out to be better than expected. The wagons could be loaded in the morning and last minute work could be finished up by tomorrow evening. They would start out the next morning very early so that they could be settled in by nighttime. Uncle Mark told Paula that her sisters and a few more neighbors were in shelters up close to their homes and that they would have to get them to the new home also before the military found them.

It got very late and Paula went down into the shelter to make up extra beds for their new arrivals with the help of Jessica. Sean and his family headed off to their shelter for the night wishing all a restful night.

Pat took Greygor by the hand and asked him to follow her; they walked down the driveway and then cut down through the yard towards what was once Daniel's grape vines. He was surprised to see a tent all set up just pass the metal poles that had been used for the grapevines that grew here.

"What's this?" He asked.

"A little bit of privacy for the two of us." Pat replied as she pulled him into the open flap.

They sat down inside of the tent and Pat turned on a small battery operated lamp, she then sat facing him holding both his hands in hers.

"I just want you to know that I love you very deeply, she said as tears glistened in her eyes.

"I know you do baby and I do the same," he said somewhat confused at where this was leading. "What's wrong baby?"

"Well, we have been together for a lot of years and I know you better than you think," she started, "I know your dying inside worrying about your family up north, I want you to know if you feel like you have to go find them I will understand."

"I don't want to leave the boys and you."

"We will be fine, if this is something that you have on your mind I just want you to know I will stand behind you on this."

"If I decide to go off searching for them it could take a long time and we haven't been apart for more than a day since the day we were married."

"I know but knowing your hurting inside in the weeks to come will hurt me a lot worse than you being away for a few months. I love you enough to let you go and do what needs to be done, I won't watch you suffer and you better not make me either!"

"I would have to go alone and travel light," He began thinking aloud.

"Dad has a lot of things figured out for you," She said. "At least I think it may be good that Luck goes with you he is very protective of you and can help warn you of danger."

"You know the boys will want to go and they won't be easy to convince otherwise."

"Don't worry dear, I have that all planned out also." Pat said, "I just want you to promise me that you will be very careful and get back to me quickly."

"I promise honey." he smiled as he leaned over and kissed her deeply on the lips.

Their arms wrapped around each other as the kiss grew deeper and their bodies slowly went from a sitting position to lying beside each other. They both could feel the passion growing as they caressed and held each other. They were lost in each other's love and let go of all their thoughts and worries of the outside world. They shed their clothing and blanketed each other and they made love to each other as time slowly went by. Their bodies intertwined and seemed to melt together into one as love took over. It was not long before the passion of their love grew to satisfy their inner most feelings and they both collapsed in each other's arms letting the sweet feelings flow through their veins. Sleep overtook them as they lay face to face holding each other tight.

Chapter 4

The ride to the Lair went slow, Greygor, Tony and Tom rode well ahead of the wagons on horseback followed by Jacob and Austin who rode close to the wagons. Daniel drove the first wagon with Paula riding next to him while Pat and Jessica rode in the back. Uncle Sean and his family drove the second as Uncle Mike and Uncle Mark drove the last two. They halted the wagons well away from the highway as Greygor, Tom and Tony checked out the highway in both directions for any military activity. They came back to the wagons and began moving them across the highway and up the road that would lead them to the lair.

Greygor was joined by his sons as they began their descent into the lair down the long curvy road. Luck sniffed the ground and walked quickly ahead of them trying to avoid the horses hooves whenever they got to close to him. The dog would dash back to the wagons occasionally and jump up into the one Pat rode in and let her pet him for a few minutes before jumping back down and running up to take the lead of the travelers. Jacob and Austin both kicked their horses into a run and headed down the road and around the curves as Luck followed them. Greygor just smiled and let them go off to have fun; he knew that the rest of the ride would be a piece of cake and a lot less dangerous. The boys knew the way to Lake Lair and it should be safe enough for them.

Jacob and Austin raced down the curvy road laughing and ribbing each other as they went; Luck passed the two of them and barked back at them as if he was laughing at the slower animals behind him. The dog's speed was amazing, he use to race Greygor's car down the road every morning that he use to drive to work and was clocked at thirty miles an hour if not more at times. The boys slowed their horses down and watched as Luck flew down the road almost a blur to their eyes.

A loud roar from the side of the road sent the horses bucking where they stood, the black bear came up from the right side and stood up on his hind legs growling and ready to attack! Austin fell off the back of his horse as it took off back up the road; Jacob's horse was frozen in fear as the bear started towards them. Austin crawled back feeling a shot of pain in his ankle that had twisted in the fall. They could see the bear had been burnt badly during the nuclear storm and was in an unstoppable rage! Jacob drew his gun but just as he aimed the bears paw went across his horses face sending them both reeling to the ground, the horse landed on top of his rider as the bear began ripping open the horses neck! It rose above the dead horse looking down at Jacob who laid unconscious and growled deeply as it got ready to attack. It roared loudly as it felt the rock crash against its snout! It shook off the pain and turned its attention towards Austin who had thrown the large rock at him. He reached for another as the bear started towards him.

It stopped in its tracks and let out another roar of pain as the yellow blur that was Luck began his quick and vicious attack. The dog came up between the bears legs and clamped his teeth into the bear's neck twisting his body around and letting his paws claw at the animal's chest. The blood began to pour as the bear attempted to swat Luck away but the dog was too fast and let loose his grip fell to the ground and shot away! He only went about six feet and then turned and jumped up at the bear once more, he practically leaped over the bears shoulder but crunched his teeth into the side of the bears face stopping him in mid air and twisting his body hard into the back of its neck. It went face first into the ground as Luck let go and flew to the ground landing on his feet and got ready for another attack. Luck growled what sounded like a warning to the bear as it attempted to stand again, it got up on all fours and started towards Luck as three shots rang out from up the road and the bullets slammed into the bears head sending it backwards and down over the side of the road.

Austin looked back to see Greygor, Tom and Tony riding down towards them. Luck went to the side of the road looking down at the dead animal and then turned to greet his master wagging his tail wildly and barking. Tom quickly jumped from his horse to assist Austin and looked at his ankle to make sure it hadn't broke in the fall, Greygor and Tony pulled Jacob out from under his horse and revived him. Luck walked up and began licking Jacobs face glad to see he was fine. The wagons pulled up and the boys were helped into them, Jacobs's horse was pulled off the side of the road and the men let it slide down over the hill. They would come back and bury both animals in a few days. The boys sat on the wagon nursing their wounds and telling their family what had happened.

"You boys are always getting into some kind of trouble." Daniel laughed relieved that they were fine.

"How were we to know some crazy bear were was going to show up and want to make us into its breakfast!" Austin asked humorously as he rubbed his ankle.

"He just knew you two boys were so sweet he just had to have a taste of you." Paula looked back smiling at them.

"Luck really took that bear down all by himself?" Jacob asked, "Last thing I remember is watching the bear slap my horse in the face."

"It was awesome!" Austin smiled. "He was all over that bear and it didn't even get a lick in on him!"

"Three bullets to the forehead ended the fight." Tom said riding alongside the wagon as they proceeded down into their new home. "But had we not shown up when we did I believe Luck would have finished it off pretty quick."

By noon the group had stopped in front of the lake deep inside the lair, they all felt the peacefulness of the area and already felt safe and at home. Greygor and Daniel walked towards the old motel they discussed his idea to make it into the initial living quarters for a few families. He looked it over from the outside already figuring how to change things to create private living areas for each family. Paula began to prepare lunch for everyone with the help of her daughters as the men took care of the horses. Luck roamed around the building sniffing and marking his new territory until he finally jumped up on the porch of the motel and fell asleep; everyone left him alone knowing he was worn out from his battle with the bear.

The days went by quickly as the work progressed at a fast pace, within two weeks they had the motel fixed for each family to live comfortably and have the privacy that they needed. The boys each had their own room and Pat and Greygor had a bedroom upstairs with a balcony and bathroom. They had fixed it so each family had an upstairs that led down to a small living room and kitchen as well. The women had washed the beds and linens that had been left for years, Paula knew all the tricks to making laundry fresh even if it had any mildew or were overly dirty. The walls and ceilings were washed as well as the floors throughout the building. In time, a lot more work would have to be done but it would keep them all busy.

Daniel also started on the plans to create traps alongside the roads to protect them from anyone who tried to attack them. He would ride out daily to check out the areas the traps would be built as well as his ideas for watchtowers. Uncle Mark along with Tom and Tony headed out to the shelters to find the survivors they had left there and to bring them into the Hidden Lair as everyone had began calling it. By that evening, everyone was greeting Paula's sister Jeri and Dee to the group as well as Mark and Mikes wives as well. There were four other men and their wives as well with them. Everyone helped them settle in.

Every morning Greygor woke up early and began his exercise regiment, one particular morning he started his run up to the lookout point after stretching his muscles out, he figured it had to be at least a half mile run up the mountain. He started at a slow jog feeling his muscles strain as he pushed himself up the mountain. He quickened his pace to an all out run until he reached the top. As he rested he looked out over the valley down below, he loved how quiet and peaceful it seemed even though the swirling clouds above kept it a bit dark. He started to stretch his body out, arms legs and torso were loosened up and readied for a long workout. He had studied the martial art of Shoatan that which included the animal styles of the orient.

Taking his stance he begin with the first of the six he had been taught be Master Phillips. The snake style was an opened handed chop and tangle attack that he began with, going through the attacks and blocks he started off slow but sped up as he allow the ability to flow through him. He switched over to panther, an aggressive partially opened palm attack that also used the elbows and knees in close quarter fights. Eagle claw was a ripping attack as well as highflying kicks and rapid hits to the neck and chest of an enemy. He then started the Crane style, the graceful fighting ability with quick hand jabs as well as kicks that seemed to come out of nowhere! Next came Tiger claw with the use of the second knuckles of the fingers. His were hard and tough and could rip skin as it hit its target. Finally yet importantly, the Dragon claw fighting ability. It mixed all the animal styles into one as well as added special moves and attacks to the array of abilities. He thought about his teacher as he moved, kicked swung and made himself into a human weapon. Master Phillips taught him very well to control his abilities in every way.

"*Remember one must let the animal's power and abilities to flow through him at all times to be able to strike with proper speed, agility, strength and precision."Phillips would say,"let your senses take over as a true warrior should, always be one step ahead of your opponent know what he has coming at you next!*"

He felt the wind whip around him as the cool sweat let him know he was working all his muscles. The snap of his strikes seemed like thunder in the air and different kicks he threw were fast as lightening. Time seemed to slow as he listened to his own heartbeat and his senses all grew more intense, he became more aware as he progressed with his workout. He stopped abruptly letting his mind and body calm down. He breathed deeply as his muscles relaxed and his heartbeat began to slow. He sat down crossing his legs he began meditating letting his mind remember his lessons from years ago. He thought back to the time of Master Phillips and how if he ever got to over confident how his master would challenge him very quickly. Normally he ended up lying on his back in a lot of pain looking up at Phillips.

"Well, Well? What happen to you my student?" Phillips would say in his mixed Korean accent, "I think ones head got a bit too big and made easy target for my fist and leg?"

"Yes sensei," He would say, "I hope you will forgive my foolishness."

"One must know the difference between over confidence and the warrior sense that you have or your enemy could easily find your head a bigger target than you want!"

He smiled as his memories flowed through his mind, Master Phillips was the wisest man he had ever met and was sad to hear of his death a few years back, though he had lived to the age one hundred and twenty. He stood up and took his sword from its hilt; he held it out from his body allowing the weight to be felt by his arms. He began practicing different swings and blocks and let the sword slash through the air as he quickened his pace. He let the sword stab out then swings back towards him and then into a figure eight swing before adjusting the weapon for a few more blocks and swings.

"Remember Greygor," Master Phillips would say, "most men get a weapon into their hands and only think of what they can inflict with it or how they can get the upper hand over their enemy. A true warrior allows whatever weapon they have in hand to become an extension of their mind and body and lets their essence flow through it to become one with the weapon.

The sword moved fast and accurately around his body, it would become a blur to the eyes. The sound it made in the air let you know it was there. The movements ended with his arms to his side and the sword back in its hilt on his back. The final movement had been so fast that even he did not remember doing it. He looked up at the sky and smiled, "Thank you Master."

He arrived back at his home and to the waiting arms of Pat; she led him in to the kitchen table and poured him a cold drink.

"Dad wants to go over the maps and your trip later," she said as she sat across from him.

"It's getting close isn't it?"

"Baby please don't worry I will be fine," she said smiling over at him. "There's plenty of work to do to keep me busy and I really do understand what you have to do."

"I know honey but I know you're going to worry and be upset while I am gone."

"Greygor, I will be worried but I know you will be careful out there and you'll be back to me as soon as you can."

"Do the boys know yet," he asked.

"Of course, they have a huge list of reasons why they should go with you and they are going to talk to us later about it."

"This ought to be interesting."

"Just remember our plan and it will all be fine." She said with a smile.

Daniel and he sat at the dining room table hours later going over the maps of the highways and shortcuts that he would have to take to reach Kentucky and Pennsylvania. Greygor would be taking the smallest wagon with Sampson, pulling it along the roadways.

"You know Daniel, he pointed. "If this tunnel here in Tennessee is not blocked it could save me a lot of time."

"You would have to leave the secondary roads to get through it but you are right, as long as there's no soldiers traveling on it at the time you are."

"Once I get through it I can travel through the forest into Kentucky and up into the Cumberland area where I can find my folks and brother."

"The small wagon should get through easier than one of the big ones as long as you're careful." Daniel said, "I would suggest sticking to the secondary roads or even old dirt roads when you head up through Ohio and into Pennsylvania."

He noticed Jacob and Austin coming through the door but acted as if he had not seen them yet. They walked over to them and waited to speak.

"Yes boys?" He said without taking his eyes from the maps.

"We wanted to talk to you about this trip you're going on." Jacob said.

"You want to wish me good luck?" He slowly looked up at them.

"Well yes," Austin said. "But we have been talking"

"And you two want to help load up the wagon for me tomorrow?" He said smiling.

"No dad," Jacob said. "We feel we should go with you to help keep you safe."

"Yea, you shouldn't be out there alone!" Austin replied.

"I'll have Luck with me."

"We know but you need us to watch your back." Jacob said.

"Then who is going to keep your mother safe while I am gone?" He asked. "I mean, everyone here has someone to protect them so far but if I take the two of you, your mom will be at risk."

"Maybe they feel that they can't keep her safe and should go with you to get out of the responsibility?" Daniel added.

"I never thought of that." Greygor said, "Maybe I am putting too much on them."

"You know if they don't have the confidence to keep me safe," Pat said walking over. "Perhaps we need to find someone else."

"Wait a minute," Jacob said, "We have no problem keeping mom safe!"

"Yea, we have learned enough to take care of anyone who tries to hurt mom!" Austin said a bit angrily.

“Perhaps we should ask Tom or Tony to help keep her safe.” Paula added.

“Hold on!” Jacob said, “We are quite capable of making sure mom is safe if anything happens!”

“We both are strong enough to do it!” Austin said standing with his hands on his hips.

“Then its settled then, he said clapping his hands loudly, “you two will stay here and keep your mother safe from harm and I will go off with Luck and find your grandparents, uncles and aunt!”

The boys at first shook their heads in unison agreeing with their father, they started to turn away but stopped and turned back.

“Understand something boys!” Greygor said firmly before they could say anything, “I appreciate what you are willing to do for me but I do need you to stay here and keep your momma safe, I will not change my mind! Is that understood?”

“Yes dad.” They both said together as they walked away whispering to each other about what had just happened..

They finished up with the map work as Paula and the girls finished getting the supplies ready to load on to the wagon outside. They all said their good nights and headed off to get good night’s sleep. Pat and him went to bed and held each other close, each in deep thought about tomorrow.

“Do you think the boys will try again?” He asked her.

“I doubt it,” she said, “I think they understand your decision.”

“You’re not going to ask me if you can go.”

“Heck no,” she smiled, “you’ll want to play around every night!”

“I will probably want to every morning as well!” He said winking at her.

“You are so bad, baby.”

He leaned over to her kissing her as she wrapped her body around him, they enjoyed the sensation of their bodies coming together as their love took over. They felt each other’s needs grow and knew that tonight would be a very emotional night for the two of them. They made love to each other bringing tears to each other's eyes as they each enjoyed the love that they always shared. Sleep eventually over took them as the night slowly went on.

Pat helped her husband get dressed in the morning, something she did not usually do; she buttoned his shirt as she gazed into his eyes the whole time. He put his boots on as she helped comb his hair that had grown longer than he normally kept it, the goatee and moustache he had let grow in the last few weeks was really starting to thicken. She really did not like it but decided to put up with it since it was hard for him to shave right now. Light began to filter through the window as he stood up and walked over to it and looked out at Sampson being hitched to the wagon, Daniel rigged the harness to be easy to take off if Greygor needed to jump to the horses back in an emergency. He also noticed that Daniel was working on the inside the wagon and wondered what he was doing. Pat came up behind him and placed his long leather jacket over his shoulders and gave him a hug from behind. They walked out of the room and down to the wagon where everyone had gathered.

Daniel took him over to the wagon and showed him the two secret compartments that he had fixed inside the wagon. On one side was a shotgun with shells and on the other was a rifle with bullets. Both were loaded and ready for use if the need would come up. Jacob and Austin came up to their father and handed him his holster and then his pistols. He put them on and hugged the boys' goodbye. Everyone wished him a safe trip and hugged him. Pat did everything she could to hold back the tears and was the last to hug and kiss him before he got up on the wagon bench; he leaned down and kissed her one last time.

"Love you baby," he said quietly.

"Love you more," she said as tears flowed down her cheeks.

He sat up and shook the reins making Sampson walk towards the road that would take him out of the lair and on his way.

"Luck!" he yelled back.

His dog ran up to the wagon and leaped into the back; he got up on the bench with Greygor and sat next to him. He waved one more time to the family he was leaving behind and went around the curve out of their sight. He made it to the top of the mountain within an hour where he stopped to let Sampson rest awhile. He looked out at the road ahead and wondered what he would find once he reached his destinations. He prayed that he would find his family safe and unharmed. He hoped that once he did find anyone he would be strong enough to keep them safe on their journey back to the Hidden Lair.

Chapter 5

Traveling along the back roads of North Carolina He traveled in a northwestern direction, it was slow traveling due to so much debris on the roads. Many times, he had to stop and move things from the road or backtrack to find a clearer way to get through. There were no changes in the look of the wooded areas or fields; he passed by looked as if they had been scorched by the nuclear storms. He could just imagine what the main cities of the world looked like from the initial explosions, probably flattened and still smoldering with no signs of life what so ever. He had not seen any military movement as of yet and had been on the road for two days now. He found a safe quiet place to camp the past nights where he would feed and water the animals and then take care of himself afterwards. He enjoyed the dried deer meat that he had an abundance of; though very salty, it was delicious. He shared it with Luck whom ran ahead of the wagon most of the time with his nose close to the ground and his ears perked up at all times.

Before falling asleep both nights He would read further into the journal that had been Bert Mellows son's diary, it told of Presidents Matthews objectives and was very in depth. Though he thought Matthews was a lunatic, he had great respect for him and knew not to underestimate his military or his abilities. The journal told of secret weapons that Matthews may have that he had not divulged to his followers, all of whom had been made promises of wealth and power in the near future for standing behind his plans. So far, all of his plans had gone the way he wanted them. It seemed that there might be no stopping him from being very successful. He wondered what it would be like to be the ruler of the world, perhaps at first, it may be awesome but after a few months, it would get very boring and monotonous. He also thought about Pat and his boys; he missed them already and only had been gone two days. He knew they were safe in the Hidden Lair as everyone had started to call it. Daniel had already started work on the traps and guard stations and with the help of what they started calling his Trapster group that which included Uncle Sam, Mike and Mark as well as Tom and Tony would have things built up quickly within weeks. The second night of camping He fell asleep a bit easier thinking about all of it.

He awoke on the third day knowing he was right at the border of Tennessee and would be heading north up on the interstate later on in the morning. He quickly washed his face and combed his hair back before having a small breakfast of canned pears and peaches. He fed Luck and then Sampson; He then secured the saddle to the horses back and then hooked him up to the wagon. He put on his long leather jacket and then loaded up all of his weapons; the two pistols across his chest were more for Pat's wishes than for his need of them being there. The leather Jacket hid them very well in case he ran into trouble.

After two hours of traveling down the back road, he had been on for the last two days he unlocked the harness from Sampson and jumped up into the saddle upon the horses back and began riding towards the interstate followed closely by Luck. He found a path through the woods and headed up to the highway that he would now begin traveling. He cautiously listened and looked around under cover of the trees before getting on the interstate; he looked for tracks along the road and listened for sounds of movement from all directions. He rode a little ways in both direction and was pleased to see very little debris along this road and he did not see any signs of trouble either. He quickly rode back to the wagon and hitched Sampson back to it and drove the wagon up on to the highway and onward north. They could move a little bit faster now but still had to be careful. He let Sampson go as fast as he wanted; the horse neighed over at Luck who barked back as if they were carrying on a conversation. Sampson began a fast trot as

Luck bolted ahead running at his blurring speed. He just laughed and shook his head at his two traveling companions, he knew that Luck was showing off to Sampson and was taunting him as he barked back at the horse. Luck rounded a curve ahead and stopped dead in his tracks! His ears perked up and he stared ahead for a few minutes sniffing the air around him. He stopped the wagon and reached into his coat placing his hand on the butt of the loaded pistol. He reined Sampson slowly forward towards Luck. As he rounded the curve and pulled along his dog, he could see the tunnel entrance.

"What's wrong boy?" He whispered to his dog.

Luck let out a deep low growl still not moving from his spot. He listened and looked into the darkness of the tunnel. He could not pick anything up but trusted his canine friend's keen hearing. He started again towards the tunnel entrance as Luck followed close to the wagon never taking his eyes off the tunnel. They stopped at the entrance and he unhitched Sampson from the wagon and grabbed the high-powered rifle from its hiding spot. Taking the horse by the reins, he slowly walked towards the entrance.

"Stay here Luck!" He whispered as the dog sat down to wait.

He remembered that this tunnel was over a half of a mile long and decided it would be safer to walk through it first before bringing the wagon. He entered into the darkness and proceeded very slowly feeling his way along the concrete walkway that maintenance men use to use years ago when servicing the tunnel. He used his keen senses to get him through the pitch-black tunnel that seemed to be curving to the right as he made his way. Going on he started to hear what sounded like talking coming from the other end, he finally could see the light at the end of the tunnel as it straightened out. He cautiously went on not making a sound. Up ahead he could see the exit was blocked by a fallen tree and its branches that would give him cover to look out at whatever was on the other side. The voices seemed to be getting louder as he got closer to the tree limbs; he also noticed that he could probably run Sampson right through the branches without any problem if necessary. He stopped Sampson a few feet back and dropped the reins as he stayed close to the wall and snuck up to the fallen limbs at the exit. He held the rifle tight as he carefully peered out under the cover of the branches.

There on the highway before him sat a M109 howitzer self-propelled artillery tracked vehicle facing away from the tunnel. Its long 155-millimeter barrel pointed in the same direction as the howitzer. On top of the vehicle sat a soldier with his M-16 rifle lying across his lap, he was watching two soldiers standing over three people kneeling with their hands tied at the edge of the road next to a deep chasm along the side of the road. Two older men and a young soldier with a bruised face kneeled there with their heads down. On the other side of the vehicle laid a body of a woman, there had to be either at least two or three more soldiers around inside the howitzer or roaming around somewhere. He could hear a female screaming and crying from within the vehicle. He listened to the leader of the group begin to speak;

"These three prisoners have been found guilty of treason against the United States of America!" He yelled loudly to his men. "The penalty for this crime is execution by firing squad!"

"You're the only criminal here Captain Frank!" The young soldier shouted kneeling before him with a mouthful of blood. "Rape and murder are still crimes!"

Captain Frank motioned to the soldier next to him who used his rifle to smack the defiant soldier in the face knocking him sideways to the ground!

He tightened his grip on his rifle as anger overwhelmed him for a few seconds at the sight of what was before him. Greygor slowly brought the rifle up to his shoulder and took aim with his scope on the soldier next to Captain Frank. He clicked his tongue and Sampson came up behind him letting the reins lie over his other shoulder. The soldier on top of the howitzer grabbed his rifle up and readied to assist the soldier on the ground in the execution as soon as Captain Frank gave the word. He surveyed the situation at hand; it had to be twenty-five yards to the howitzer and to the prisoners that were at least ten yards apart. He would have to take out the two primary targets that had rifles and then Captain Frank. He could feel his awareness and senses begin to peak as his finger began to tighten on the trigger.

The shot rang out as the rifle bucked against his shoulder and the first soldier's body fell hard against Captain Frank, He aimed again at the soldier up on top of the vehicle who was attempting to stand and he shot again hitting him in the chest and sending him backwards off the front of the howitzer. He leaped backwards grabbing Sampson's reins as he dropped the rifle to the ground, as the horses started forward hard through the branches. He was already in the saddle as they penetrated what they had been using as cover; he had both pistols in his hands and readied himself for the attack. One of the prisoners leaped up and tackled Captain Frank to the ground as He rode hard towards the howitzer. A soldier started out of the top of the howitzer as another came out of the back door and used the huge metal door as a shield. The soldier on the ground began to fire at Greygor who fired back; the bullets ricocheted off the metal door causing the soldier to take cover. He fired at the soldier on top of the vehicle hitting him square in the forehead sending him reeling to the ground. A shot was fired from his left as he looked over seeing Captain Frank shoot the man who had knocked him to the ground.

Greygor aimed at him as the bullet from the other soldier's gun hit his forearm knocking the pistol from his hand. He felt the burning sickening feeling run through his arm as the bullet went through. Sampson was about to go pass the howitzer as he jumped from his back and let both his feet slam into the heavy metal door! The force of his leap slammed the door close on the screaming soldier who was crushed within it. He flew to the ground and rolled to the side of the howitzer and began to stand up. The shot ricochet off the metal side of the vehicle and he turned towards where it had come from. Captain Frank had his pistol trained on him and Greygor stopped and lowered his arms to his side as he stared at him. He was a tall muscular soldier with jet-black hair and a wicked smile. He let his left wrist muscle tighten and twist and felt the cold metal of his large throwing knife slip down into his hand from its sheath in his leather jacket.

"Now, wasn't that invigorating?" Captain Frank said snidely. "You did rather well up until now traitor, you took out all of my men and came close to finishing what you started!"

"You never know Captain I may just finish it in a few seconds!" He said with a slight growl in his voice.

"You are a cocky little fellow!" Captain Frank laughed, "It is a shame that I have to kill you for treason."

"Nah, it's a shame I have to kill you for just being a total asshole!" He replied nonchalantly.

"You really believe that don't you!" He laughed.

Time seemed to slow as from the corner of his eye Greygor noticed the yellow blur heading towards Captain Frank from the tunnel.

"Can I have the name of the man whom I must kill now please?" Captain Frank asked.

"Greygor Josephs!" He shouted.

"Farewell, sir!" Captain Frank raised his pistol and took aim.

Greygor saw the yellow blur speeding towards the Captain. From six feet away it leaped up and he watched as Luck's mouth clamped down on his enemies right wrist and the gun flew up in the air as Frank screamed in pain! He threw his knife and heard it sink into Captain Franks shoulder deeply, he leaped behind the dead soldier as Luck and the Captain rolled on the ground towards the hill, Luck let go of his wrist and jumped away as Frank rolled over and down the hill! The gun landed and went off with a loud bang! He felt a sinking feeling as he heard a loud yelp come from Luck. As he looked over, he saw him crumple to the ground. He jumped up and ran over to his dog and picked him up in his arms, tears filled his eyes as Luck raised his head and licked a tear from his master's cheek and then breathed his last breath. He held his old friend tight as he tried to compose himself.

"You did good dog." He whispered against his ear. "Thank you."

He stood up and looked over at the two surviving men who were both kneeling with their hands tied behind their back. He pulled a knife from his belt and walked over to the men, cutting their ropes he helped them up and the older of the two ran immediately over to the howitzer.

"His daughter is on it," the other man said as he rubbed his wrist to bring back the circulation. "Thanks for saving us."

Greygor, who had been watching the man help his daughter out of the vehicle turned to the other man and stared at him. "You're a soldier?"

"Yes he was, he risked his own life to try and save my family and ended up being marked a traitor," He said coming up to his side. "My name is Phillip and this is my daughter, Anna.

He reached out and shook his hand and then shook Anna's hand as well.

"I am Private Jenkins, but my friends call me Kent!" The younger man stated as he reached out his hand. "Thank you for saving us."

They shook hands and Kent began telling Greygor about what happened. The soldiers had been a few days out of their shelter heading to the meeting area up north when they ran up on the small group of twelve survivors. They initially had been helpful and nice to the group but by the next morning, orders were given to kill the weak and keep the women and the stronger men. The orders were carried out and only two women and two men survived and were brought on the trip north. On that same night, the soldiers tied up the two men and took the women into the vehicle. The soldiers including Captain Frank took their turns with Phillips wife and Anna the fourteen-year-old daughter. Kent had grown angry and refused to follow the orders of the captain. The soldiers subdued him and added him to the other prisoners. During the attack on the women, Anna's mother attempted to escape and was shot as she ran from the soldiers. This morning the order to kill all the prisoners and the traitor was given. Greygor began looking around at the area accessing what needed to be done. Weapons and supplies needed gathered, bodies buried and the howitzer disposed of.

"We need to clean up this place before we move on." Greygor stated.

"I need to bury my wife and my brother," Phillip said sadly. "She is lying on the other side of the howitzer.

"I will help you." Kent placed his hand on his shoulder.

"My wagon is on the other side of the tunnel," He replied.

"I'll go get it!" Kent said walking away, "Be right back."

He disappeared into the tunnel and Greygor looked over at Phillip, "You sure we can trust him?"

"I believe so," Phillip replied. "He almost died with us for what he believed in."

The four of them worked together burying Phillips family and then the soldiers that had been killed. He took Lucks body over to the tunnel entrance and buried him away from the other bodies as Phillip, Kent and Anna began gathering up supplies and weapons.

He patted the dirt down and knelt by his dog's grave. "You saved me pup, I will always remember that. I will miss having you around my friend!"

He got up and walked over to help the others, on the way he found his pistol and rifle that he had dropped. He winced as pain shot up his arm from the bullet he had taken. He dropped to his knees holding his arm. Kent ran over to him and noticed the blood; he grabbed the arm and held down on the wound to stop the bleeding.

"Phillip!" He yelled, "Get the first aid kit inside the howitzer and bring it here!"

After a few minutes, Phillip came over and handed him the kit, Kent began cleaning the wound on the arm and bandaging it. Kent pulled out his canteen and made him drink.

"You're lucky the bullet went all the way through and missed bone," Kent said, "You need to rest; you lost a lot of blood."

"You sit here," Phillip told him. "We can gather everything and finish up, and we can camp here tonight and move on in the morning."

By sunset, everything had been gathered and the howitzer had been destroyed. So that it could never be used again. They had collected seven M-16 rifles and 2 pistols all with ammunition. The food supply was minimal but it would be useful. Anna had cooked a pot of stew for everyone and they all sat around the campfire eating.

"You three can have whatever food that was found and I would suggest you take some rifles as well." Greygor said feeling a bit stronger now that he ate.

"Perhaps we all should stick together," Kent, replied, "There is strength in numbers."

"I don't think it would be too safe for the three of you, I am heading north to find my family and get them to a safer place south of here."

"Perhaps we can help you?" Phillip asked, "I am pretty good with a gun, and Kent here has a lot of backbone from what I can tell."

"I appreciate you all wanting to help but I can't endanger your lives," He said, "You need to get to a safer place yourselves."

"Well, as you can see we really don't have any idea where a safer place would be and we don't want to end up in the militaries hands again," Phillip said. "You saved our lives and we could be a great help to you in finding your family and getting them safe."

"I don't know." He said back."

"Listen Greygor," Kent added. "The military are heading north to a meeting point, they are capturing and killing survivors as they go, I don't want to be the one to tell you this but your family could end up like we were. Their groups will merge and there will be more than just six or so soldiers together. There will be hundreds and eventually thousands together. You are one man against a growing danger that will kill you if you don't start using your head a bit."

"What did you say?" He said a bit angrily.

"You seem like a good fighter," Kent kept going. "And to be perfectly honest you got lucky this time, you almost got killed and had it not been for your brave dog we all would be lying dead here instead of sitting here around a campfire."

"I see what Kent is saying," Phillip said. "We do appreciate what you did for us but you need some help to get through this. To be blunt, four heads are better than one. Kent knows the ins and outs of the military and has been a trained in fighting. I am a bit older and wiser than you are and may be able to offer you some advice. My daughter can help with the cooking and camping and though young can handle a gun. Honestly, we would be more help than you may think."

Greygor sat there pondering the idea of letting them travel with him, both men made a good point and they both seemed willing to help him. "I do hate to admit it but you both have some valid points, I don't want you do this because you feel you owe it to me for saving you but because of the reasons you said."

"We want to help you because you need help my friend." Phillip smiled.

"Alright then," he said. "You can travel with me but you have to do as I say at all times!"

Both men agreed Greygor looked over at Anna who had said nothing so far; she was looking down with her arms folded in front of her. He could see she was shaking and she began slowly shaking her head no.

"NO!" She yelled shocking everyone around her, "I will not be used again! I would rather die than have to go through that hell again!"

Greygor stood up quickly and went over to her and knelt in front of her, he knew what she was already thinking.

"Listen Anna," He said quietly and calmly, "No one here or anywhere will treat you in that way again, I will make sure of it. I know you trusted those soldiers and thought you were safe. Then they attacked your mother and you in horrible ways. It won't happen again."

He reached into his jacket and pulled out a pistol and handed it to her, she stared down at it with her tear-filled eyes and then looked up at him.

"I want you to take this and if you feel threatened by anyone around you I want you to shoot them." He said to her. "Even if it's me, it will be understood why you did it!"

He stood up and walked back over to where he was sitting and sat down. He finished his drink and then got up and walked over to the wagon, grabbing a blanket he crawled under it and laid down to get some sleep. He closed his eyes and listened as his three new friends found places to sleep as well and went to bed for the night. He slowly fell asleep and the dream came once more,

Up on the ledge once more he looked down on the masses going about their lives safe and happy. They all had done well he felt. He felt Pat's hand gently touch his shoulder.

"You did it baby." She said softly. "We are all safe at home."

Urgency, Came upon him as he drew his sword and raised it up! He blocked the oncoming blade and struck out with his other hand knocking his foe back! Swords clanged as he lunged out and sliced the air trying to stop his attacker! They came face to face as their swords locked up!

"They are mine!" He said with a deep voice!"

"Never!" He yelled back unlocking his sword and swinging it out feeling it slice against the enemies ribs!

He could hear him scream in pain as the dream went black!

He awoke to the flashes high in the sky; he wiped his sweaty brow trying to figure out why he was having these wild dreams. He closed his eyes once more and fell into a deep sleep once more.

Chapter 6

Deep within the national forest of Kentucky the small group made their way slowly and cautiously. They had traveled another day on the main interstate and now had gone two days through the trees and brush of the woods. Greygor was still wondering about what had happened to the body of Captain Frank. Kent and he had searched for hours for him at the bottom of the hill before they moved out but could not find any sign of his body or of him running off. They hoped wild animals had dragged him off but were concerned that no signs had been found of that as well. Kent and he had been talking a lot about the military and after he had shown him, the journal Kent confirmed a lot of what had been written in it. Kent told him how Matthews had sent out word to his military forces of the date the nuclear storm war would happen, the soldiers were dispersed to shelters in different locations called cells. Each cell was to emerge at different times and then meet at the rally points in different locations. Kent and his group were one of the first set to exit and meet in the north. The order was to capture and detain any survivors. Captain Frank had been given the secondary order after they had left the shelter.

"So, who is leading the military now?" Greygor asked as they walked through the woods.

"What do you mean?" Kent replied.

"Well, with Washington D.C. getting hit so hard Matthews has to be dead."

"He is alive and well waiting for his soldiers near Somerset." Kent replied, "His last transmissions came from his secret hideout up north."

"I should have known he would run and hide, he knew D.C. would get hit the hardest so he split leaving his followers there to die."

"He wants world domination." Kent said sadly. "He had to make our enemies think he was there so he taped his last speech days before he left and then played it while he went to his hideout, most of his closes followers didn't even know he left till it was too late."

"So he pretty much has the upper hand then." Greygor said more to himself than to Kent.

"He did have a big glitch in his plan that he had not planned on." Kent replied.

"What glitch?" Greygor asked.

"Well, he didn't count on the ANA hitting our ammunition dumps as hard as they did, unless the cells had the weapons, tanks or artillery pieces within their bunkers there is nothing else left."

"That could be a plus for us!" Greygor said with a smile.

"Yea but he is now trying to find other weapons to use along with the weapons the cells have, swords, bows, knives." Kent added.

"I know someone who may be able to help us then." He said. "Guess I may have to find him and pay him a visit."

"The chances of other survivors up north are pretty slim." Kent replied.

"Oh believe me if I made it he definitely made it!" Greygor said patting him on the shoulder with renewed hope!

They continued traveling through the forest finding the best route for the wagon which was never to far behind, Anna had been driving the wagon as her father lead her along the trails that Greygor and Kent had found or made. Being deep in the woods, they relax a bit knowing that the soldiers would be traveling the main roads and staying out of the forest. He knew that they had to be getting close. Kent and he stopped to rest and wait on the wagon; they drank from their canteens and grabbed a bite of beef jerky.

He had started to get use to having Kent around and actually started to like the younger man, he seemed to be very informative and very social. His basic training had built him up pretty well and he stood at least five-foot-seven. He kept his dark hair military style and his face clean-shaven. He had a friendly personality but could probably take care of himself in a fight. Phillip also seemed very friendly as well. He was about ten years older than Greygor and had the same stature as Daniel. His hair was graying and short and he was tough when need be. Anna of course was shy and at fourteen that was unusual. He felt most of her quietness came from what happened to her and after talking with Phillip had been correct in his thinking. She had a small muscular like frame of a body and long dark hair. She was a farmer's daughter for sure. He did not talk with her much unless she initiated the conversation. He knew she needed time to get over the things that she went through, if she ever would, was the question.

They saw the wagon coming up the path with Phillip guiding it towards them. He waved when they came in sight and Anna actually did to for once. Both men must have been thinking the same thing and smiled at each other hoping she would be ok. Greygor handed Phillip his canteen once they stopped the wagon and he took a quick drink to quench his thirst before handing it to Anna who jumped down off the wagon and walked over to Sampson and began petting and praising him for traveling so well through the woods.

The three men began gathering firewood as she fed and watered the horse; they figured that stopping early would not hurt. They talked as they worked, Phillip began telling a story about a fishing trip years ago that had turned bad. They laughed at the outcome that left Phillip falling into the river and having to be saved by his daughter.

"That was bad!" Kent laughed as he picked up another piece of wood.

A high-pitched whistle broke the laughter as an arrow splintered the wood in Kent's hand! He dropped his armful and dived for the nearest tree and readied his rifle. Both Greygor and Phillip dived for the closes tree as two more arrows flew into the ground close by!

"Anna!" Greygor yelled looking back towards the wagon as an arrow hit the side of it! "Take cover!"

An arrow slammed into the tree that he was behind as he tried to look out and up the hill.

"They're shooting from that high line of brush up the hill!" Kent whispered over to Greygor, "They have us pinned down!"

"I can't get a shot on anyone!" Phillip replied. "Whoever it is keeps moving after they fire."

Another arrow hit close to Phillip, he ran for another tree as arrows hit the ground behind him as he went. He dived behind the tree and kept low. Greygor jumped out from behind his tree and ran a few yards up the hill firing his pistol up at the bushes; he dived behind a large rock as an arrow nipped his boot and slammed into the dirt. He looked down at where Kent and Phillip were trying to figure out a plan.

"Kent." he whispered loud enough for him to hear, "I need you to run to the second tree to your right while I give you cover fire."

Greygor twisted to his left and began firing up at the brush as Kent dashed right and went pass the first tree and dove behind the second as arrows followed him along the way!

"When I give the word I want you both to begin firing above the bushes straight up from where you are!" He whispered the orders to them.

Looking back at the wagon he saw Anna under the wagon and beside the wheel with a rifle in hand, she gave him the thumbs up that she was going to help surprise whoever was up there.

"Now!" Greygor shouted.

The three rifles began firing in unison as he began running up the hill using whatever he could for cover as he went and fired his pistol along the way! Whoever was up there had been surprised, as Greygor had hoped, as he got closer! Finally, he could see a shadow moving quickly behind the thickets, he ran up to the bushes and began a mad dash to catch up to the shadow behind them. He caught up and as he did he dived into the bushes and into the body that he had been following! The gunshots stopped as he rolled down the other side of the hill trying to grab hold of their attacker! The wrestling match was not going as good for Greygor the man flipped around and landed on his back slamming his face in the dirt! He swung his elbow back catching the man in the cheek causing him to roll off! He rolled the other way drawing his other pistol and aiming at the man! The attacker already had his bow cocked and ready to fire, pointing right between Greygor's eyes!

"Thought you didn't like guns?" The man replied with a smile.

"I always thought you were a better shot? Greygor smiled back. "Especially with that thing."

"What can I say?" He answered, "oh by the way, sorry about your canteen!"

He looked down and felt the wetness down his leg and saw the four arrow sticking through the water vessel on his side. "Damn bro, you are good at that stuff!"

"How are you brother?" He said standing up and helping Greygor up.

"I am doing well, Arthur!" He took his hand and let him pull him up. "How are the kids and mom and dad?"

The brothers hugged each other happily as Kent Phillip and Anna came around the bushes.

"Hey there," Greygor smiled at them. "I want you to meet my brother, Arthur."

"He was trying to shoot us?" Kent asked confused.

"Nah," Arthur shook his hand, "just trying to scare you a bit, didn't realize it was my brother till he tackled me in the brush."

"You could have been shot young man!" Phillip replied.

Nah, you all shot too high even before you started laying cover fire for my big brother." Arthur took his hand as well in friendship. "Where's the wife and boys G?"

"They are in North Carolina in a hideaway with Pat's family." He answered. "How many survived on Xanadu Mountain?

"We have Mom and dad, my three girls and two sons, four uncles, three aunts, eleven or so cousins and about three hundred people or more." Arthur said. "It could be four hundred."

"You must have had a huge shelter."

"Uncle Jake does know how to build things!" Arthur answered back with a smile and a wink. "Guess we should get your wagon and head to the camp."

It did not take long to get moving, Arthur listened as Greygor told him of the events that he had gone through since leaving the shelter in North Carolina up to saving Kent, Phillip and Anna.

"Wait a minute G," Arthur said to his brother. "You attacked and killed soldiers, twice?"

"They had the first group of civilians in chains bro," he answered, "and had already killed two people in their group and were going to kill them as well!"

"That's not good!" Arthur stated.

"Are you defending the soldiers?" Kent stopped walking and stared angrily at Arthur.

"No, Kent," He said, "It's just that if that's what the military are doing then our family and the people on the mountains are in deep trouble!"

"Why do you say that?" Greygor asked.

"Because we found their meeting area and were about to go meet up with them," Arthur replied. "We are running out of food and water up there and didn't know they were doing that kind of thing."

"They will all be slaughtered!" Phillip added.

"You don't understand Arthur," Kent said "The soldiers are under orders to enslave or kill any survivors that they run into!"

"We got to get them to the Hidden Lair in North Carolina!" He stated more to himself than to his brother.

"What is the Lair?" Arthur began to ask.

"Yes the Hidden Lair," He replied. "It's a large valley we found surrounded by mountains and it has three roads in or out. It is easily defendable and hard to find. Pat's father and the other survivors there are working on making it even safer as we speak."

"Is it big enough for all the people on Xanadu Mountain?" Arthur asked.

"You should remember the area brother; we use to go there every summer."

Arthur thought, "Yea, now I do, you're talking about Lake Lair aren't you?"

"That's it brother!"

"Hell, that place could hold triple the number of people if not more."

"Only problem is moving all those people there." Greygor said.

"No brother, the first problem is convincing them all that the military is doing all these evil things!" He replied, "The council is voting on heading down there tomorrow evening and it's not if to go, it's when to go!"

"We got to let them know it's dangerous!" Kent said. "We can't just sit back and let them walk into a slaughter!"

"I agree Kent," Phillip added, "If we could talk to the people perhaps they will listen."

"What is the council and who is in charge of it? Greygor asked.

"Uncle Jake is the leader of it and dad is on it as well," Arthur told them "We can talk to them first; they will let you speak at the meeting tomorrow and tell everything you know."

"Still, the problem is moving all these people safely south." He said.

"Hey bro, you're always telling everyone to take things one step at a time," Arthur patted his shoulder "Its time for you to follow your own advice."

He knew his brother was right. Arthur had always been the one who talked sense to him when things got difficult and stressful throughout their lives.

"We will help you too," Phillip said, "whatever you need we want to back you."

"If we work together we can make it." Kent added.

"I will help you too!" Anna yelled from the wagon, "I don't know how but I will!"

Hearing her say that meant a lot to Greygor, he looked back at her and smile. She smiled back at him and that made him feel even better inside.

They continued traveling through the forest as they talked; Arthur told them it would probably take another three hours to reach the camp. The brothers were the same in stature, both short but muscular except Arthur was an inch or so taller. He had blonde hair that he kept cut short and brown eyes. He was a single man now with four kids to care for, choosing to use his skills with the bow and arrow working as a forest ranger in Kentucky. Arthur felt his children would be safer in this area with all the things going on in the country. He began practicing archery as a child, over the years his aim and abilities grew better and even began creating his own bows and sets of unique arrows. Greygor knew he would be a great asset in a fight.

He felt some of the weight lift from his shoulders but his mind was still on his older twin brother and sister as well as his youngest brother and their families. He hoped that they had survived and were all right. He would have to find them before the military did. He wondered how he was going to get all the people on Xanadu Mountain safely down to North Carolina as well as find his siblings in Pennsylvania.

Arthur placed his hand on his shoulder knowing he was thinking of everything. "You have to take one step at a time bro, one step at a time."

He smiled at his brother and shook his head. That would have to be his way taking things a step at a time until he reached his wife and children again. Doing it would keep him alive and all those around him safe and hopefully out of danger.

Chapter 7

Greygor hugged his mother Darla and his father Robert tightly very happy to see them, as they were he. He then greeted his brother's children as well. Kayla the oldest was first, she was fifteen with long blonde hair, blue eyes and was blossoming into a beautiful young teenager. Kandace hugged him next, she was fourteen with brown hair, blue eyes and medium build unlike her sister who was very skinny. Arthur's thirteen-year-old son came next. Eric with his long blonde hair was about as tall as his father was already and was muscular like his father as well. Last but not least was Trenton; he was ten with blonde hair like his brother and father.

They all had come running up to him yelling "Uncle Grey! Uncle Grey!"

He smiled and felt very happy as he hugged each one of them. He introduced his friends and then explained about Pat and his boys being safe down in North Carolina. Uncle Jake Trotter came up to see him next and hugged him followed by Greygor's cousin Beth and her husband Dutch, his cousin Donny, Danny and Rich. Other people came up to welcome them all to the mountain, happy to know others had survived after the bombings. Uncle Jake showed them where they could set up the wagon and camp. After settling in Uncle Jake told Greygor to meet him and his parents over at Robert's cabin. Arthur walked with his uncle towards his parents place as the four new arrivals fixed everything up. After about an hour he walked over to his parent's cabin.

The cabin was small but an adequate place for his mom and dad. Both had retired from the retail business years ago and settled here in the Kentucky forest. Darla was a very small and skinny woman of around sixty-eight; she was very strong willed, loving and caring person. She had reddish brown medium length hair, brown eyes and an angelic face. Her children and grand children all had her facial features. Robert at seventy-two looked to be fifty at the most; he was short like his sons with a medium build as well. His white hair had disappeared from the top of his head but he still had it on the sides. He had been a great salesperson before he retired and taught his children the retail trade even though all of them went their own ways. Greygor and his siblings had grown up in a very loving home where their needs were met throughout their lives.

Darla was waiting at the door for him when he arrived kissing him on the cheek and hugging him again as she welcomed him into the cabin. He went into the dining room where his father, Uncle Jake, Arthur and Uncle Jake's oldest son Danny sat around the table talking. He sat down next to his father as his mother stood behind her son placing her hands on his shoulders.

"Well son." His father started. "Your brother here told us a little about what's been going on with the military and as you know we were about to go and join a camp a few miles away."

"Could you fill us in on what you have seen and know so far?" Uncle Jake asked.

"Well, I guess the best place for me to start is this journal that was given to me." He took the book out of his pocket and handed to Uncle Jake. "It tells a lot about what the military and President Matthews have been doing to prepare for world domination."

He then started telling his family about the military he first encountered in North Carolina and how he led an attack on them to free the survivors that they held captured. He then told how he rescued his traveling companions from the soldier's seconds before they would be executed at the hands of the soldiers at the tunnel. As he told them, Uncle Jake read the journal. He was shocked at what he read. He handed it over to Robert who put his glasses on and began to read as he listened to his son.

"We need to figure out what we should do," Uncle Jake said. "We can't go down to that camp, it would be a slaughter."

"We could move the people here down to the Hidden Lair," Greygor replied. "There should be room there for everyone, water and food supplies might have to be built up but that can be done as we go and once we get there."

"What are we going to do cousin, walk there?" Danny asked. "That's a long way for the kids and the older folks."

"We could convert all the boat trailers into horse wagons," Uncle Jake answered. "We have close to fifteen horses here in Xanadu and Arthur had seen a large herd of horses southeast of here that we could go and get."

"We need to talk to everyone tonight and let them know that there is a change of plans and why." Robert said. "We need you to speak to them son, and let them know what has happened."

"I'll ask my new friends for some help in that." Greygor replied.

"What about the military that are camped over by Somerset, how do we know that they aren't going the same way?"

"Well," Greygor said, "I have a plan to sneak down into the camp and get information about their plans and then we can go from there."

"And who exactly is going to sneak into their camp?" Darla asked staring over at her son. "Well mom, the only one who could actually get away with such a stunt is me."

"You have a wife and children to think about!" She said angrily. "You can't risk your life like that!"

"Arthur can lead me down to it and my friend Kent can help me get in." He said, "We have to know their plans mom to be able to get out of here safely."

"I'll go in with you to help keep you safe." Danny replied.

Robert looked over at his wife, "honey he is right, he is the only one who is capable of getting in there and out without getting caught."

"I watched the goings on at the camp," Arthur said, "New arrivals to the camp have to pull guard duty on the same night they arrive, he could get in the morning find out what ever information he can and then sneak off while on guard duty that night."

"Seems like we have a few good plans going," Jake said, "Robert and I will go talk to the council about the meeting tonight. Arthur you need to gather a group of men and go after those horses that you mentioned. Danny you need to get a group together and start working on the boat trailers, lighten them up and make them easier to pull. Greygor can go talk to his friends and see if they will speak tonight to the people."

They all got up from the table bidding each other farewell. Greygor was the last to leave and had gotten to the middle of the yard before he turned to see his mother coming out the door she walked out to him.

"Can we talk?" She asked.

"Sure mom," He smiled at her.

She walked over to him and took his hand in hers; he felt her warm dainty hand squeeze his gently as she smiled back at him.

She looked into his eyes. " Honey, I know your taking on a lot right now, and you think you have to do all of it yourself to make sure everything goes right and nobody gets hurt or worse. You need to remember though that everyone around you will do what they can to lift some of this weight from your shoulders."

"I still need to find our family near Pittsburgh ma." He said looking away and up into the sky.

"You will Grey." she said placing her finger against his chin and making him looks at her. "Out of all my children, you would be the one I would trust and want to find our family and protect them from harm. You are strong and have abilities others can only dream of having, I know you will use them well and get our family together again and safely away from the military."

He took her in his arms and hugged her. "Thanks mom, I love you!"

"I love you too honey." she said with tears welling up in her eyes.

He released her and began walking towards his camp. His heart seemed to swell and feel very warm, her words echoed in his head as he caught sight of Kent and the rest waving at him as he approached them.

The people of Xanadu Mountain gathered at the meeting place rapidly that night. Greygor and his three traveling companions sat in the front row with a few of his cousins. Up on the makeshift stage sat the council, his father Robert and his Uncle Jake sat facing the crowd along with Uncle Jake's brother B.J. and four other men who had been introduced to Greygor before the meeting. Phillip, Anna and Kent seemed a little nervous about speaking in front of the crowd. Phillip placed his hand on top of his daughters and patted it reassuringly. Greygor looked over at his cousin Beth, she was a small woman with red hair, dark eyes and she was always very pleasant. She sat next to her brother Donny, using sign language to talk to him. Greygor knew sign language and noticed the conversation. She was telling him about Arthur, Dutch her husband, and a group of men went out to find horses for the upcoming move. Uncle Jake stood up and walked over to the podium, he looked down at the papers that were sitting there and then looked out to the crowd waiting as the people became silent. He cleared his throat and smiled at everyone.

"Good evening to all of you!" He spoke in the microphone just loud enough for all to hear. "Today my family welcomed my nephew and a few friends of his into our camp. We were glad to learn that they had made it through the nuclear storm and that Greygor's wife and children are safe down in an area of North Carolina awaiting his return."

The crowd began to clap and again Jake waited for all to quiet down once again.

"Well as most of you know." Jake began again. "Tonight we were to vote on when we would present ourselves to the military so that we could receive their help and get food and water. The soldiers were to be our saviors and protectors."

Uncle Jake's face grew grim as he looked out at the people he had help save from the nuclear storms that had ravaged the world. The crowd could see the upset in his face and the night grew very silent.

"Fortunately, the council has learned that the military has become a threat to all survivors that they meet up with!"

Uncle Jake fell silent as the people talked amongst themselves, their disbelief and worry about what they were to do now could be heard as the voices grew louder.

"This can't be!" One man yelled from the crowd. "How do you know this?"

Many in the crowd joined in shouting for more information, the voices growing even louder as Jake raised his hands into the air trying to calm everyone so that he could speak again. Once more, they became silent.

"I know this is a hard thing to understand," Jake started, "I know we all feel let down and very angry to hear of such things but it is better to learn it now than to walk into the military camp and be attacked and captured!"

The murmurs throughout the crowd began to rise again as Jake raised his hand once more to silence them.

"Please, if everyone will try and calm down I will bring up Greygor and his friends to give you information on what the military has been up too!" He said waving them up on the makeshift stage.

The four of them got up and walked up and stood next to Jake and faced the crowd who once more fell silent. Uncle Jake shook all of their hands and then walked back to be seated with the rest of the council.

Kent walked up to the podium and looked out at everyone, "My name is Corporal Kent Jenkins, and I was stationed with the 23rd Armored Division out of Fort Gordon. In the last two years, my unit was used for missions to help stop terrorist acts from actually happening on American soil. About a year ago we were called up into Alaska to guard the pipeline, it was reported to us that the ANA forces were on their way to capture the pipeline. My unit was ordered to fire upon the pipeline and destroys it before it could be taken from us. We did as ordered and we demolished it with our tanks. After returning to Fort Gordon we learned that President Matthews was telling the world that terrorist had destroyed the pipeline!"

Kent went on to tell of numerous attacks that the military had done that were blamed on the terrorist of the ANA. He then went on to tell about the orders that they received a week before the nuclear storm missiles were to strike. The soldiers were to gather up their weapons and supplies and enter the bomb shelters at each fort. Numerous cells throughout the country were to exit their shelters at specific times and make their way to rally points designated by the commander and chief of the military. His unit was one of the first to exit the shelter and began moving north to their meeting area that which was close to Somerset Kentucky. Orders were given that any civilian survivors found were to be evaluated and then made use of or destroyed. Kent stopped at this point and let the information sink into the people's minds.

"No more than a few weeks ago my unit came upon Phillip's camp." Kent continued. "We were ordered to befriend them until further orders."

With that, Kent took a step back and allowed Phillip to step up to the podium. He stood looking out at the crowd and then began to speak. "When the military arrived in our camp we were very happy to see them."

Phillip went on to tell how the soldiers sat and had dinner with the twelve survivors and made small talk. Phillip invited them to stay in the camp overnight and all seemed well. In the morning the soldier's leader, Captain Frank gathered his soldiers next to their tank and gave them the order. Within fifteen minutes, the soldiers had slaughtered eight of the twelve civilians in the camp! Phillip and his wife, his brother and his daughter Anna were put in chains and led off by the soldiers who were suppose to be protecting them. That night after making camp, the soldiers dragged his wife and daughter into the tank and began raping and beating them. He tried to help them but Captain Frank bashed him in the head with his rifle. All he could do was lie there and listen to his families screams.

"That is when Kent here shoved his Captain back and began yelling at him that the whole thing was unmilitary!" Phillip said looking back at him. "Kent began walking towards the tank, Captain Frank ordered him into the tank to take out his aggressions on the women! Kent turned and punched him in the mouth! Two soldiers grabbed him from behind and the Captain got up and ordered him to be shot by firing squad the next day! The screams from the tank grew louder as the women inside were attacked!"

Phillip stood there with tears forming in his eyes. Anna walked up to him and hugged him. She then let him take a step back as she took over the podium. Anna stood there and took a deep breath and closed her eyes tight. When she opened them and looked out at the crowd, she knew that she had to be strong and tell her story.

"My name is Anna," She started, "The soldiers were cruel and as they beat my mother and I, my mom tried to get them to leave me alone and offered herself to them. She fought hard against them and tried to pull me out of the tank with her! A soldier hit her in the face with his rifle and then let her fall outside as he laughed; he then pointed his gun at her and shot her in the back as she tried to get up. I was attacked throughout the night. Soldier after soldier beat me and raped me, by morning I was close to death. Then as the sun beamed through the crack in the door, I could hear the leader yelling at the men to shoot the traitors! The next thing I heard was a horse running across the camp and gunshots!"

Anna looked back at Greygor and smiled at him though tears filled her eyes, she turned to look back at the crowd and pulled out her pistol and held it up in the air.

"He saved our lives and then saw his dog shot by the military. After all that had happened to me, I could not trust him and I wanted him dead because of what had been done to me! He understood my feelings and he gave me this pistol to protect myself if at anytime I felt in danger by him or anyone else! I wanted to shoot him right then just to keep myself safe! I am glad I didn't because after traveling with him these past few days I have grown to trust him and know he will keep me from harm!"

With that, she walked over and handed the gun to him, she then hugged his neck and kissed him on the cheek. He smiled at her and patted her on the shoulder as he walked up to the podium. He looked out at everyone.

"Since leaving the shelter down in North Carolina," he said, "I have had to rescue civilians from the military three times! The first time was successful and yes, I had to kill soldiers to do it! The second time, I ended up being shot but these three people behind me are now safe. Again, I did have to take the lives of the military to do it! For me to have to take the life of another human being is heart wrenching, I pray that God will understand that I only did it to save innocent lives."

He lowered his eyes and then gazed out at the people in the crowd. Everyone remained silent and waited for his next words.

"Now, I am faced with my third attempt to save people from the military." His voice grew stronger. "I am now here letting you know what the soldiers are doing and what awaits you if you decide to go to their campground just miles away! I know all of this is unbelievable but President Matthews is using his military to enslave and kill all of us so that he can become the master of the earth! He wants to be the conqueror of the world!' He will destroy anyone and anything to get what he wants!"

The crowd began to talk amongst themselves; many of them shook their heads in disbelief. He stood silent letting them talk to one another knowing they were concerned about what to do about water and food here on the mountain that was eventually going to run out.

"Listen!" He shouted. "I know things look bad and we all are scared of future possibilities! Yes, we are all in danger! We all must find the hope within us and do what we can to protect each other and find a safe place to go! I know our world as we knew it has been burnt to a crisp and all that is left is the ashes of our former lives! Together we can work things out one-step at a time! I know of a safe place that we can go to but we have to work together to make it there! In North Carolina, there is a place large enough to protect us all! I call it the Hidden Lair! It is surrounded by mountains and has only three protected roads that can be traveled in and out! Together we can make it there and live protected from the military!"

"What about food and water!" A woman shouted from the crowd.

"The lake there is filled by hundreds of springs coming down off the mountains that are clean water, my family and friends already there are gathering food as well as hunting for food and placing it in storage."

"How are we going to out run the military?" A man asked in the third row. "What if they are heading the same way?"

"In the next few days we will be taking a group down into the military camp, we will then infiltrate the camp and find out the information we need. Then we will figure out the best roads to take to reach the Hidden Lair."

"How do you expect us to travel all that way?" Another man yelled.

Greygor smiled as from behind the crowd came his brother Arthur and Dutch, they led a herd of horses up over the hill, everyone looked back to see.

The crowd turned back to the stage and began clapping and cheering for Greygor. He smiled and turned to see the council standing and clapping for him as well.

"How did you time that just right?" Kent leaned towards him and asked.

"I didn't." He smiled back at him.

Arthur rode up to the stage and jumped on it from the back of his horse. He walked over and shook his brother's hand. "I figured I would show up now before you bored these people to death."

Everyone began laughing loudly and continued to clap.

"We have a lot of work to do!" He yelled. "Get those trailers and such ready to move out!

Everyone began to scatter with renewed hope, heading off to get things done. The council left the stage as well. Uncle Jake walked up to Greygor with Danny by his side. Dutch jumped up on the stage too.

"When do you plan on heading out nephew?" Uncle Jake asked.

"Early in the morning before sunrise," He replied. "Kent you will be in charge of our trip inside the camp."

"What?" He asked surprised.

"Hey, Dutch I was wondering?" He turned to his cousin ignoring Kent. "Think you can handle acting like a soldier for a day?"

"I think I can handle that!" He smiled. "Never hurts to have an extra hand."

"Kent," Greygor turned back to him. "You will need to teach your men as much as you can on military dos and don'ts, as well as lend out some of your uniforms and equipment tonight. You will be in charge of the whole mission."

"Yea, ok." Kent said still in shock.

"Arthur?" He turned to his brother, "I want you to go around and find our best archers and marksman with rifles, get them together and find as many bows, arrows, crossbows firearms, and any other possible weapons you can find! I want every man, woman and child old enough to fight to start to train even before we get back have Richy and a few others help you gather people up.

Arthur shook his head, turned around and then jumped on to his horse and rode off. Kent and Greygor led the other two men off the stage and up to their camp.

Kent grabbed Greygor by the shoulder stopping him from going on and waving the other two on.

"What's up?" He asked.

"What did you mean that I was in charge of this mission?" Kent asked.

"It's just what I said." He answered. "You have the knowledge to get us safely in and out of the camp."

"That's true but you won't listen to a word I say." Kent replied. "You seem to be in charge of everything so far. How can I get you to listen to me?"

"Come on Kent, what are you really trying to say?"

"Well, when we get into camp for example. You are going to see civilians that the military have captured. Knowing how you are so far you will want to rescue them and jeopardize the information finding mission and get us all killed!"

"What if I promise to listen to your orders?" He smiled and placed his hand on Kent's shoulder, "I swear to keep to the plan and to listen to all orders given by you during this mission."

"You do realize that the military is nothing like it used to be, it isn't all about honor and protecting the weak. It is all about the strong destroying the weak and who can gain higher rank by destroying anyone in your way."

"That is why you're going to go over everything that you can with us tonight before we head out in the morning." He patted his shoulder. Then two of them headed up to the other men who were waiting patiently for them.

Chapter 8

The four of them began walking up the road two miles away from the military camp where Arthur had led them. They had left Xanadu Mountain at 3:00 A.M. and had reached this point around 9:00 A.M. with no problems along the way. Kent had trained the three men on everything he could think of and told them more as they made their way to the road. The uniforms they wore were fitted to them the night before by a few of the women in camp. Greygor remembered how neat and proper the uniforms had to be when he was in the armed forces. The uniforms now were ripped and torn; there were no gig lines because the shirts had no buttons. All rank was ripped of three of the uniforms and Kent's rank was still on his. The boots were no longer spit shined, they were scuffed and dirty. The only thing the soldiers now cleaned was their M-16s. Kent made them all carry their rifles on their shoulders barrel down, and had made sure Greygor had no other weapons on him. If the guards searched them and any other weapons were found and that could spell a quick end to the four of them. As they walked along the road Kent quietly went over how they should act while in camp and to follow every order given to them no matter what.

They had traveled a mile and a half on the road and saw horsemen heading towards them. They rode fast at first and then slowed the horses down and then stopped waiting for the soldiers to reach them.

"Halt!" The leader of the soldiers shouted at the four.

They stopped and stood at attention. They waited for the soldier to speak to them again. He looked them over slowly as his men kept their rifles aimed at them.

"What unit are you from?" He asked loudly.

Kent took a step forward. "We are part of the 23rd armored division out of Fort Gordon sir! I am Corporal Jenkins sir reporting for duty!"

"There are only four of you left Corporal?"

"Yes Sir!" He replied. "We met with resistance and the rest of my squad was killed!"

"Damn civilians!" He grumbled. "Sorry to hear that corporal. There have been other reports of attacks on soldiers."

"We will avenge our fallen soldier's sir!" Kent replied.

"By the way Corporal," He started, "at dawn the winds blow west."

"By sunset the winds shift and blow north." Kent answered with the password.

"Take your Men into camp, Sergeant Sanders here," He said as he pointed. "Will lead you to the main tent to be briefed by the general."

"Thank you Sir!" Kent said as he walked forward and the other three followed.

They followed Sanders down the road knowing that the other soldiers were behind them watching cautiously until they were out of sight of them as they went around the bend. They finally entered the camp and were astonished at the many tents both large and small that there were. The soldiers who were already there watched the new arrivals with suspicious eyes. They numbered in the hundreds possibly over a thousand. They were amazed to see the long hair, beards, moustaches and the worn uniforms. It was nothing like the old military Greygor had been in. They saw a fenced in area filled with civilians that soldiers had captured on the way to the camp. Kent knew that it was tough on Greygor just to walk on and not do a thing. The sergeant stopped at the large tent in the center of the camp, he dismounted his horse and walked up to the flap and went inside and announced that he had new arrivals, the four of them waited outside at attention. He came out of the tent and motioned for them to go in. They marched into the tent and stopped, letting their eyes adjust to the low lights within. At the table ahead of them sat General Snorpaly. He was a tall stout man with a balding head and small beady eyes. He looked up at them and then motioned for them to come forward. They took a few steps forward and then stopped and stood at attention.

"I am Corporal Jenkins of the 23rd Armored Division out of Fort Gordon reporting sir!" Kent said saluting.

The General saluted back, "At ease men and welcome to Rally point foxtrot. I will make this as brief as possible.

"Thank you Sir!" Kent replied.

The general went on to tell them that all new arrivals will stand guard on the outer perimeter beginning at 2300 hours tonight. He then told them that supplies and weapons were not to be used for gambling, all ammunition and weapons should be checked and wiped down before anything else. The mess tent opened at 11:00 A.M. for lunch. Tents were to be put up before sundown. He then explained to them the thing that they needed to hear. The camp would be broken down in 45 days and start moving north east into the Pennsylvania area to secure a large mass of civilians that have been sighted there. The general went over a number of other things that he considered to be important.

"Will there be anything else, sir?" Kent asked.

"Oh yes." He said. "You will be happy to know that Captain Frank from your unit made it here. He was pretty banged up and lost a hand but he is in the sick bay recovering."

"Can we go see him sir?" Kent asked hoping that the general would actually say no.

"It won't do you no good corporal," He replied, "He is unconscious and on very strong pain killers."

"He will be all right then?" Kent asked.

"He was pretty well out of it when he arrived; he was talking about being attacked by giant horses, a rabid wolf and a Wildman from a tunnel before blacking out."

"We hope he is all right sir!"

"Were you together when he was attacked?"

"No sir," Kent said. "We had been ordered by the Captain to search out civilians that had escaped from our capture. We were attacked and lost three men before we killed the civilians. When we got back to our unit everyone was gone. We searched for them and could not find anyone so we headed here."

"That's very good corporal." General Snorpaly said, "You are excused."

With that Kent returned to attention and saluted him, the four of them left the tent and started walking across the camp.

They had their tent up within an hour and rested while they waited for the mess tent to start serving. Soldiers came over to their area and welcomed them to camp. Greygor sat near the fire that they had made thinking. Kent walked over and sat beside him acting like he was cleaning his rifle.

"You do remember your promise?" He asked Greygor quietly.

"Yes corporal I do." He whispered back.

"Well then." Kent continued, "I am ordering you to stop thinking of ways to get to Captain Frank in the sick bay right now!"

"Yes Corporal Jenkins!" He said a low growl in his voice.

"I understand G that he killed your dog and those other people you were trying to save but we can't risk your friends and family up there on revenge. There will be a time and a place for everything that is going through your mind."

"Are you getting to know me that well already?" Greygor smiled.

"I promise you if you do anything to jeopardize this mission I will shoot you myself!" Kent replied firmly.

"That includes trying to rescue the civilians over there in those pens!"

"Yes sir!" Greygor said snidely.

"I am serious!" Kent said as sweat began to bead up on his forehead.

"I need your promise that you will not kill anyone within this camp!"

"I promise Kent." He whispered and shook his hand seeing how nervous he was making him. "I am sorry."

"Let's go get some food. "Kent smiled. "I am starving."

They got their food and Dutch and Danny sat away from Greygor and Kent to listen to soldiers talking on one end of the tent. Greygor and Kent talked and listened to soldiers as well. A medic who had been taking care of Captain Frank was telling the wild story to the other soldiers at his table. Frank had been out of it most of the time but he told the medic about the attack. It seemed that his unit was attacked by a wild man and he rode on a giant horse that trampled anything in its way. He had told the medic about the wolves that helped his attacker and how he sliced one of the wolf's head off with one stroke of his bayonet!

Greygor could feel his anger grow inside him but also started to grow concerned that the story that was being told was going to get him killed.

"Don't worry about it." Kent whispered against his spoon of soup he had been blowing on.

"That isn't how it all happened." Greygor quietly replied, "He is going to get me killed."

They continued eating listening to other soldiers talking. Another soldier was talking about the Commander and Chief giving a speech tonight at 1900 hours. He was going to let everyone know how things were going and let everyone know the next step in the military plans.

"Excuse me sergeant." Kent leaned over towards him. "My squad just got here today, are you saying that our Commander and Chief Matthews is here with us in camp?

"Yes corporal." The sergeant answered happily, "He arrived 2 days ago from his secret bunker up north!"

"That is fantastic!" Kent smiled.

"That is great!" Greygor added. "Thank God he made it here safe!"

They finished their meal and left the mess tent. Kent seemed concerned at what he heard but did not say a word once outside. They arrived at their tent and restarted the fire that had gone out. Kent was too quiet.

"Okay now?" Greygor finally asked, "What is wrong with you?"

"I think we need to get out of here when everyone starts heading over for that speech." Kent answered.

"Why?" He asked.

"Because, this adds another reason for you to slip up and get us all killed!"

"Oh come on Kent, I didn't even think about anything like trying to kill off Matthews!"

"Don't even tell me that it didn't cross your mind G!"

"I made you a promise! Greygor said, "I always keep my promises. I will not try to attack, kill, or free anyone while we are here."

"I expect you to leave your rifle in the tent the rest of the time we are here then." Kent added.

"No problem corporal, it's your orders!" He said getting up and placing the rifle in the tent and then returned to sit by Kent. "I am more concerned about that story told by Captain Frank, it is going to get me killed!"

"That is actually a good thing G." Kent replied.

"What do you mean?" Greygor asked raising an eyebrow.

"Don't you see," Kent answered. "If rumors and exaggerations are created by people around you and your enemies hear them they are more likely to want to seek you out and see if they are true. If they are started by your enemies and grow within their ranks they will be a little less willing to search you out to find out if they are true."

"I don't know if I believe that." Greygor smiled and shook his head.

"Look at all your heroes throughout history Greygor." he replied. "When I was in college I had a professor whom showed us how tall tales worked on the enemy's minds and how it helped the hero in battle and wars."

"Really, I never really thought about it that way."

"I am smarter than I look my friend." Kent smiled.

"Thank you, Master Kent," Greygor replied jokingly.

"Oh yes my pupil." Kent joked back making reference to an old martial arts show of the 70s. "And when you can snatch the pebbles from my hand you will be ready to leave!"

They both began laughing at each other's humor until they noticed three soldiers walk over to them and stop. They stopped laughing and looked up at them.

"Are you laughing at me?" He growled at Greygor. "I don't like people making fun of me!"

Greygor stood up and looked at the large soldier. "We were actually just telling jokes to each other as we talked."

"You're making joke about me!" He said angrily as he crossed his huge arms across his chest.

"I heard your name mentioned Corporal McKinney by this private!" The soldier on his right replied.

"Yeah I heard them!" The one on the left added, "I heard them, call you pebbles!"

"Whoa now nothing was even mentioned about you!" Greygor said trying to calm the problem down as a crowd began to form, "I apologize if you overheard us and thought you heard something you didn't!"

"Are you calling me a liar?" He raised his voice.

"Stand down private!" Kent stood up next to Greygor. "We were having a conversation between each other that did not involve any of you so let's leave it alone!"

"What did he call me?" McKinney asked.

"I think he called you a cow dirt taster!" The soldier on his left antagonized. "It sounds like they want to challenge you!"

"How the hell did you get cow dirt taster from the word conversation?" Kent asked looking at the soldier on the left.

"Are you challenging me private?" McKinney said angrily to Greygor. "Let's do it then!"

"There is no challenge!" Kent yelled, "Both of you need to stand down!"

"What is going on here?" General Snorpaly came through the crowd as everyone came to attention.

"This private here initiated a challenge to me!" McKinney angrily replied. "He called me a liar, and was telling jokes about me!"

"That is not true Sir!" Greygor said

"See sir!" He said. "He is calling me a liar!"

"The private and I were just talking and he misunderstood what we were talking about and his two friends here egged it on sir!"

"That is not true sir," Said the one soldier, "we were just minding our business when this private started making jokes about Corporal McKinney!"

"I have been challenged and demand satisfaction!" He shouted.

The crowd grew larger and started chanting challenge! The general looked around and shook his head.

He then backed away from them and shouted, "A challenge has been made. Let the stronger man win!"

Kent grabbed Greygor back towards the tent as McKinney's friends backed him away.

"Listen to me Greygor!" Kent said as he helped him pull his shirt off and then helped him with his boots and socks. "There is no way I can stop this so you're going to have to fight him."

"Don't worry I will just knock him out and be done with it."

They looked over at him as took his boots and shirt off, his muscles rippled on his arms chest and back, his stomach was the only thing fat on him. Greygor and Kent both gulped in awe at him.

"Hate to tell you this G. Kent replied, "A challenge fight is to the death!"

"I made that promise to you though!" Greygor said. "You ordered me not to kill anyone here in camp."

"Forget that order right now! Kent whispered, "My new order to you is get out there and you kill him as quickly as you can! Don't give an inch, you hit him hard and fast and take him down for good!"

"Yes Corporal!" He said.

"I am serious Greygor," Kent replied concerned. "Anything goes and do not play around, this is for rank and soldiers take that very serious."

Greygor turned and walked towards McKinney and the General, his eyes looked his enemy over trying to see any weak points that he could work on in the fight. He noticed a scar above his left knee and watched as McKinney rubbed his right shoulder. He made a mental note of the possibilities that he could take with the two areas. The general stood between both men holding his arms out to each of them.

"You both know the rules," General Snorpaly stated, "this fight is to the death, anything goes and the winner claims the rank of the deceased. McKinney, you will receive the rank of Sergeant First Class if you win and private you will be promoted to Corporal if you are successful."

He backed up a few steps and saluted them and they returned the salute.

The two men turned towards each other with their fist up and ready, they began circling each other as the crowd began yelling at them to start. McKinney took a swing at Greygor who ducked out of the way.

"A little slow there big man!" He shouted at the soldier.

"I'm going to rip you apart!" McKinney growled at him as he swung again.

Greygor brought his fist out hard and fast slamming it into the soldier's fist! Both their knuckles crackled on impact but McKinney was the one to pull back and shake his fist in pain.

"What's wrong big boy, did that hurt a little?" Greygor smiled at him as he backed up a few feet and readied for his next attack "Maybe you should go soak it fat boy!"

McKinney's face turned red from anger, Greygor knew that if he could get him mad enough he would get him to attack in a frenzy of anger. He could hear soldiers in the crowd laughing at his remarks towards the bigger man. It worked.

McKinney launched himself hard at Greygor bringing his fist around as he closed in on him; Greygor grabbed the soldier's wrist and let his body twist backwards flipping the McKinney over him and into the ground as hard as he could! McKinney landed on his back with a loud thump and rolled a few feet. He began to get up on his hands and knees but Greygor was already on him and landed a kick into the man's ribs sending him tumbling a few feet more. He backed up as McKinney slowly tried to get up again holding his side from the pain.

He got up and looked over at him. "I am going to kill you!"

Greygor didn't let him finish as he ran a few steps and did a jump kick up and into the big man's chest! Both his feet hit into him sending him flying backwards into the crowd of soldiers behind him. Greygor landed on his side but was back up ready for another attack. The soldiers who had caught McKinney pushed him back up and into the center of the circle formed by the yelling soldiers. Greygor again ran straight at him and brought his left fist across the man's right temple and his right open hand into his solar plexus, knocking the air out of him and bowling him over. He backed away from McKinney taking up a defensive stance a few feet back waiting for him to get up on his feet.

Greygor could now feel his warrior sense begin to kick in. The adrenalin in his body began to flow and he could feel all the sensations growing stronger. Time seemed to slow down around him; his concentration grew as the noise from the crowd faded. His enemy was finally back on his feet and tumbled as he walked towards Greygor. They began circling each other again.

"You look a bit tired big boy?" Greygor said, "Maybe I should put you down for good this time!"

"You are a little asshole!" McKinney yelled swinging his fist hard at him.

He blocked the punch and punched the soldier in the mouth and then spun on his heals bringing his other fist around hard hitting him again in the face! McKinney stumbled back as he spit blood from his mouth. Greygor jumped at him aiming for his face again but at the last minute went low and brought his foot into the soldier's knee as hard as he could. The strike bent his knee inward and toppled him to the ground. His huge body landed on top of Greygor who struggled to get out from under him. McKinney finally had the upper hand and brought his fist up and into Greygor's jaw knocking his head against the ground. The soldier crawled on top of him punching him as fast as he could as he did. Greygor attempted to block the punches as he fought to get away. McKinney was on top of him before he knew it and pinning his arms with his knees as he brought a fist down and across Greygor's face!

The punch sent an electric shock through his mind as his teeth ripped open his inside cheek. He tasted the metallic taste of his own blood filling his mouth. McKinney slammed his other fist down and across the other side of his face! Darkness began to take over in Greygor's head. The pain began to fade as well as the sounds of the crowd around them. Another fist came down into his face sending a flash of pain through him. The strength in his arms began to disappear as McKinney's legs crushed them into the ground. He faded deeper into the darkness as McKinney raised his arms up in victory laughing as the crowd began to clap and shout his name.

Within the darkness of his mind something began to form, blonde hair and the lovely face of his wife came to him. She smiled at him and he could feel her love build up inside of him.

It felt like a shot of electricity hit him! His eyes flew open and he felt his warrior sense once again!

He could see McKinney raising his arms up and felt the weight on his left arm loosen up. With all his strength he pulled his arm out and brought his fist up to his chest! He let his fist spring up and into the soldiers groin hitting it hard! His eyes bulged out as the pain knocked him over and to the side of Greygor who rolled a few feet away and jumped up on his feet! His warrior sense went wild and he let out a blood curdling scream sending the blood from his mouth spraying up in the air! He leaped up into the air towards McKinney who was on his knees attempting to get up! Greygor let his body twist around performing a roundhouse kick to the soldiers face. It sent the bigger man reeling to the ground as Greygor landed next to him and reached down and grabbed the man by the back of the hair and lifted him back up to his knees. His fist began pummeling the soldier in the face crushing his nose as blood sprayed out. He threw him to the side like a rag doll and jumped up in the air letting his feet come down with a hard thump on top of McKinney's chest and then leaped off of him and to the side. He looked out at the crowd with his back to his main enemy who struggled to get up on his knees. His warrior sense was at its peak as he turned back to McKinney, he walked up to him and wrapped his arms around his head and used all his strength and twisted hard! The loud crackling sound from the man's neck could be heard by the crowd as Greygor threw his now lifeless form to the ground and stood over him with his arms raised high!

The soldiers all cheered and clapped as Greygor hollered back to them in victory! He could feel his warrior sense telling him to finish this, he felt his enemies all around him and he readied to attack and destroy them all! His adrenalin began flowing wildly as his body tensed up ready to attack all of them!

Kent could see that more was about to happen, he jumped through the crowd and hugged Greygor hard congratulating him and then got as close to his ear as possible.

"You need to cool down G!" Kent whispered harshly. "We need to get on with our mission!"

The pain finally hit him as he came out of it. He reached up and lightly touched his cheek, it had already begun to swell and he began to slump to the ground. Kent grabbed him and held him up as General Snorpaly walked over to them.

"Congratulations Corporal."The General said looking down at the dead man and then at Greygor, I am glad you're on our side, now go clean up and you might want to go see a medic while you're at it."

"Thank you, sir!" Kent replied.

Kent placed Greygor's arm over his shoulder and they walked through the crowd over to their tent where Dutch and Danny were waiting. Kent poured water on a cloth as Dutch got a first aid pack out of his back pack. Greygor rinsed his mouth with cold water, it stung horribly. Tears welled up in his eyes as he swished the water around and then spit it out.

"I think we should try and get out of here as soon as possible." Danny whispered to the others.

"I think he may be right." Dutch agreed. "One of us could get killed."

"We need to finish this mission." Greygor whispered slurring his words through the pain. "It's too dangerous to leave before nightfall. We need to listen to what Matthews has to say and wait till after we report for guard duty tonight."

"Greygor is right," Kent added, "we have to let things settle down anyway after that fight and any information we can get from Matthew tonight might help us in moving those people off the mountain."

"Alright then," Greygor said, "Kent and I will hang here for a little bit, while you two walk around and get more information. Be very cautious as you do."

Danny and Dutch shook their heads in agreement, got up and walked off towards the mess tent.

"As for you Corporal," Kent said sternly. "All orders are now back in force!

"Yes sir!" He said lying his head down on his makeshift pillow. "Wake me when it's time for the speech."

He must have slept a good couple of hours before Kent had waked him up. Greygor washed his face again and could feel that the swelling had gone down a lot. The pain had calmed down as well but he could still feel the throbbing and a slight sting from the cut within his mouth. Bonfires had been set around the camp to make up for the light of the sun fading for the night. He put his shirt and hat back on as he watched the soldiers walking over to the large tent in the center of the camp and sitting on the ground waiting for the seven o'clock speech Matthews was about to give. Kent patted his sore shoulder and motioned for him to come on and they both walked towards the crowd. Kent had been especially quiet the whole time.

"You do realize I didn't enjoy killing that man?" Greygor finally broke the silence between them.

"I know G." Kent stopped and turned to face him. "There was no way around it but you need to try and get that warrior sense thing under better control. I am not upset that you had to kill that jerk, it was what you about did afterwards that could have got all of us killed. You need to think deeply about that!"

They continued walking with the crowd and met up with their other two friends and sat down beside them. Everyone was talking as eyes were on the tent front awaiting their leader's appearance. At 7:00 pm sharp, 1900 hours military time, the General came out of the tent and walked up to the podium. Everyone stood up and saluted. He returned the salute and then cleared his voice.

"Good evening to all," He started, "I have a few things to go over with you before we hear from our Commander and Chief. First off, as of today we have reached the two thousand mark of soldiers who have found their way to the camp. Two squads have returned to camp with a fresh herd of horses to assist us in our movement north into

Pennsylvania. We will begin packing up camp in twenty five days and marching northeast. There has been word that a large mass of survivors have been sighted and we must subdue them as soon as possible."

The crowd began to clap and wail their approval, and then quieted down once more. Greygor felt a sickening feeling in his stomach. He wondered if any of his family could be in the group the General had spoke of. Even if they were not it could get dangerous within that area.

General Snorpaly shouted sternly, "I am honored to present to you our Commander and chief, President Matthews!"

Every soldier snapped to their feet clapping and cheering as the General stood to the side awaiting their leader. From the tent he walked out wearing his military uniform. He raised his hands up high waving to his followers. President Matthews, through his black moustache and goatee smiled with such intense evil Greygor thought the devil himself had just walked out of the tent. He stood six feet tall and looked buffed in his uniform, as he walked to the podium his deep dark eyes peered out at his military as if he were looking into all of their very souls. Greygor clenched his fist, fighting the urges of his warrior sense to destroy the evil that had just emerged from the darkness. The military saluted him and he returned their salute with a snap! Everyone sat down and the crowd hushed.

"Good evening!" His loud baritone voice hit the crowd like a hammer, "We have embarked on a journey together unlike any in the history of the world! Alexander the great, Caesar or even Napoleon could not imagine the wonders and the treasures that our journey will eventually yield for all of us! Not only the treasures of Fort Knox, but we shall share all of the treasures of the world together! The world as we knew it had grown weak and ripe for the taking and that is what we have decided to do! Together we shall rule this world for we are the strongest military force known to man! We shall seek out any survivors throughout this world and they will succumb to our will and our might or be destroyed where they stand!"

Greygor not only listened to the words of Matthews but he also listened and watched the crowd's reaction. The soldiers were taking it all in and were on the edge of their seats with each word that came out of this man's mouth! How could they believe this bullshit? Matthews sounded like a madman and seemed to enjoy comparing himself to the most evil of dictators and leaders of history. He had no compassion for the billions of people he killed with the nuclear war he unleashed and only cared for his own personal gains! Greygor could feel his anger growing within him but did all he had to do to keep it from taking him over. The crowd finally began to calm down as Mathews waited to continue.

"In every journey such as this my soldiers," He stopped and glanced around the crowd, "there will be those who may try to oppose us! They may attempt to gather their own forces to try and stop us, attack us when our guard is down or even attempt to infiltrate our camps and destroy us from within! Together we must keep such things from happening! We will be traveling North in twenty five days to investigate reports of survivors gathering together and attacking our soldiers as they travel to our meeting points! Whatever we find as we go we shall destroy!"

The crowd began yelling and screaming for blood their approval to their mission! Matthews stood there with his wicked smile as the soldiers hailed his words. Greygor and his men followed along trying to keep up their disguise. Matthews raised his hands up into the air taking it all in as if he thought he was a god! The hair on the back of Greygor's neck sent a shiver down his spine. He knew this was going to be even more dangerous than he had thought. He was going to need extra help in making it to the Hidden Lair!

"All of you must ready yourselves for what is to come in the following weeks and months!" Matthews shouted, "We shall keep to our mission and take this world for our own!"

The cheers went up again from the crowd as Matthews turned and walked into the tent disappearing into the darkness. General Snorpaly walked back up to the podium and waited for the crowd to calm down.

"Everyone is dismissed for the evening!" He yelled over the murmuring of the crowd "We will begin recreating platoons and squads tomorrow as well as choosing leaders of these groups! We will have formation at 0600 hours! Corporal Jenkins and his squad and Sergeant Wilson and his squad will report to me at this time!"

He saluted all of them as the crowd began to disperse. Kent led his three men up to the podium followed by another group of four men. They all stood at attention in front of the general who was looking through papers that he had on the podium. He finally looked up at the two groups and told them to at ease.

"Your squads will be pulling guard duty for the night. Corporal Jenkins you will be taking the southern roadway and Sergeant Wilson will be covering the northern roadway. There are to be two men awake at all times and they will report to their squad leader at the ends and beginning of their shifts. Sleeping while on duty is punishable by execution. Any discharge of your rifle will be immediately reported to your squad leader and then to myself. The challenge and password will change at 0200 hrs to the next one scheduled. You are to report to your stations in one hour with full combat gear. That will be all, go to your tents and get ready, you're dismissed."

They all walked to their tents. The sergeant walked next to Kent as the other men followed.

"Be careful at that Southern check point I heard there has been a few attacks there." Sergeant Wilson told them.

"Thanks for the warning Sergeant we appreciate it." Kent replied as they parted ways.

By two o'clock in the morning they were following Arthur back to Xanadu Mountain and were miles away from the military camp. Not a word had been spoken as they made their way. Arthur as well asked no questions the whole way. He figured they were all trying to pull their thoughts together and didn't want to take no chances of getting caught. Their escape would probably not be noticed till sunrise and then they would have no idea what happened to Corporal Kent Jenkins squad. They had left the guard station as if some type of skirmish had happened. They left it for the military to come up with their own stories of what happened. Whatever, the story may be.

After traveling over several mountains for miles Arthur halted everyone to rest. Greygor sat next to his brother and drank his water still feeling the sting from his wounds inside of his mouth. He couldn't get over how crazy Matthews and all those soldiers were. He feared for anyone who might come in contact with the power hungry military. He placed his face in his hands trying to keep himself calm as well as figure out what he had to do to get his family to safety.

"It's all going to work out bro," Arthur said patting him on the shoulder. "Just take it one step at a time."

"We need some major fire power," he whispered as he thought out loud. "I got to go through Ohio to get to Pittsburgh anyway!"

"You're thinking of trying to find him?" Arthur stood up looking down at his brother. "He's too dangerous G!"

"You don't know him like I do Arthur!" Greygor looked up at him. "He isn't scared to kill if he has to and he has the weapon stash to do it!"

"You're too close to him bro!" Arthur replied. "Cole Cramer is a cold blooded killer and he doesn't care who he has to go through to do it, even you!"

"Cole is the best thief and assassin that there has ever been brother dear!" Greygor said sternly. "We need someone like him to watch our backs and get us through this!"

"He's dangerous bro," Arthur replied. "But if you feel we need him I'll help you find him if he is even alive."

"If anyone could have made it I know he had too." Greygor smiled.

Chapter 9

It had taken four days to get the people on Xanadu Mountain ready for travel. On the morning that they had got back Uncle Jake called a meeting of the people there. He quickly filled them in on the information that the four men had brought back with them. He had already put together a few groups of men to assist people in readying for the trip. Boat trailers and such were remade into wagons as best as possible, everything needed began to get packed up and readied for the trip. Greygor went over maps with the council and the men who would be assisting in the move. Kent and Arthur began assembling groups of people who would help protect the people during the move. They would be traveling east all the way into West Virginia to a meeting area where they would wait for Greygor and whomever he was able to find in Pennsylvania. Along the way and once there groups would check out vacated sporting good stores shopping malls and such for weapons, supplies and food and drinks to add to whatever they had.

Greygor had decided that he would head northeast with a small group on the day the people of Xanadu mountain started off. He chose Arthur, Kent, Dutch and one other man named Pete to ride north with him. Jake and Robert wanted him to take more but Greygor knew that the horses were needed to draw the wagons. He also felt they could travel faster and safer with a smaller group. Greygor had studied the maps for hours and figured he would make a beeline up through the Ohio area he felt Cole was probably holding up in and then head straight into Pennsylvania. His calculations gave him five days to travel, three days to search for Cole, five days to reach his search areas around Pittsburgh, ten to twenty days to find his family and then enough time to get them out of there and then three day tops to meet up with Uncle Jake and his people in West Virginia. Then they could head down into North Carolina and get to the Hidden Lair. Once the military started out on the twenty fifth day it would take them at least eight to ten days of constant marching to reach the Pennsylvania border. Greygor figured that he would stay at least four days ahead of them, hopefully more.

They had already been riding three days and were already ahead of schedule. Greygor thought fondly of the farewells he had given to his relatives and friends as they all started on their trip off of Xanadu Mountain heading east. Arthur and he had given their parents hugs and kisses goodbye and told them they loved them before they left hoping that they would see them soon. Arthur sadly said goodbye to his children who would be traveling on the wagon with their grandparents. The five men waved as the last of the people left out before getting up on their horses and heading northeast. They had mainly used old forest trails that Arthur had learned about most of the way up into Ohio. They traveled at a steady pace and rested the horses as needed. At noon they all stopped for a break once they reached one of the major roadways they had to travel on for part of their trip.

Pete and Dutch rode their horses up the road to check out the areas ahead to make sure all was safe while the others watered their horses and rested. Greygor looked around the area, a large mound of dirt sat in the middle of the road ahead and the woods on both sides of the road ran up the small hills on both sides of the road. He watched as Pete and Dutch disappeared around the curve up ahead. Sampson drank his water as Greygor petted his neck and then walked over to Arthur and sat against a large rock with his brother.

"We must be at least ten hours or more ahead of schedule bro." Arthur said handing him a piece of beef jerky.

He took a bite out of it and chewed it, the salty taste was good. He took a sip of water to wash the meat down. "We keep going at this pace we should be in great shape."

"You still having those dreams you told me about?"

"They hit practically every night bro." Greygor replied. "They always end differently and they seem so real."

"It's just your stressing on everything and your mind is playing tricks on you." He said, "Everything will be fine G."

"I think your brother has a point there Greygor, you stress out to much." Kent said smiling as he sat down beside them.

"I guess I do." He smiled, "I think about the things that Matthews has planned and it scares me to death. I don't understand how those soldiers can believe in his plans and can follow him the way they do."

"Power and treasures can make most men do anything." Kent replied.

"Is it really that simple?" Greygor asked. "How can one man promising them all those things actually get people to follow him?"

"Think of it this way G." Arthur said. "Your promising people a chance to be safe and secure in a place none of them have ever seen and somehow they are all following you to this place."

"That's different." He said and then stopped thinking about it. "I guess you're right, but what I am promising is life over death or slavery."

"It's the classic battle of good and evil!" Kent said raising his fist up in the air and laughing.

"Don't be so melodramatic." Greygor laughed.

Machine gun fire from around the curve caused all three men to jump up and look over in that direction! They could hear men yelling and then Dutch and Pete came riding hard around the curve towards them! Arthur grabbed his bow and arrows and his rifle and headed up the hill and into the woods. Greygor and Kent grabbed their rifles and jumped behind the mound of dirt in the road on either side!

"We got trouble!" Dutch yelled as he jumped off his horse and headed behind a tree on the other side of the road as Pete did the same! "A group of soldiers and a tank headed our way!"

"Arthur! Greygor yelled out to him. "As soon as you see them rounding the curve hit them hard! Pete! Find better cover!

As he yelled gunfire erupted ahead of them and before Pete could move his body shook as he was hit by a number of bullets! He fell to the ground lifeless! An arrow slammed into the chest of the soldier who had shot Pete knocking him backwards! Greygor saw soldiers rounding the curve and taking cover behind trees and rocks along the way! He shot one of them as he tried to dive behind a log on the side of the road. They could now hear the engine of the tank slowly making its way towards them. Kent fired a shot at a soldier behind a tree and then took cover behind the dirt. Arthur was shooting and moving in the woods on the hill, he fired another arrow into another soldier who was trying to get a shot off at Dutch. He twirled and hit the ground! Dutch moved and fired as he ran to a rock a little farther off the road. He rose up from behind the rock and fired his rifle! The bullet hit a soldier in the leg! He fell and took cover behind a tree and fired his rifle hitting the rock Dutch had ducked back behind. Greygor rolled to the side of the mound and fired at the soldier hitting him in the cheek! He fell dead. Greygor got a glance of the tank coming around the curve with soldiers behind it using it as a shield as they fired. He ducked back behind his cover as a bullet ricochet off the spot he was looking out from!

"Kent! We need to move back!" Greygor shouted over the gunfire. "Dutch and I will start firing giving you a chance to get back and find better cover! Then you two can do the same for me!"

With that both the men rolled out and began firing rapidly as Kent crawled back and away from the dirt mound. He jumped up and over a large rock about ten feet back! Greygor and Dutch took cover as Kent got ready to do the same for Greygor! Arthur was picking off soldiers behind the tank one after another. The tanks engine roared louder as the driver hit the gas and headed straight for the mound of dirt Greygor was hiding behind! The soldiers fired rapidly at Dutch and Kent not allowing them to give cover fire for Greygor!

"Greygor look out!" Kent shouted watching the tank hit the mound of dirt and start going over it!

He looked up as the tanks front end came up and over the dirt smashing it down! He felt his Warrior sense kick in and felt the flow of adrenalin! Greygor leaped up and under the raised front end. He rolled under it as the back end leaped up as it went down the other side of the mound! Greygor rolled down the other side of the dirt and rose up on one knee and drew his pistols! He fired at the soldiers that were around him! An arrow hit one to his left as Kent shot another to his right! Greygor saw something fly high over his head and watched it as it flew into the tanks back door!

The explosion from within the tank was deafening! It knocked Greygor forward and to the ground! His pistols were knocked from his hands! He got up and came face to face with the barrel of a rifle and the smiling face of a soldier! His finger began to tighten on the trigger as time slowed! The huge blast of the gun sent Greygor reeling backwards as the soldier fell on top of him dead! Blood dripped on him as he pushed the lifeless body off of him and looked up in shock!

"This saving your ass is getting really old friend!" The dark haired man in black clothing smiled and held out his hand to help him up.

He pulled him up and they shook hands and then stood there as a smile grew on Greygor's face. "I can't believe we found you!"

Cole stood there with his sawed off shotgun in one hand and another strapped to his chest. He stood a few inches taller than Greygor. His jet black hair was cut short and it looked like he hadn't shaven in a few days. His eyes were also very dark, almost evil looking. His face was thin but he was muscular.

"I would duck!" Cole said calmly drawing his other shotgun from his chest and aimed it at Greygor's head.

He dropped to the ground right as he fired and blasted a soldier trying to come out of the back of the tank! He stood back up after picking up his pistols and putting them back in their holsters. Cole's men finished off what was left of the soldiers and began cleaning up the mess. Arthur, Kent and Dutch walked up behind Greygor.

"What are you guys doing up this way?" Cole asked. "Thought you were living in Carolina?"

"I do Cole, we are heading up into Pa. to find our family and get them to safety." Greygor told him.

"There aren't any safe places my friend, the military are all over the place hunting down people and killing them!"

"I found a place in North Carolina called the Hidden Lair, my family is there and it's secure enough to keep the military out." Greygor said.

"You better hope it is G." Cole said as he placed his shotguns in their holsters across his chest. "As for Pittsburgh, I hope you know it got hit pretty hard and the chances of finding your family alive are slim."

"Have you been up that way yet?" Arthur asked.

"Not yet," he answered, "been busy trying to keep the military off our back, moving camp every couple days, finding survivors along the way and killing soldiers as we go!"

"Why don't you head down to Carolina with us?" He asked. "There's plenty of room and we could use the extra help."

"I don't know G," he said, "I have like five hundred people and my family as well to keep safe. I can't be taking them up into Pittsburgh and then move them all south."

"We have a large group heading to a meeting point. We can send all your people down there as well and a few of us can head north and find our families." Arthur said.

"I could help lead them down if you want." Dutch put in.

"This area is going to be very dangerous in a couple weeks," Greygor told him, "Matthews is leading over two thousand soldiers up this way and into Pa. to find massing groups of survivors and destroy them. He plans on killing anyone he finds along the way!"

"That's not good." Cole said, "Let's get this clean up finished and head to my camp; we can talk more when we get there. I don't like being out in the open too long."

They all worked together gathering rifles and ammunition, burying the dead and they drove the tank up into the woods and set it on fire. They gathered their horses and headed to Cole's camp. Greygor and Cole rode together in front.

"Thought you didn't like guns?" Cole reached over and tapped his pistol.

"Why does everyone say that to me?" Greygor chuckled.

They traveled a good five miles before leaving the road and heading down a path that lead into the woods. Greygor told Cole more about what had gone on with him after the nuclear war and more about the Hidden Lair. Cole seemed very interested in possibly getting his people to a safe place after he told him more about it and about the idea of forming some type of fighting groups to help protect everyone. Cole told him that he had already started working out with a lot of his people, teaching them as much as he could about thief combat as he called it. They arrived at the camp after two hours of riding. Cole was greeted by his wife Lori and his daughters, Mandy and Jess Anne. Greygor smiled at them hugging each other tight. Lori was a beautiful lady of thirty four, with long brown hair and a petite body. She was the same age as Cole. They had married right out of highschool and had their first child Mandy who was now fifteen. Jess Anne was thirteen. The mother and daughters had all the same features and very sweet personalities. They all greeted Greygor as well asking about his family.

"I am so glad you're here G," Lori smiled at him, "Perhaps with you here we can find your friends sense of humor again."

"What's wrong old friend?" Greygor smiled at him. "Thought you loved living in the woods and getting the chance to take down soldier now and then?"

"All he does is growl like a bear all day," Mandy added, "and barks orders at everyone!"

"I'm really not that bad." Cole replied, "I just got a lot on my mind. Let's go for a walk G before dinner your friends can set up camp over there where they are."

"It should be ready in about an hour or so dear." Lori hugged him again

The two friends started walking through camp. Cole introduced him to a few men as they went along. They finally reached the end of camp and walked a few hundred feet to a creek. They both sat on rocks across from each other.

"So what is going on with your old friend?"He asked reaching in his pocket and throwing Cole a round green can.

"Where the hell did you get chew?" He asked as he opened it up and took a pinch and placed it in his mouth enjoying the taste and burn of it on his gums.

"Got it from a dead soldier," he smiled back at him as he took out a small cigar and lit it; he puffed it letting the smoke rise up into the air. "So tell me why you seem more up tight than you normally are?"

"It's just too damn hard to train these people to fight; they don't know how to do anything I swear!" Cole replied spitting out his darkened saliva. "I have tried everything to teach them the thieving abilities but they just don't get it!"

"Perhaps you're pushing too much on them at one time."He told him. "Are you starting with basic fighting?"

"Hey G, there really isn't much time to work on that, if you haven't noticed the military are out to kill everyone!"

"Stop going out looking for fights and concentrate on training these people more!" He said sternly, "start with the basics , from there you pick out the few or more who can handle fighting like a thief and double your efforts on them as the others keep practicing! Another thing would be to only attack the military if there are civilians in danger."

"Maybe I am just not cut out to train men and lead them." Cole said after spitting the juice from his mouth.

"Perhaps you just need to quit letting your anger build up inside every time something doesn't go right." Greygor replied. "If you remember right, you taught me your fighting ways and the ability to shadow walk, it took me two years and I am still nowhere close to as good as you are at it."

"Yea, I do remember how pissed off I use to get with you." Cole chuckled, "but you got better after your martial arts training after you joined the army."

"Everyone has the potential in them to fight; we just have to draw out their abilities and then hone them into whatever type of fighting they can do. Whether, it's my ways, your way or some way different. Not everyone can be a thief or warrior."

"I suppose this is your way of putting me in my place again?" Cole asked with a smile.

"I wouldn't call it that," He smiled back, "Let's just call it a best friend saving your ass again."

"It's going to be great working together again," Cole replied, "remember the joint missions we did for the military?"

"Unfortunately yes," He replied. "There were only two and I really wanted to forget them both!"

"Oh come on G, it wasn't that bad. We completed them and we made it out alive."

"We barely made it and you don't listen to orders to well." he answered, "When you were ordered to keep to the shadows it didn't mean to fire those damn shotguns of yours from those shadows!"

"Had I not fired on that one Cuban soldier he would have shot you in the back!"

"You could have knifed him, like normal thieves do!"He said, "We spent the rest of the night dodging bullets, out running the enemy, and then spent hours swimming out into the ocean waiting for our pickup helicopter to finally reach us. It's all because you love the excitement!"

"We got the defector out." Cole said nonchalantly. "All was good in the world."

"You are lucky you didn't get a court martial for your overzealousness."

"You kept that from happening old friend."

"It's only because I am a better bull shitter than you!" Greygor replied.

They both could remember the day they were called in to work together on that mission. Cole was a marine given a mission to infiltrate Cuba and assist a defector in leaving his homeland and getting him safely to United States soil. Greygor was asked to lead his team in with the assistance of a marine with very unique abilities. Greygor agreed without knowing it was his old high school friend. When he found out whom it was he knew there would be trouble. All was going well, they were dropped close to the Cuban shore by helicopter and swam in. within two hours they reached the house that Juan Ramirez was hiding in and extracted him quietly. Cole and Greygor were in the lead cautiously making their way through the shadows of the city heading back towards the oceans shore. Greygor went pass a door way just as a soldier came walking out, the soldier ordered him to halt from behind. The shot gun blast slammed the Cuban soldier into the wall and that was when the sirens began to sound.

They all bolted through the streets running hard and taking out anyone who got in their way. Military and police vehicles were all over the streets. They reached the shore and dove into the ocean and began swimming out to their extraction point. As Cuban boats searched for them, they held their breath underwater trying not to be detected. They were finally picked up and flown to safety. The mission debriefing was harsh, the General wanted to know what went wrong? Why were shots fired? Why were there six dead Cuban soldiers? Greygor protected Cole stating that the Cuban soldier had fired first at him and Cole was just protecting a fellow soldier from being shot in the back. After hours of questioning the General finally decided that force had been necessary. Cole was clear of any charges against him.

"Glad I had you to speak up for me." Cole said.

"Be glad I lied for you!" Greygor told him.

"Anyway, so how do you want to do this next step of ours?" Cole asked.

"We get your people ready to move out in the next few days, we have my cousin Dutch lead them to the meeting point while Kent, Arthur, you and I head up into Pa. and find our families as planned."

"Do you really think my sisters and mother could still be alive?"

"We have enough time to search around for anyone we can find, there is always a possibility."

"Don't you think the chances are slim?"

"Maybe so but I have to at least try my friend." Greygor said optimistically.

"As always, I got your back!" Cole replied. "If anyone is still alive up there I will help you find them."

"Let's go eat." Greygor smiled getting up and walking back towards camp followed by Cole. "By the way, how is your weapon stash?"

"I have a lot of rifles with ammo, swords, knives, axes, shields and such." Cole said," I also have a bunch of crossbows, bows and spears."

"We definitely are going to need all of it." Greygor smiled, "I knew you would come in handy somehow."

The two friends laughed out loud as they walked through the camp. It was good to laugh and smile.

After dinner they built a bonfire and discussed the move with a few of Cole's main fighters who were to put the word out the next day. Dutch again agreed to help lead the camp to the meeting area and wait there for Greygor and the rest to join up there also. They discussed working out with the people and build their fighting skills to protect each other. A few men volunteered to travel into Pa. to assist in searching for survivors but all eventually agreed to keep the group down to four so they could move faster and less inconspicuously. They would go over maps the next day to find the safest routes for both the large group and the smaller group. Greygor felt tired and dismissed himself from the group so that he could get some sleep. He walked over to his horse and began removing his weapons that he seemed to keep on him all the time now. He looked up at the flashing sky thinking about Pat as always. He heard someone walking up behind him and turned.

"Hi Greygor," Mandy startled him.

"Hey darling," He smiled, "What are you up too?"

"I just wanted to say thank you," She said smiling, "My dad seems a lot happier since you got here. He is actually smiling."

"He just needed to relax and get things off his mind my dear."

"Well whatever you said to him worked," she replied. "He had us all scared he was going to end up getting hurt or even killed."

"Your daddy's a lot tougher than that." He smiled. "Don't you worry any, he will be alright now."

She walked over to him and hugged him tight and then kissed him on the cheek. "Thank you Greygor."

He hugged her back and she went back to the campfire. Greygor smiled knowing that he had made her happy and that things were going pretty well. He went to bed and closed his eyes thinking of Pat still so far away. His dream came once again.

Up on the mountain he looks out at the people below safe and secure in the Hidden Lair. Pats hand touches his shoulder as he hears her beautiful voice.

"You made this all happen, baby."

He turns to tell her it wasn't just him, as he does a sword comes down towards his face! He ducks and draws his sword just in time to deflect another attack. The blades ring out as the clash again and again!

"These people are mine!" Matthew shouts at Greygor. "You have no chance

against my forces!"

"I will keep them safe from you!"He shouts back knocking Matthews's sword back once again!

He counters another swing and then let loose a figure eight attack bewildering his enemy! He lets his sword thrust go low and then brings it up under Matthews swing, plunging his blade up into his belly, feels it scrape the chest bone and penetrate out his back taking Matthews up and off his feet! Matthews lands on his back in agony! Greygor places his foot on the man's stomach and drawers his sword out and raises it high!

He sat up off the blanket as sweat poured from his brow and breathing heavily! He saw Arthur kneeling in front of him looking at him concerned.

"Are you alright, bro?" He asked.

He waited a few to respond, "Yea, just another nightmare."

"You want to talk about it?" He asked.

"No, I'll be okay," Greygor said reassuringly, "go ahead back to sleep."

Arthur went back to his blankets as Greygor lay back down and letting his mind and body calm down. At least in the dream he had won he thought. Why do these dreams keep ending differently? He nodded back off to sleep knowing that tomorrow would be another busy day.

Chapter 10

The mountains of Pennsylvania were a lot smaller and more hills like than the larger Appalachian mountains of North Carolina. As boys, Cole Arthur and Greygor had roamed, explored and had fun in the wooded hills of their neighborhoods. They made camp at the foot of several of the hills each of which led up to the neighborhoods that their friends and they had lived in. This was where they played as boys, partied as teenagers and it was a safe place to hide when needed. They had traveled two days to reach this spot, still many days ahead of the military. They all hoped that Cole's people were having no problems heading down to the meeting area led by Dutch and a few good men Cole had chosen to help him get them there. They had built a fire in front of was once known as the Indian caves, though everyone knew that there had never been any caves there. It was just a rocky formation at the bottom of one of the hills that had been a meeting place for many friends throughout the years. The creek still flowed through the woods but it seemed a bit smaller than it did in their childhood days. Many good memories were made here it made them smile as they thought about better times.

They setup camp and built a nice fire to heat up their food. The horses were fed and watered and the four friends sat around the fire finishing up their meal and talking to each other. Greygor discussed the training of all the able bodied people in fighting and weapons. He felt it was necessary to begin with the basics and then separate them into separate fighting groups of some sort depending on the individual's abilities and talent. Each group could be trained by the person or persons with the best abilities in that area. Arthur talked about naming a group the Sharpshooters; this group could be trained in the use of rifle and archery to assist the other fighting groups from afar. Cole could train the thief group, much like Special Forces who literally attacked out of nowhere. Kent asked about forming a group of Calvary like fighters whom would ride in on horseback to fight alongside the other fighting groups. He wanted to name it the Rapid Riders. They all thought it was a great idea due to Kent's knowledge and training within Matthews Military. Greygor had a few more ideas for other fighting groups that they could form along the way. They largest of the groups that he wanted to name the Warrior group was already beginning to form within the two groups that were heading to the meeting place. It would need a leader with extra special talents. The group that he had been calling the Trapster group was already forming in the Hidden Lair by his father in law, Daniel.

As nighttime fell they left the talk of fighting and began discussing old times here in their neighborhood. Kent and the others enjoyed hearing Arthur telling old stories of Greygor their youngest brother Wayne, their dog Roger and himself playing in the woods. One of the brothers would run off through the woods and the other two and the dog would track him down. Their dog was a Shetland sheepdog that was the smartest of dogs. He use to catch ball and Frisbee around the house, followed all commands very well and had been a very loyal and close friend to the whole family. It made Greygor think of his buddy, Luck whom he had just lost a few weeks back.

Cole and Greygor began telling a few of their crazy teenage stories that had happened to them over the years. He told of the one girlfriend whom both Greygor and he had liked and had fought over. They ended the fight with both of them leaning against their cars, in front of her house, both of them bloody and worn out. She ended up walking out of her house and right pass them shaking her head and cussing them. She walked up the road to a waiting Trans Am. It was another guy she knew and started dating after the two of them fought over her.

They all laughed at the story. It felt good to all to be laughing and smiling in such a dangerous new time. Kent told a story or two about his fun as a teenager that which brought more smiles to everyone's faces. This area made them all feel safe and secure for now. Cole began another story of a wild night that Greygor and he had. It was a Friday night and it was Cole Greygor and another close friend of theirs, Chad. They were cruising around town in Greygor's old blue Buick Station wagon. They had been checking out three hot girls at the mall and were now following them down the highway. Greygor was driving, Chad was in the front seat and Cole was in the back. The girls were leading them on waving and beeping to them to follow so of course they did. The girl driving the other car signaled that they were getting off an exit and tricked the guys into getting off the exit and then took off up the highway! Greygor stopped at the stop sign as they all grumbled about being tricked. Cole yelled switch, (because out of the three he was really the best driver.) Greygor moved to the passenger side as Cole jumped over the seat and put the car back in drive as Chad jumped out of the door and went to the back seat. Cole hit the gas and flew up the ramp back on to the highway after a major 360 degree turn around. The Buick which was known for its speed hit seventy miles an hour before getting on the highway. They were all laughing and shouting as they caught up to the girl's car. Greygor looked to the backseat to high five Chad! He wasn't there! Both of them looked back and then at each other and then began hollering for him. He wasn't back there. Again they looked at each other and simultaneously looked up towards the roof. (Chad had the wild habit of riding up on the roof holding on to the luggage rack!) Both Cole and Greygor rolled down their windows and both attempted to look up on the top for Chad. Greygor came down shaking his head that he wasn't up there. They quickly did a turn around on the highway and headed back to the exit thinking the worse! They exited and found Chad lying on the side of the road laughing as they pulled up unhurt! When he had jumped out of the passenger door Cole had took off before he could get back in the back door and had thrown him into the grass on the side of the road! For years Chad would never let them live that down! They all laughed at the story.

"I really hate when you tell your version of that story!" A voice came from out of the darkness.

Everyone went for their weapons as the man came closer to the fire. Arthur already had an arrow notched and ready but didn't pull it back once he felt the point of a blade at the back of his neck!

"Chad?" Greygor smiled.

"You two about killed me that night by the way!" He answered taking Greygor's hand and shaking it.

"Ease up on that arrow buddy." A man said from behind Arthur.

Greygor looked over to see another old friend of his from high school. "Hogan, I can't believe it is you!"

Hogan Randolph and his brother Rider stood beside each other looking as different as night and day. Rider stood six foot just as his brother with blondish brown hair and a big clean shaven smile on his face. Hogan on the other hand sported a full beard and moustache with dark brown hair. Hogan had that same look throughout high school. Both of his friends were pretty smart through high school but Hogan though rough looking was more into studying and believe it or not philosophy. Chad walked over to Cole and shook his hand as well. The light from the fire showed of the man's red hair and moustache. Chad was very big into technology and worked for the government on different inventions that he created. Another red headed man walked out of the darkness.

"Will?" Arthur smile at his best friend from high school.

"Hey there bud!" Will smiled shaking his hand. "Glad to see you alive!"

Greygor introduced his old friends to his new friend Kent and then they all related their survival stories and the happenings of the last few months. Rider, Hogan and Chad along with a bunch of other survivors had been finding people whom had survived and they were all camped up in the old grade school neighborhood just a few miles away. They told Greygor and the rest that they had a few attacks on the military but had found survivors within a thirty mile radius so far. There had to be at least eight hundred to a thousand men women and children. Arthur and Cole asked about their family, Will let them know that they had found their older twin siblings as well as their families. Cole's mother and two sisters were amongst those found as well. This information brought smiles to all their faces. Greygor asked about their youngest brother and his wife and children. Will sadly told them that he had taken a group out to the area where they lived and found their house demolished to the ground. There had been no signs of them anywhere. Greygor and Arthur looked at each other knowing that they had to at least try to find them eventually. Greygor told his friends of the threat of the military who were heading this way from the south. The military knew of a massing of survivors up this way and they all figured that it was their group that they were talking about.

"What can we do?" Rider asked. "We have weapons and a few men who can possibly fight but we can't take on the whole military yet!"

"If we double our efforts perhaps we can get these people ready for a fight" Hogan added.

"Have these people been shown anything yet?" Greygor asked.

"We figured that we might have to defend ourselves eventually so we all have been working out with weapons and such trying to be ready if we need to be, but to go against a whole force of soldiers is way to much!" Hogan replied.

"How much more time do you need to get them ready?" Greygor asked.

"It would take months my friend!" Chad added.

"These people come from all walks of life and none of them have ever used a gun, sword knife or anything!" Rider said.

"Well guys," Greygor looked at them all, "If anything we can buy us all some extra time. The military won't be heading this way for another thirty days. Then it will take them at least ten or more days to reach this area search you out and attack. My thought is when they arrive here we are all going to be long gone heading south as we all work out and train in case we all have to fight. That will give us at least another week to stay ahead of them. We can meet up with the other groups and keep moving south staying far ahead of them!"

"Where the hell are we going to take all these people too?" Rider asked.

"We can take them to the Hidden Lair where we can set up a defense against the military if they decide to follow us that far!"

He then began telling them about the Hidden Lair as well as his plans to create different fighting groups along the way to help keep everyone safe. He went in depth with the help of Arthur, Cole and Kent about how they could train along the way starting with basics and then putting the people with different skills in different groups. Everyone listened intently to his ideas and Greygor could see renewed hope in all their faces. He told them about how the Lair was surrounded by the huge mountains with only three roads in and out and how his Father in law was already working on traps to help protect anyone within. He also told them about the other two groups who would be waiting for them at the meeting point who was already training to protect them.

"We only have a few weeks though?" Will questioned.

"Yes we do my friend," Greygor replied, "but what other choice do we have?

"Though our chances are slim," Hogan said, "I would rather go down fighting protecting those around me."

"We have to at least try. I don't intend to give up that easy." Rider added.

"The trick is going to be staying one step ahead of the military in every way possible!" Chad said.

"I think I can add a few helpful tricks to that." Cole smiled.

"You're not going to tell me any of your possible plans are you?" Greygor asked.

"Now G that would spoil the surprises." Cole laughed.

"No, it will keep me from worrying and having a blooming heart attack."

"Ok then," Rider said, "Will and Arthur I want you two to head up to the camp with Chad and begin letting everyone know what has to be done."

"No problem." Will said.

Arthur grabbed his gear and headed off with Will and Chad. He walked his horse along with them. Greygor and the others began talking about what was needed weapon wise as well as how to begin training everyone who was able to fight. They began breaking down and gathered everything. Rider led them as they talked along the way. It felt good to be amongst old friends again. It also felt strange the way things were falling into place. The trip took them up one of the hills that led up to Rider's neighborhood, most of the houses had been demolished but a few still stood. It was explained to him that they were able to use a few of them for shelter but most of the people were in tents around the old school building that which also was being used for shelter. By the time they reached the camp it had to be twelve in the morning. Hogan showed Greygor and his team where they could set up while Rider went off to find Arthur and Will. Greygor got settled in and fell asleep instantly feeling like a lot more weight had been lifted from his shoulders.

Chapter 11

The aroma of fresh brewed coffee caused Greygor to awaken and sit up. He thought he was dreaming but was delighted to see a curly brown haired woman sitting on the ground close to him. She was of medium build and was a beautiful sight to see. Next to her was a man of the same size and hair with a bushy moustache. She handed the wide eyed Greygor the cup of coffee.

"Thank you," He said still wondering if he was dreaming or not. "Are you really here?"

"We are really here G," Charles said smiling at his younger brother.

"Glad to see you safe Grey." Marie smiled at her brother as well.

The twins looked great for being five years older than Greygor. It was easy to tell that they were twins but they each had their separate personalities. Marie was sweet and caring with a flare of looking after others no matter what. Charles had a good heart but was the type who looked out for himself more. Both had been very good role models for the younger brothers as they were growing up.

After sipping his coffee He hugged his brother and sister. They began talking about the family Greygor had found and his wife and kids in North Carolina safe in the Hidden Lair. Marie and Charles began telling him the family that was here in this camp. Maries husband Gary, her daughters May and her husband Lou, as well as Maries daughter. Janice. Charles had his wife Angel and son Jack. Marie also mentioned seeing her ex-husband Carl in the camp as well. Greygor asked about their youngest brother Wayne but they had not found his family yet. Greygor told them that before he left this area he would try and find them. Greygor saw Rider, Chad and Arthur walking towards them and stood up to greet them.

"How are you guys doing this morning?" Greygor asked.

"We are doing well." Rider answered. "We need you and Charles to come with us. We are having a meeting over by the school."

"Is anything wrong Ride?" He asked.

"We are just trying to get things situated for the days to come!" Chad said.

"Arthur and the rest are waiting for us there." Rider said.

"Let's go then!" Greygor said slapping older brother on the shoulder as they all began walking.

A large group of men and women were assembled in the old school gym. Cole and Arthur were standing at the entrance talking along with Hogan and Will. Kent was talking to a short haired tall blonde woman who Greygor recognized as Cole's sister Toni. Rider led them into the gym and to the table in the center that was covered with maps and papers. The elementary school gym was large and at one end was a stage where school plays were once held years ago. This part of the building seemed to be untouched by the devastation of the war. Through the early morning the people in camp were told of the coming events and different men and women were asked to come to this meeting to represent larger different groups in the camp. Greygor, Rider and Charles were joined at the table by Arthur, Hogan, Kent, Will and Chad. Other men walked up to the table to hear the discussion. They began by going over the maps trying to figure out the best route to take south. Different side roads ran along the major interstate 79 but everyone felt that to move so many people it would probably be a good idea to travel the interstate at least to the meeting area in West Virginia. From all calculations if they left this area even in fifteen days that would give them a good twenty day head start over the military.

Rider suggested that they began teaching people how to fight as well as use different weapons. They all would assist with the workouts and training and then the leaders of each group would begin choosing and separating the men into the different groups. Rider and Hogan would have the largest group that which they would call the Warrior group. This group would be filled with able body men able to fight with different types of weapons.

Cole would lead the second group. This group he wanted to call the thief group, they would specialize in the art of shadow fighting as well as martial arts.

Arthur's group he chose to call the Sharpshooters. They would be using bows and rifles to give cover fire to the other groups from behind and also from the sides of the fight.

Kent had the next group he named the Rapid Riders, Calvary like group that ride into battle on horseback assisting the other groups. They talked about another group made up of larger men who would use broadswords, mallets Axes and such who would cause crippling damage to the enemy.

Charles was given the last of the groups, the Guard group. This group would be in charge of the defense within the camps and along the way south. This group would be in charge of getting all the people to safety if a battle happened and it didn't go well for the fighting groups.

They all hoped for a straight and easy move down to the Hidden Lair with no confrontations but they wanted to be ready just in case. Supplies, horses and weapons were needed as well for the trip. Will offered to set up a few teams who would go out and find what all was needed. He would lead a team south towards the race track to try and find any horses that may be left in that area. Chad offered to take a team out in search of more bladed weapons, bows and other types of weapons. Arthur mentioned to him about a warehouse he used to work at years ago that the owner kept a stockade of bladed weapons.

Questions began coming from the crowd, Greygor tried to answer as many as he could. It started to get very loud within the gym; the people were concerned about the military, the supplies needed and the trip itself. Rider and the rest tried to get things to quiet down but to no avail. Cole leaned over to Greygor and whispered in his ear. The two men walked away from the table and up on the stage. Cole got a big smile on his face and pulled out his shotguns and raised them in the air. He pulled the triggers firing them. The explosion rocked the room! Everyone became silent and all eyes were on the stage now. Greygor stood silent letting them all calm down. He looked over at Cole and shook his head in approval and then looked out at the crowd as more people began coming in after hearing the shots fired.

"We understand that these are confusing times and you all have many questions that you want answers too! Greygor raised his voice for all to hear. "I will try to put all things into perspective for all!"

The crowd seemed to calm down and everyone turned their eyes and ears to the stage. Rider Arthur, Kent and Hogan walked up on to the stage and waited for Greygor to go on.

Greygor began to tell the crowd about President Matthews' whole plot. He told of the terrorist acts that were actually carried out by our own military. How far back that they went he did not know. He then told of the promises that he made to his soldiers and the orders that the military were given pertaining to any civilians found on their way to the staging areas. Greygor added his own stories of stopping the military from enslaving and killing survivors. He let them know about his sneaking into the military camp and seeing how they were and hearing the speech Matthews gave to his military that night.

After that he began telling them about the Hidden Lair that they all could escape to after meeting up with the other two groups already waiting for them in West Virginia. He told of the layout of the Lair and how it was surrounded by large mountains and that there were only three roads that could be used to enter or exit from there. He then explained how the people already there were setting up traps for security on each of the roads to assist in protecting all within the Hidden Lair.

His next point involved the trip down to the Hidden lair. He let them know how by using mostly secondary roads and even by moving south they all could possibly not run into any military. But for the protection of the whole group most of them would have to be ready if they would have to fight their way to the destination they hoped to reach. He told of Rider's and Hogan's sword fighting abilities, Kent's military and fighting knowledge, Arthur's and Will's archery skills and even Charles fighting abilities that were well honed.

He told them that these men would train them and help them over any obstacles! The training would begin in a day or two, and would continue as they traveled south to the Hidden Lair. He wanted them to know they would gather whatever weapons that they could and that Cole had a good supply already. He then went on to tell them that due to the Mediterranean War and because of the nuclear bombardment the military was in short supply of firearms and were in search of other weapons such as swords and other weapons.

He also told them that due to that war and the nuclear storm the soldiers who were in the Mediterranean were the best of the best of the military. From the navy seals to the Special Forces, all of whom were both now dead and gone or left over there in the desert. The soldiers Matthews was leading were brand new and had no real fighting abilities or they had no battle knowledge!

He went into great detail on all these points hoping to answer as many questions that could have been presented. He stopped talking so to catch his breath and give his voice a rest, feeling the strain from talking so loudly for so long. The people seemed quite satisfied with what he was explaining to them.

Rider came forward and began clapping for Greygor. The whole room followed suite and began clapping as well. Once it died down Rider began telling everyone to go talk to their groups and let them know what was going on and what was needed of them. Everyone began to leave as they talked amongst themselves. It took a few minutes for the gym to empty out leaving the eight of them alone on the stage.

"Well brother do you think we have a chance?" Charles asked.

"I actually believe we do." Greygor replied. "It's going to take a lot of work but honestly I believe we can make it!"

"Well then my friends, we better go get things ready!" Hogan walked over and patted Greygor on the shoulder.

They all jumped off the stage and walked towards the exit. They discussed a few things as they went and then once outside parted ways. Greygor silently walked along with Arthur.

"So when are you going? Arthur asked.

"I am taking a search team out in a few days." Greygor answered. "The Barbarian group we have will need its leader!"

"Will, told me they searched everywhere for them."

"I know our brother is alive!" Greygor stopped and looked sternly at Arthur. "I know Wayne and his families are alive, I can feel it."

"Well bro your gut feelings have done well so far so hopefully your right."

Charles and Marie joined them and they sat around talking. Marie's husband joined them as well as did Charles wife Angel who invited them for dinner at their camp. It felt great to Greygor to be amongst his family and friends. He knew that in the days to come he had a lot to do so some relax time was a good thing.

Chapter 12

The first few days of training went well. The group leaders and Greygor started the first day with exercising, aerobic conditioning and stretching. On the second day they did the same but as evening approached they started some minor hand to hand combat. Unlike the military training that Kent and Greygor went through that was made to break a man's spirit then rebuild him into a fighting machine, The group leaders trained by praising the peoples abilities as they went along. By the third day weapons were added at the end of the day. Arthur began picking out a few people to try out for the sharpshooter group he was forming. Cole also began taking a few that showed thief possibilities and began working with them. It started to look as if the largest of the groups would be the warrior group. Greygor assisted in the training every day. He saw potential in many of the men and women. Cole's sister Toni was one who showed great strength and ability. She was a tall blonde nicely built woman who fought fiercely with a staff or sword both of which she was very good with.

As the days went on he met up with a few different old friends from the Joseph men's younger days. Dale and Pete Uran were best friends with Greygor's youngest brother Wayne. Both were big muscular men like Wayne. They both were great to have near you in a scrap. Dale had picked out a large double bladed axe to practice with and Pete worked with a large aluminum bat and a broad sword. Another friend he met up with was his old coworker Landon Yonder and his brother Mick. They both seemed to be catching on rather well with short swords. He walked around helping those who needed it and complimented those who showed their abilities well. In the evening of the third day the team sent out to find horses returned with about twenty horses found around the old race track and at a few small farms along the way. They figured that between the group here and the people down at the meeting place that they now had close too sixty reliable horses. Supplies were being brought in by different teams practically every day.

Greygor and his family sat around a nice campfire that night after enjoying the meal that was prepared by Marie, Angel, May and Janice. Gary, Arthur and Charles were talking about different things that had been happening in camp while Greygor sat talking to Jack about different types of weapons and fighting styles. Jack had been watching Rider with his double sword style and was interested in how he was able to do it. All Greygor knew was that Rider was into martial arts years ago just like he was and that he must of picked it up through that. Finally after a while everyone was sitting around relaxing and watching the flashing lights from above and the swirling clouds. Greygor got up and walked a few yards over to the edge of the hill and looked down into the darkness.

"What's on your mind?" Cole's voice came from behind.

"I wish I knew what the military was doing." He answered quietly.

"Well, we can always find out if you like?"

"I know you said you could sneak down and get information my friend but I don't want to put you in danger."

"You are talking to me G!" Cole smiled.

"What about your group?"

"I got a few good ones who can train while I am gone."

"When do you want to take off?"

"You know me." Cole shrugged, "I will be gone by three in the morning!"

"Please buddy," Greygor placed his hand on his friends shoulder, "you just be careful."

"I will meet up with you on the way down."

With that Cole walked into the darkness. Greygor knew Cole would be fine but he was fearful for everyone knowing that the military could be anywhere. He stood there enjoying the silence just staring up into the night sky thinking about Pat and his boys and wishing he was with them. He also began thinking about the other two groups at the meeting place and hoped they were alright as well. His shoulders felt heavy with worry as did his heart.

"There's too much on your mind, as always young man?"The older ladies voice came from beside him.

"You read me like a book Mrs. C." Greygor looked over at her frail form and smiled.

He could see her gray hair and the wrinkles upon her cheeks. She took his hand and smiled at him. Her hands were still soft but he could feel the loosened skin of age. Her big blue eyes looked up at his face and they smiled at each other.

"I take it my son is taking off tonight?" She asked.

"Knowing him, he will be leaving any minute now that he talked to me."

"He respects you as a good leader." She replied. "He would never admit that but he does."

"I'm not the leader here." Greygor laughed.

"Oh hog wash!" She nudged him. "You have always been a special person Greygor, even in your teenage years you were excellent at taking care of people around you and keeping things in line."

"I don't have any leadership training; I wasn't even a boy scout when I was young."

"You have a natural leadership ability that can't be learned or trained for." She placed her hand on his shoulder. "You lead with your heart and soul young man; your compassion and love of life are what makes you a natural born leader."

"Mrs. C. I am not that good at this stuff." Greygor turned to her. "I don't know where to begin!"

"Greygor my dear," she said. "You are just too modest and paranoid as well. The day you left your wife and children, in search of family and friends to rescue and get to safety was the day you began the process of being a leader of these people. When you began delegating your authority to those who would listen and follow your orders was another step of becoming a leader. You naturally listen to those who follow you for their input and their ideas and use what they give you. Use what you already have and let yourself grow into these peoples leader as you are destined to do. Quit fighting what is to be and go with it."

"I think you have too much confidence in me" Greygor replied.

"Look around you young man, everybody you have come in contact with believes in you. Stop fighting with your inner turmoil and start getting ready for the real enemy! That would be Matthews and his military."

"You're always trying to build my self-confidence aren't you?"

"Not really," She smiled as she took his hand warmly, "Can't build something that's already there. But I can be supportive and let you know that so far you have done a fabulous job. Keep taking it a step at a time and you will be fine."

They stood there in silence for a while as he pondered her words of wisdom. Though he tried to find a way around it she was right about everything as she always was. He had to smile and let out a small giggle.

"I know what you're thinking," She said with a smile, "Oh darn she is always right!'

"I guess I was." He smiled back.

"So tell me about these dreams that you have been having?" Mrs. C asked.

"I see my friend Cole still gossips."

"He is just concerned for you."

"Well the dreams always begin the same but always have a different ending."

"Tell me about them then."

"It always begins in the Hidden Lair atop a cliff that looks down at the valley below. I can see all the people coming in and I can actually feel how safe they feel. Pat has her hand on my shoulder and tells me what a good job I did protecting everyone. Next thing I know she disappears and I am fighting a dark figure with a sword! The ending is always different, I win killing him with my sword or he wins by killing me."

"Well, I would have to say it's a type of premonition type dream," She said, "Seems to me that this adventure that you're on now will be good for everyone and you will face the evil that you are up against. Not just once or twice but more than likely many times. Death is always a factor in any great conflict of course both this dark shadow and yourself may have many conflicts ending in what both of you think is the others demise but in actuality later each will be surprised to find the other alive."

"Have you always been so philosophical Mrs. C?" He laughed.

"Oh yes my dear," she smiled, "but when you were teenagers I had to stay with the K.I.S.F.S program."

"What in heaven's name is that?" Greygor asked.

"I had to keep it simple for stupid!" She laughed even louder as Greygor did too.

They both walked back to the camp hand in hand as they continued talking. She asked about his boys and wife as well as his family he had found so far. She kissed him on the cheek and headed off to her little gathering as he went back to his.

He went back to the fire and realized someone new had arrived at their sight. Carl had stopped by. Greygor cringed as their eyes met. Carl was Maries ex husband and the father of Janice, over the years he had treated both of them horribly physically, mentally and not mention emotionally. Greygor greeted him and then went over and sat by Marie and May.

"Remember your promise to me." Marie leaned over hugging him and whispered in his ear.

He shook his head acknowledging her words and tried to pretend that he wasn't there. Carl was a big man height and weight wise. He was of Indian decent with long grayish black hair down his back and a large moustache as well. He was running his mouth about how good he was with an axe and how he should be made a group leader as well. Greygor bit his tongue trying to keep his word to his sister as well as to his niece. In his mind he imagined letting his knife slide down his wrist into his hand and letting fly into the big mouths neck! He smiled at the thought and felt his sister's elbow hit him in the ribs.

"Stop that!" She muttered under her breath. "I know what you're thinking about."

"I wasn't thinking anything!" He whispered back.

The night went on with stories and laughter amongst the family and friends. A couple of questions were asked about the Hidden Lair which Greygor answered. Most of the family had been there and remembered it from vacations down to North Carolina to visit the parents, Arthur and Greygor when they all lived there. Time seemed to fly and everyone started heading off to bed. Greygor got up and started walking to his tent to get some sleep. His body was a bit achy from today's workout as well. He went to bed and thinking about the words of Mrs. C. He felt better about things since talking to her and understood what she was saying. As he faded off to sleep he told himself he would do everything in his power to get all of the people to safety.

Greygor woke up at dawn; he cleaned up and got dressed before meeting up with Arthur, Marie and Charles for breakfast. While they ate they discussed the search for their brother Wayne and his family. All the searches so far started and ended at the house they had lived in for many years. It had been demolished by the winds of the nuclear storm. Marie mentioned that she had talked to Wayne's wife Jan the day before and that Wayne happened to be on vacation that week so he wasn't downtown when the missiles started flying. She told Marie that the family was going to be relaxing at home and not going off on a trip like they usually did. She also mentioned that the three girls didn't have any events during that time so more than likely they had to be close to home when everything happened. They talked and decided that they would take a search team out tomorrow and began their search at the place where all other searches had begun and ended. Arthur asked who should go. Greygor felt Marie, Arthur, Will, and Charles to start should go. Charles mentioned Wayne's best friends Dale and Peter had asked him if they could help. Arthur got up and said he would go tell them that they were taking the team out in the morning. Greygor would let Rider know what was going on today during the workouts. He finished his food and drink and left to help out with the forming fighting groups. He felt his adrenalin flowing just thinking of the search for his brother the next day.

He seemed to flow smoothly through his own workout feeling his strength and speed growing. He sparred with Hogan showing the men and women proper form and a few special tricks of his own to gain victory. Rider challenged him afterwards and gained advantage over him with his double sword abilities. They shook hands and patted each other on the back. Greygor went out in the crowd and helped teach different people offense and defense in a fight. Everyone seemed to be coming along fine for only having a few days to train so far. Arthur came by later in the day to tell Greygor that both Peter and Dale would be going with them in the morning. They would pack up a few things tonight to get ready for an early start in the morning. Marie had already started getting a few things ready and Arthur was about to head over to get a few horses for the morning. Greygor of course told him that he wanted Sampson for his ride.

The day seemed to go pretty fast. Greygor ate shared some family time and then hit the bed right after dark so to get goodnights sleep. He prayed that he would find his brother the next day before fading off to a deep and much needed sleep. He slept soundly without having his recurring dream.

Chapter 13

They all searched the neighborhood for hours. Only a few houses still stood out of the hundreds that had once made up this neighborhood. It was a horrible scene that no one should have to look upon. Everyone knew that beneath the rubble most of the people whom once lived here were buried and gone from this earth. After hours they all met up in front of what was once Wayne's and his family's home. It had also been leveled and blown to pieces. Greygor took a drink of water from his canteen staring blankly at the yard that his brother had kept so nice and was now burnt to a crisp. Arthur walked up to his side and stood there in silence as the others walked around thinking the worst.

"There isn't any way that anyone could have survived this G." Arthur said silently to him.

"I know that." He said.

"Perhaps we should get everyone back to camp; we are too close to the highways here." Arthur replied, "If any military happen to be in the area they could spot us easy."

"Yes, your right." He said.

"I will start telling everyone."

"Wait a minute Bro," Greygor said, "Remember the saying that you can't teach an old dog new tricks?"

"Yes, what's that got to do with anything?"

"Before the gas shortages and everything Wayne's family made all kinds of trips to amusement parks, Vegas, Florida and even on weekends took off on little trips around this area."

"You don't think they were home when this started G?"

"They weren't home bodies, if he was off all week he would have taken his family somewhere fun even if he had to walk or ride bikes."

"So where do you think they would have gone?" Arthur asked. "I mean there aren't many places around here that close by."

"What about the school?" Marie came up to them and asked. "It's only about four miles away."

"That's what I was thinking sis!" Greygor smiled. "Let's mount up and get out of here."

"Let's go then!" Arthur replied.

They traveled down to the secondary road and began riding steadily in the direction of the school. Pete and Arthur rode ahead keeping an eye out for any dangers ahead. Greygor kicked Sampson into a fast trot followed by the rest. Charles rode up next to him keeping pace.

"Have you thought about what we might find or not find Grey?" He asked.

"I'm always thinking about that Charles but I just have a feeling that they are alive."

"I am not talking about that; I am talking about wild animals or possibly some crazed starving people out for blood!"

"You're not getting paranoid on me now?"

"No, just wouldn't you think some type of things like that would happen after the nuclear war?"

"Oh you mean like radioactive creatures, zombies cannibals and things that go bump in the night?" He laughed.

"What about that bear you told us about that attacked your boys?"

"It was injured and starving and I really don't think it intentionally attacked."

"I just don't want anyone to get hurt or killed." Charles replied.

"That's what we are around for bro to find those who need us and protect those around us!" Greygor smiled.

It took them an hour to reach the top of the hill that led down to the high school. They stopped the horses in a small wooded area off to the side of the road. Marie, Charles and Will stayed with the horses as the rest grabbed their weapons and began walking down the dirt covered driveway towards the school. Arthur went into the woods staying out of sight as he went down. Greygor stayed to the middle of the road as Peter and Dale followed behind at a distance. They could see that the Junior high school building that was smaller had been collapsed in by the storm as they reached the large parking lot. The larger and much older High school had not suffered as much except for a few large holes in the side of the building and all the windows had been blown out. They all stopped at the rubble that had once been the middle school. Looking around and listening for any sounds of life. Arthur walked out of the woods and came up to them. The four men advanced towards the large gray and red brick building ahead. The walls were now blackened and covered with dirt that had been blown against it. They made their way to the side door that would lead them to the center of the building where the gym and pool were.

"I want you to find some cover." Greygor pointed at Arthur, "Do you think you can get on top of the building and cover us from the windows on top?"

Arthur looked at his brother with a smirk on his face before letting out a laugh, he took off running towards a burnt out tree next to the building. As he ran he slung his bow on his back and leaped towards the lowest branch flipping his body upward towards the next one up. He was on top of that branch within a second and jumped up to the next. Greygor thought he heard him laughing as he went up the tree and then leaped to the roof of the building. Arthur sat down on the edge of the building and waved at his friends below. Greygor stood with his fist on his hips shaking his head.

"Quit goofing off." He said silently up to him.

He looked back at his other two companions who were standing there in amazement of what they just saw Arthur do.

"Oh come on guys!" Greygor replied. "You have seen him do that before, back in high school and harder climbs than that!"

"Yeah, but he isn't a teenager anymore." Peter said. "Can you still do it?"

"I don't need too." He smiled. "He is the one covering us!"

"In other words, no he can't." Dale chuckled to his brother.

"You guys are a laugh riot!" He smiled at them.

He motioned to his brother to go as they walked over to the door. Arthur waved and took off across the roof at a steady walk. They reached the door and Greygor pushed it slowly open as the other two stood ready. They looked down the long tiled hallway littered with glass, sand and rocks. It darkened quickly due to no windows within it. Dale blocked the door open with a rock as Greygor started forward down the hall. He took his sword from its place on his back and used it to tap the walls and floor along the way. The other two started in after the fifteen steps he had taken within the building. They could hear a low humming sound ahead. The slow walk into the darkness seemed to take forever; He could feel the layers of dirt on the wall and felt the grit and rocks beneath his feet. It was cold and dank inside the building and he was glad he had worn his long leather jacket. Not only did it keep him warm but it gave him security knowing he had enough weapons in it to take care of most things that could come along.

The hall went down and then back up as Peter and Dale used the side hallways for cover as they advanced. The humming sound grew louder as they got closer to the gymnasium. They could smell the chlorine of the pool already as the hallway began an upward incline. The sight of two small windows of the gyms door came into view, very faint light showed through them. Greygor attempted to use his ability of shadow walking that Cole had taught him years ago to adjust to the darkness of the hall but also felt his warrior sense slowly growing. He knew that beyond the doors ahead something was going to happen, His ears picked up a slight whirling sound ahead that seemed to be separate from the humming sound. The vibrations he felt with his heightened sense of touch finally told him a generator was being used ahead but for what? His eyes focused on the light from the windows, it let him know that it was very minimal. He closed his eyes trying to focus on what may lie within the gym and for some reason within his mind he saw white flashes and felt the warrior sense growing but not to maximum advantage as he called it. Reaching the door he raised his hand to the other two to stop.

He reached and grabbed the door handle that he would pull to open to enter into the gym. He waited a few seconds before going in; he tried to look up to the ceiling through the window to see if he could catch a glance of Arthur above. No such luck but something told him he was up there waiting for Greygor to enter. He looked back towards his friends behind him and motioned that he was heading in but to wait till he yelled to them to follow. They acknowledged his request with okay signs.

The rush of air from the quick opening of the door took his breath away for a second as he moved rapidly into the huge gym! Something told him to run forward quickly once inside! He heard a loud poof sound and saw a white flash head towards him! Greygor dodged the oncoming object and ran to the left as he heard the object slam into the door behind him! Another object was launched towards him, he reeled to the right feeling the rush of air of the thing go pass his ear and then heard it hit the wall! He raised his sword up as another came at him! It hit his forearm of his left arm hard causing him to let the sword fly out of his hand and across the floor into a darkened corner! Two white flashes came at him and he dodged one as the other hit him hard in the thigh! He fell and rolled too the right trying to find something he could hide behind.

Above Arthur tried to focus in on what was being fired at his brother and finally caught sight of one of the flashes being launched! He fired an arrow at the object, the arrow hit right on target causing the one machine to squeal to a halt! It then exploded sending sparks and smoke up into the air.

Greygor got up from the ground running hard in the direction of the small blast but felt something slam right into his stomach bowling him over unable to breath! Arthur fired another arrow at the second flash hitting the second machine just as he had done to the first! It also exploded the same way! Greygor was able to slowly get up from the ground and reached to the small of his back for his flying G. Loud running footsteps came towards him fast and he felt a foot slam into his left shoulder sending him flying backwards and on to the floor! He felt someone's knees land on his arms and felt a blade at his neck.

"Don't do it!" Arthur shouted down to the person on his brother. "My next shot hits you right in the back of the head!"

Dale and Peter came running through the door headed towards Greygor and person on him axes ready for action!

"Stop please!" A young girl yelled from the darkness! "Don't hurt my daddy!"

"We give up!" An older woman's voice shouted. "Please just don't hurt him he was just protecting his family!"

"Get the girls out of here honey! The man yelled. "Do it Jan!"

Dale and Peter stopped in their tracks as Arthur above withdrew his arrow after hearing that familiar voice. Greygor looked up into his youngest brother's face and though in a lot of pain smiled.

"How are you doing Wayne?" He was finally able to get out though winded as well. "Think you can get off of me now?"

"G?" Wayne asked in shock as he got up off his brother and gave him a hand up. "You're alive?"

He easily pulled Greygor up into the air and he then landed on his feet off balanced but held up by Wayne's strong arm, he then pulled his brother to him hugging him tight. He squeezed what little breath he had left in.

"Wayne!" He whispered barely. "Let me catch my breath!"

Wayne let him go and helped hold him up as Dale and Peter came up to greet their high school friend. They all hugged happily as

Greygor bent over with his hands on his laps shaking his head and trying to catch his breath.

"Thank god you are alive, Grey." Came the voice of Jan from his side and she hugged him as well but not as tightly. "I hope we didn't hurt you to bad with that machine."

From the darkness he heard more footsteps coming towards him. "Uncle Grey! Uncle Arthur you're here!"

The three girls came up and hugged their Uncle and then hugged Dale and Peter. Arthur came through the double doors and greeted everyone as well. Another happy reunion had begun! They all decided to get out of the school and walk up and see the other three on the hill. As they went they told their stories of how they survived. Charles, Marie and Will were very excited to see the family safe and sound. They all hugged and began to talk to one another. Wayne was the youngest of the brothers but the tallest and he had the biggest muscles. His short brown hair matched his oldest siblings and he had the same facial features as his older brothers. Jan was a very petite woman with blondish long hair and a very sweet face. Their oldest daughter Dorina resembled her mother very much. The middle daughter Ashley had blonde hair and looked like her father as did the youngest that also had blonde long hair. 15, 13 and 11 were their ages and they were growing up to be very beautiful young ladies.

Greygor walked over to Sampson and took a swig from his canteen. He was feeling better now though the hits he took were rough.

Wayne walked over to him and placed a hand on his shoulder. "Sorry about the gym attack Bro I was just trying to protect the family."

"No problem, I have been hit harder than that in the last few weeks." Greygor smiled at him. "What the heck were you shooting at me anyway?"

"That was a baseball machine set at its highest speed; we had two of them firing at you and only hit you three times! Wayne laughed. "You're still pretty fast for an old man! Ha-ha!"

"Thanks a lot Bro!" Greygor cracked a smile handing him the canteen. "I am just glad everyone is safe."

He began telling him about the military and the plans that they have. He told him a quick recollection of his exploits and brought tears to his eyes when he told him that their parents were safe. He then told him of the two large groups of people and how they were forming fighting groups to assist in their travels back down to North Carolina and to the Hidden Lair. He was quick and to the point on everything and finally ended with the search that had just ended with finding his family.

"So, we are going back over to Moon and meeting up with this large mass of people?" Wayne asked. "Then after doing some training and me taking a group of men for my group the Barbarians as your calling them, we are heading south to meet up with mom and dad's group of people who are also training I take it.? Then we are all traveling to this safe place and hoping not to have any problems from the military on the way? If we do hopefully our people can defend themselves and we can all make it to the Hidden Lair where the military will have one hell of a time messing with us?"

"You seem to have the general idea so far!" Greygor laughed at how crazy it all seemed.

"It sounds pretty crazy to me!' Wayne said sarcastically. "You have come up with some wild ideas in the past my brother but this takes the cake!"

"If you would rather stay here and take your chances Bro, I will understand."

"I dont think so!" Wayne laughed, "you need someone like me to help watch over our family because if a couple of baseballs can about take you out God only knows what could happen to you!"

"That's not funny!" He replied rubbing his thigh where he knew he had to be badly bruised.

Greygor turned to Sampson's saddle and grabbed a stiff blanket from his back and handed to Wayne. "I was saving this for you."

He unfolded a blanket to show a double edge battle axe that belonged to Greygor for many years. Its blades were sharp and wide and it had a three foot handle on it. He felt the weight of it in his hands and shook his head affirmatively. He began swinging it around his body and letting his muscles get the feel of it, he kept a tight grip on it even when he switched hands and twirled it. He finished up by sinking the blade into a log close to him just to see just how sharp it really was.

"Thank you Bro!" He smiled at him. "I know this axe means a lot to you. It's like you knew that you were going to find me."

"You and the family mean more to me than some silly weapon Bro!" Greygor smiled, "I wasn't giving up on you being alive."

They hugged and then began getting everyone ready for the ride back to the camp. It didn't take long before they were on their way.

Chapter 14

Supplies were being brought in on a daily basis into the camp as they all readied for the move south. They teams had found several stores in the area that they were able to get into and get canned foods, rice, pasta, bottled water, and other long life food items. From demolished sporting good, hardware and larger stores they found clothing, survival gear and more weapons that would be useful along the way. More horses were found and Chad had formed a group of people to create makeshift wagons.

Training in the last four days since they had returned from finding Wayne was going very well. He had jumped right into creating his Barbarian group and started working with them the next day. Rider's Warrior group was achieving great strides in their workouts.

Arthur and his Sharpshooters aim were getting better every day. Kent chose several very strong horses for his Rapid Rider group and he worked out with his people teaching them attacks from horseback. The Thief group exercised with the warrior group since Cole was still away. Charles was getting his Guard group together and keeping them busy with guard duty for the camp as well as training.

Greygor's coffee was perfect this morning; the bitter brew was hot enough where he had to carefully sip it. He sat talking with Arthur, Rider and Chad about the things that had been developing as well as the move that was taking place in the days to come. They were still a week or more ahead of the military and their plans. Greygor kept wondering how long Cole was going to be out investigating the military camp. He knew that his friend was good at this but still worried. He looked up from his coffee cup and looked around slowly taking in the area around him. Something was missing but he couldn't put his finger on it.

"What's wrong G?" Rider asked. "You seem to be in your own little world this morning."

"It's nothing Ride." Greygor smiled after sipping his coffee. "I must be getting a bit edgy about this move and everything."

"Don't worry G." Chad replied, "We will get everyone safely down to the other group and then get to the Hidden Lair."

"I know Chad."

He smiled at them but still couldn't shake the feeling that something just wasn't right. He took a quick swig of his coffee letting the hot liquid flow quickly down his throat. He tossed the cup into the wash bucket and stood up and stretched his muscles ready for a new day of exercise.

"Well guys it's always a pleasure to have you around but its time to get busy." He said as he began to walk away as the others followed for a few yards and then headed off to their different areas.

Greygor had promised to help out Kent for a while and try his hand at Rapid Rider training. He wanted to be ready for anything that could present itself at any time. He felt practicing with each group would hone his skills. Though every night his body was sore and achy it made him feel stronger each day. He reached Kent's area after a few minutes and got a huge smile on his face as he watched Kent going through an exercise while his group watched.

He rode hard at his first target, riding low with his long sword in hand he sliced down low cutting the dummy where the thighs would have been sending it flying up into the air and then to the ground! He turned his horse around rapidly and headed towards the next target! He began to pass it on the right bringing his sword straight into the center of the dummy! He plunged it in and then let his arm swing back so that the sword would not get stuck and cause him to lose it! The horse bucked and he pulled hard to the left on the reins! The horse once again did as his rider wanted and took off at a dead run at the next target! Kent sheathed his sword and pulled a spear from its holder on the side of the horse. As he headed towards the next target he threw the spear hitting it in the center! He rode a little ways pass the target then brought his horse to a stop and turned him towards the group. He stopped a few yards in front of the men and women.

"We have to remember when we attack we are mainly out there to quickly wound the enemy and then go to the next target as quickly as we can!" He shouted though winded. "Those wounded will be handled by the other fighting groups as quickly as possible. Keep control of your horses and your weapons at all times! When thrusting a sword into a target make sure you can bring it back out the same way as it went in or you could end up being pulled off your horse and breaking your neck! When slicing an enemy do not go for a deep cut because if the sword hits bone it could stick and take you down! Keep your reins tight at all times but especially when you're attacking the horse needs to know you are in charge as well as know you're not going to let it get harmed!"

Kent saw Greygor behind the crowd and got off of his horse and handed the reins to one of the men.

"Get to your horses and run a few exercises with them but be careful!" He shouted as he walked towards his friend.

"That was some great riding my friend!" Greygor said shaking his hand. "I didn't know you could ride like that, let alone use weapons that accurately. I am impressed!"

"Thanks Grey." Kent grabbed his canteen from his side and drank some water. "Looks like we may have some good fighters here, they learn fast!"

"I have to agree with you there friend." Greygor said. "You had asked me to come down to give some fighting pointers but it seems you're doing a great job yourself."

They began talking about different attacks and the possibility off adding some different weapons to the attacks, Kent listened intently to a few ideas he had and had many of his own that which they both agreed were really good. The group went through their drills as the two men watched pointing out things as the workouts went on. From behind they heard someone yelling and turned to see what was going on. Coming down the hill was his niece May!

"Uncle Grey!" She yelled. "Uncle Charles needs your help! He's been hurt!"

He took off at a dead run followed by Kent across the small field and then up the hill following May whom had started running towards the trouble. A large crowd was circling whatever was going on. He pushed through the people and finally made it to the center of the crowd. He found Charles on the ground cradled by Angel as Jack stood holding his sword out protecting the both of them! His brother was holding his side and Greygor could see the blood. Anger filled his mind as he looked over at the man yelling at the crowd!

"No damn Joseph man is going to give me orders!" A loud voice exclaimed. "I'll kill every one of them!"

Greygor stared at the long faced dark haired man. He stood a good six foot tall and was built very muscular. It was Ray, a person Greygor and everyone else knew way too well as an ignorant trouble maker when he was in high school and within his own neighborhood. Beside him as he walked around was his younger and much smaller brother Matt! He followed his brother around like a lost puppy looking for a bone. He also was a little weasel of a man, always in and causing trouble.

"Yeah!" He yelled after his brother would speak. "Who are they to give us orders?"

Greygor rushed over to his brother and checked his cut, "how bad is it bro!"

"About three inches deep and five long." He answered with pain in his voice.

"Ray!" he yelled with a growl in his voice turning around and drawing his sword! "What the hell do you think you're doing?"

Greygor backed Jack up and made him put his sword away and help his father and mother as Ray made his way towards him. He held his sword out ready for whatever could happen.

"Well! Well!" Ray spit out his angry words. "Here's the leader of the punks now! Ha-ha. Come to try and tell us what to do yourself since your big brother ended up split opened."

"Chill out Ray!" He shouted. "We don't have time for your ego trip!"

"You're the one with the ego!" Matt said sarcastically from behind his brother. "The big bad Greygor Josephs is trying to give orders!"

"Will you please shut that little brother of yours up?" Greygor said as Ray stopped a few feet in front of him holding his sword in front of him!

"I'm going to tear you apart you piece of shit!" Ray again spit as he shouted.

Through the crowd came the other leaders of the groups, all of which pulled their weapons out! Arthur notched an arrow and aimed it at Ray! He smiled wanting so bad to fire! Ray looked around at them and turned to Greygor again!

"So, still can't fight your own battles?" He growled, "Going to let your friends take me down like the piece of shit that you are!"

"Everyone back down!" Greygor yelled. "Put your weapons away I will handle this!"

He thought back to how they had once known each other from grade school and through high school. They weren't the closes of friends but still talked to each other for years. After Greygor got out of the military for some reason or another Ray had grown hatred towards him that to this day he could not figure out.

"Come on Ray let's try and work through this before anyone else gets hurt!" He said letting his voice calm down a bit. "We have to put whatever differences we have aside and get our families to safety!

"You can kiss my ass G!" Ray said immediately.

"Yea kiss his ass!" Matt repeated him like a parrot. "Mine too you asshole!"

Greygor cringed at the sound of that crackly voice and just wanted to put his fist through the little man's face! He kept his composer and tried to calm things down. "Listen Ray, I apologize for anything that I did to you as well as for anyone trying to order you around. Can't we let things ride and get on with what we got to do?"

"Slice him up Ray!" Matt cackled behind him. "He thinks he is the boss around here and he wants to push everyone around!"

They began circling each other as Greygor tried to calm the situation but the two men kept ranting and raving using every swear word that they knew. Everyone backed up a few steps not wanting to get caught up in the fight. Ray poked his sword towards him letting their blades clang together.

"I'm not doing this Ray." He said as he lowered his sword and began walking away.

"Don't turn your back on me!" He screamed and jumped towards Greygor swinging his sword down at his back!

He turned rapidly and raised his sword to deflect the attack! The blades rang out loudly and Ray pulled back and attempted a sideways swing that Greygor easily deflected! They started a rapid succession of attacks on each other; Matt did all he could to stay behind his brother taunting Greygor as the fight continued! He caught Ray's sword with his and used all his might to push it straight up and then swung his blade at Ray's midsection! He jumped back bumping into Matt who almost caused him to fall to the ground! The sword fight escalated as they attacked and defended their selves. They parried and thrust each gained the upper hand at different times and then had to block attacks from the other. A few times Ray about tripped over his brother who did all he could to remain safely behind his much larger brother. The murmurs from the crowd seemed to fade as Greygor's warrior sense began to kick in now. He could hear his friends in the crowd yell to him to be careful. He went forward attacking once more with a figure eight attack that Ray had trouble defending his self and about lost his sword! They locked up and came face to face!

"I am going to kill you!" Ray growled through clenched teeth as the two men pushed into each other with their locked swords.

Greygor unlocked his sword and stepped to the side twirling on one foot as Ray went forward off balance! As he spun around he let his sword slice into Ray's back who screamed in agony! He turned around one hand reaching back; he looked at his blood covered hand and rushed Greygor again! He picked up running foot steps behind him as he readied for Rays attack from the front! Time seemed to slow as he raised his sword up to deflect the rapid attack as Rays sword came in he let the edge of the sword scrape his as he dodged to the left and twisted his body away as he did this Ray went off balance and kept running forward! Greygor heard a loud thump and turned to see Ray and Matt slam into each other! Ray's momentum knocked both men to the ground!

Everyone saw that when the two men impacted the sword had plunged into Matt's chest and the knife that Matt was trying to stab Greygor in the back with had entered Rays left shoulder. As they collided their heads had cracked together! Greygor dropped his sword and walked over to them and was joined by Rider and Kent. They helped the larger man roll off of his brother and knew immediately that Matt was dead. His wide opened eyes showed the shock on his face from the sword penetrating his heart. The blood flowed from his body dampening the ground under him. Ray was barely conscious and Kent drew the knife from his shoulder and applied pressure to the wound. The wrist of his sword hand was mangled horribly from the blow of the attack. Bone stuck out from the fracture he had received from the crash. Rider placed his hand over Matt's eyes and pulled his eyelids closed. Ray started to come around and yelled in pain from his wounds. Greygor stood above him saddened that it had to come to this. The rest of the group leaders came up and looked down at the two men.

Rider who was kneeling looked up at Greygor and asked. "What do you want to do with him?"

"You're a bastard!" Ray said through gritted teeth. "I'll get you for killing my brother!"

"You're the one who started this!" He yelled angrily. "I tried to get you to stop! You tried to kill my brother and me and then ended up killing your own brother! If anyone's a bastard you are! To top it off your brother lies dead next to you and you show no remorse! You are such a lowlife and deserve to die yourself!"

The crowd became very quiet as both men stared at each other. A shot of pain ran through Ray's arm causing him to wince and tear up. Greygor turned and walked over and picked up his sword and put it back in its sheath. He looked around at everyone knowing he probably shouldn't have said that Ray deserved death but the man had just killed his own brother and that bothered him that he didn't even care!

"What do you want to do with him?" Kent asked from behind him.

"You want us to finish him off?" Wayne asked raising an eyebrow.

"Fix and stitch up his wounds, set his arm so that it heals right and then give him a horse and supplies." Greygor said loud enough for everyone to hear. "Send him riding North away from the military and us. Have a small team travel with him for about twenty miles. Then let him keep riding! If he shows his face anywhere near us again I will personally kill him myself!"

They helped Ray up and led him over to the medical tent. They kept their weapons at the ready in case he tried anything stupid. The crowd began to clap for Greygor and for his decision not to take Ray's life. He went over to where Charles had now sat up while a woman stitched up his wound.

"Are you alright brother?" He asked smiling down at him.

"Yes, it will heal." Charles said. "He was fine till he found out you were my brother and then he went all crazy. What did you do to him?"

"Believe me brother if I knew I would tell you."

"You don't have any more enemies that we should be aware of do you?"

"Well other than Matthews and his military?" He said as he started to walk off. "I really can't think of anyone off the top of my head!"

The crowd began to break up and get back to work as Greygor walked off to be by himself. He still felt like something was just not right but just couldn't put his finger on it. He stood at a hillside just looking around wishing Cole would hurry and get back with some news. Perhaps that would ease his uneasy feeling.

Chapter 15

The first three days of travel had been slow but steady. Though they had gone over all the maps and over every plan for the move and the training along the way these first few days had been a shambles. Everything that could go wrong did and the things that might have gone wrong did so as well. Wagon wheels broke; horses came up lame, a number of people ended up sick or hurt. They all wondered if they never would make it pass the Pennsylvania border. They eventually did and as the trip progressed into West Virginia things seemed to progress a bit better. Everyone began getting up about four in the morning having breakfast and then began moving out about six. Each day they pushed to make it at least eighteen to twenty miles. It had been figured out that the trip down to the meeting place would take sixteen days and then twenty or more days from there to the Hidden Lair. The days were going by quickly and they were about three days away from Berkley West Virginia. The people seemed to be doing well with the move now and getting use to the early morning start and then setting up camp around seven at night. People took turns riding on the wagons or riding horses while others walked and then they switched throughout the day. Greygor let his three youngest nieces all ride on Sampson most of the trip south. A few men had been chosen to ride ahead to let the people waiting in the meeting area know that they were on their way.

Every night the group leaders got together and discussed their progress so far in the training as well as the movement south. So far the efforts they made to keep training as they went was going very well.

They had all ate dinner and were relaxing around bonfires as nightfall came and went. Greygor and the Joseph family sat around discussing the trip and watching the night sky above light up with the lightening. It wasn't long before Greygor decided to turn in and said goodnight to all. He went off to his blanket and made himself comfortable. It had gotten to the point that the night flashes actually helped him fall asleep.

"Don't you ever worry about being sneaked up on and killed in your sleep?" A familiar voice silently said from the shadows a few feet away.

"Not when it's my best friend trying his hardest to sneak up on me." He whispered back smiling as he sat up. "Are you okay?"

"I am fine but our people might not be." Cole answered as he sat down next him.

"What did you find?"

"Well, the military started moving out just as they had planned too for one."

"Well that was already known my friend." Greygor smiled.

"I am curious as to why the majority of the military is being led south and a smaller group is actually heading north my friend?" Cole asked.

"What did you say?"

"For some reason Matthews is leading his men down to the North Carolina border where we will be greeted by their smiling faces!"

Greygor placed his forehead against his hands shaking it in disbelief. Cole reached out and placed a hand on his shoulder. He just sat there letting different scenarios go through his mind. All of which did not look good.

"While you were in camp did you see or hear anything extra strange?" Greygor looked up at him.

"Actually I did see a messenger was sent out on horseback every couple days and then the soldier would return and report directly to Matthews's tent. I couldn't get close enough to hear anything. It was weird to the messenger seemed be heading towards the North at first then the last few times they seemed to be going East to West."

"I wonder why?" Greygor asked as if he already knew the answer.

"You're about to tell me we have an informant in this camp aren't you?"

"I know there is Cole." He said with a hint of anger in his voice. "I have felt like something wasn't quite right in camp but couldn't put my finger on it."

"Who would betray us and their own family?" He asked.

"Well, we know that it's not Ray or Matt." Greygor chuckled.

"Hell, I wouldn't put it pass those two back stabbers!"

"I would have thought so too but since the messengers started heading East to West as we began traveling down I really doubt it."

"Why couldn't they, G?" Cole asked, "They are both capable of it!"

"Well since Matt is dead and Ray is pretty busted up and heading north I really don't think it's them!"

"What the hell did you do while I was gone?" Cole looked at him confused.

Greygor began retelling the story of the events that happened with the two of them and then explained the outcome of the fight. Cole now seemed to be in a shocked state as he listened in disbelief.

"You let that slime ball get away? Cole asked.

"Yes, I didn't want his blood on my hands."

"He could heal up and hunt for you or try and help the military find us though." Cole firmly said. "Do you want our blood on your conscious?"

"Lighten up my friend he really isn't that smart."

"Revenge can make the stupidest man a genius."

"Can we get back to the military please? Greygor replied.

"We need to have a meeting with the group leaders first thing in the morning." Cole said.

"No, we need to get them together now!" Greygor stood up and stretched. "We have to let them know what's ahead of us and then get these people down to the meeting place and get things figured out!"

"Let's go gather them up then!" Cole said standing as well. "Looks like its going to be a long night!"

"You got that right." Greygor said as the two friends began to walk together. "Let's keep the informant thing between the two of us for now."

"You have a feeling of who it is?"

"I might Cole but I don't want to say anything yet."

"My lips are sealed!"

By ten o'clock all the group leaders were sitting around the fire Cole had built yawning and trying to wake up. Landon Yonders and his brother Mick had been asked to come as well since they had been assisting in the thief group training while Cole had been away. Wayne and Arthur were the first to arrive followed by Chad, Rider and Hogan. Kent, Will, Charles and Jack were last to arrive.

"Listen up everybody!" Greygor started. "Cole has just informed me that we have a problem that we have to figure out immediately."

"I kind of figured it was something since you woke us all out of a sound sleep Bro!" Wayne laughed.

"The military has somehow figured out that we are moving South and are planning on setting up a trap at the borders of North Carolina as well as sending soldiers North to follow us down from behind." Greygor told them.

"I was there with you when Matthews said he was moving his troops north." Kent said. "How does he know we are moving the people south?"

"For all we know he could have had soldiers watching our movement, but that isn't important on how he knows it's more important that we figure out what is best to do!"

"Cole, how many troops would you says he has heading North and South?" Rider asked.

"Mathews is moving close to two thousand men towards the border at this time and the rest towards the North. Ammunition is in short supply and they are doing the same as us gathering up swords bows and other assorted weapons along the way. Horses as well are minimal for them as well." Cole responded.

"It looks like we may out number them. Chad added. "That's with the fighters we have with the other group. But with them having so many rifles at their disposal they have the upper hand in any kind of fight."

"How long before they reach the border Cole?" Arthur asked.

"The way they were moving I would say a few days before us giving them time to set up a field to stop us."

"Do we know about where they are going to set up their camp?" Kent asked.

"I was able to draw up a few maps that show where they are heading." Cole answered. "Why what's on your mind?"

"Well, if we can check out that area." Kent stood. "Get the details of the area and perhaps arrive at that point before the military we could have a chance of surprising them before they get settled in."

"We could set up the Sharpshooters, Rapid Riders and Thief group early and have the element of surprise." Greygor added to what Kent was saying.

"We could go ahead and get the fighting groups moving down faster than the main party." Hogan said. "We could meet up with the other group and get whatever people able to fight from there and go ahead of them and get there before the military does and be ready!"

"That is a possibility." Rider replied. "Even if the soldiers would get there a day ahead of us we could use the night to our advantage."

"What about the rest of the people?" Charles asked. "I mean yes we are willing to give it a good fight and we may have the possibility of getting the upper hand but we have to be ready to get them somewhere safe if all falls through."

"The only option is to begin moving them East towards the ocean." Greygor said. "Once we meet up with the other group we get them going to the ocean and then move them south into North Carolina and then back West towards the Hidden Lair if the fight goes bad."

"If we win though don't we stand the chance of any surviving military following us to the Hidden Lair?" Landon asked.

"After, we win this fight." Greygor said firmly. "Any soldiers left alive or who attempt to flee will be hunted down and killed to assure the lair stays hidden!"

"You're sounding a little cruel there Bro." Wayne replied.

"The military wants us all dead and buried!" Greygor stated. "We need to feel the same for them!"

"I have to agree with you on that G." Arthur said.

"We are going to let all the people know what's going on." Chad asked.

"Of course my friend but first we have to get everything figured out." Greygor said. "In the morning Kent Arthur and Cole are going to take a few men from each their groups and ride to the area at the border and map it out. You're going to need to find the best places for you to set up your groups."

"You're going to want me to have part of my group their ready to infiltrate before dawn to add to our advantage right?" Cole asked.

"Your too take out as much of their ammunition and rifles as possible. You know who your very best are in your group use them! We can go over this once you three get back from your ride."

"Tomorrow morning we will get the word out to everyone about what is going on. We will then gather all the members of the groups and take off ahead of the main party to get to the meeting area and gather the rest of the people and place them in their groups."

"Are you going to use my Guard group in this?" Charles asked.

"Yes but your men will be in charge of getting the people down to the meeting area and then I want you to get everyone ready to move out. We will send word to you to begin moving the masses south after we win or too make a mad dash to the east to escape the military."

"You want me to get to the coast travel down into South Carolina and then head northwest to the Hidden Lair?"

"That's exactly what I want you to do Charles." Greygor replied. "Here is the thing, we are going to let the people know that Matthews is heading to the border and planning on catching us there. As of now the word to go out is that we are going to use the groups to fight so that the people can move Northwest to Canada and hopefully to safety!"

"Thought you said we were heading south or east depending on the outcome?" Hogan asked.

"There is a chance that the military has somehow infiltrated our people." Greygor told the leaders. "We have to keep our actual plans between us for right now my friends."

"The people are going to be wondering why the groups are heading out ahead of them." Chad added.

"For now we just tell them the plan about Canada." He stated. "Cole noticed messengers riding in and out of the military camp and the only thing that we can think of is either they have soldiers watching us from afar or they have a man or two in our camp."

The rest of the group leaders agreed to keep the plans silent as well. They began going over the plans for getting the groups moving ahead of the rest of the people. Everyone gave their input on the plans that they were making. After a few hours they all headed off to get a little sleep before dawn.

In the morning Arthur, Cole and Kent packed a few supplies and rode out of camp with a few of their men. The other group leaders began gathering their people as they put the word out about what was going on. Greygor packed up his weapons and gear on Sampson and rode out with Rider and the rest leading the fighting groups south. They were going to travel throughout the day as well as the night as to reach the meeting area quicker as planned.

Chapter 16

The fighting groups had made it to the meeting place in a day and a half The leaders began adding the people from Xanadu mountain and from Cole's camp to their groups while Greygor greeted his parents and other family members. Darla and Robert were very happy that all their children and grandchildren were safe. He then talked to the council that had been created on the mountain and a few of the leaders from the camp. He explained to them about the military and the plans that had been created so far.

Charles lead the rest of the people in, three days later and Arthur and Kent rode in the same day with all their information from the border area. They let Greygor know that after they had gathered their information about the area Cole had decided to ride off with one of his men and check the progress of the military. He told them that he would meet them back at the meeting area in a few days. The group leaders got together to look over the maps and information brought back. The area that the military were heading for was along the main highway. They figured that Matthews had decided on this area because of the mountains on each side would keep the people from any escape. The mountainous terrain wasn't really too steep and were covered by woods. Between the mountains the width of the highways and including the brush covered center were two hundred yards of flat terrain. Before reaching the area this highway area the highways sloped down for about five miles. In Matthews mind he felt this was a great place to trap all these people and wipe them out.

In Greygor and the group leader's minds this place was perfect for an all out assault on the military. The mountains on each side gave great cover for the Sharpshooters to fire down on them! Kent suggested that the Rapid Riders could carefully make their way around the mountains and attack the soldiers from the sides and from behind. The Warrior and Barbarian groups could use the incline of the hill to the north to cover their attack as well. The thief group could use the bushy terrain in the center to launch their assault on the soldiers. As the meeting progressed Cole rode into camp and joined the meeting. He let them know that the military would probably reach the area within six days. The meeting ended with word to keep training everyone and to be ready to move out at anytime. As everyone went off to take care of their groups Greygor and Cole stood around looking at the maps and discussing a few other plans.

"You're definitely sure about the six days?" Greygor asked

"They aren't moving all that fast as if they are waiting for something." Cole replied. "They are more than likely waiting for word from their stool pigeon."

"I have to agree with you on that."

"When do you think he will make his move and try and get to the soldiers G?"

"I have a feeling he is just biding his time till he thinks no one will notice his disappearance. Things are getting real busy now and it will happen soon."

"So are we taking him out before he can let them know anything?" Cole asked.

"No way my friend I want him to feed them all the information that he has been collecting and then get back here to our camp."

"Alright now I am utterly confused my friend," Cole scratched his head. "You are going to let him get out of camp and go to the military and tell them what he knows and then come back into camp?"

"That is my plan my friend." He smiled wickedly.

"Wait a minute G; you're not planning on following him are you?" Cole asked concerned.

"Both of us are following him to their camp and then we are going to find out what he tells them and what Matthews has planned." Greygor said nonchalantly.

"I don't think that's a good idea buddy!" Cole said. "All he really can tell them is what we let out to the groups that the fighting groups are going to hold this ground while the larger mass heads west!"

"I have to get in there and see what we are up against as well as know if what we really have planned will work! I need your help on this Cole."

"Wait a minute my friend what are you working on inside that head of yours?"

"Come on Cole if we get in there and see that our groups can't handle this battle there is only one other alternative!" Greygor stared at him. "These people deserve the chance to live!"

"You're planning on assassinating Matthews and as many of his top leaders as you can before you get killed off while you send the people east!"

"You left out the best part then as I lead his military West to assure the peoples escape I get to silently attack soldiers every night till none of them are left!" Greygor said.

"That will never work!" Cole told him. "What makes you think they will follow you that far?"

"Revenge my friend." Greygor smiled again. "These soldiers who follow him have actually never seen a day of combat in their life and are hungry for the gold that he has stashed for his followers. Without Matthews everything that they want vanishes! They will know I was the one who killed their leaders and want me dead! I will make sure they follow me all the way to the end!"

"What if we get in there and see that the groups can handle what is about to come?" Cole asked.

"Then we go back to the initial plan, we set up our people and destroy the military as we have planned too and then we high tail it to the Hidden Lair!"

"I really do hope you remember everything I taught you about shadow walking!" Cole said shaking his head.

"I'll be fine Cole, you are a good teacher remember?"

"I am starting to regret teaching you this stuff." Cole added jokingly. "We got to get some practice in tonight for your sake."

"We have two nights to hone my skills my friend." Greygor patted his shoulder.

"How do you figure?"

"Our little friend is going to be given his opportunity three nights from now." He smiled again.

"How is that going to happen?" Cole just had to know.

"Charles's is putting him on double outer perimeter guard duty that night."

"So you're going to make it easy for him then?"

"Oh why not let's give him what he wants?" Greygor replied. "It will take him a few days to meet up with the military and tell them what he knows and then we can have the group leaders tell everyone our true plans while we check out the camp and follow him back here. By the time he learns the real plan he won't have time to reveal it to the military."

"He could sneak off again." Cole mentioned.

"No way, he is going to be kept very busy afterwards."

"On another matter Greygor, what is your plan for my thief group before the shit hit's the fan?"

"Let's just say that your group will be doing some real special infiltration for two nights before the battle."

"So I need to pick out about twenty of my best shadow walkers and be ready to steal weapons and ammo?" Cole asked. "Luckily on their march down they have been keeping their weapons in the ammo tent and only handing out rifles to soldiers on guard duty."

"Actually, I was thinking more along the lines of you stealing the firing pins from most of the weapons in the tent." Greygor replied,

"And yes you taking most of their ammunition. But I want you to create a firework show from their ammo tent as well."

"I don't know G messing with weapons around sleeping soldiers could get someone killed. What about the guards on duty?"

"You're the master at handling little things like that, just do what you do best."

"Is this your way of telling me that you would rather not want to have to perform that plan C?" Cole asked letting out a small laugh.

"I really don't think you want me to actually have to do it either." He said. "You would miss me way too much."

"Not really, I would just start hanging with one of your brothers!" Cole laughed loudly.

"You're an ass!" He said seriously. "I have to go talk to Charles about a few things, meet you tonight."

The two friends shook hands and headed on their way to prepare for the coming days. Greygor had his talk with Charles and then talked to each of the group leader's one on one letting them know the plan as well. Cole met with Kent and asked him to sneak two horses out of camp on the day of their ride to the military camp. They set up a place that he would leave them. During the next few days Greygor worked out with the different groups but at night Cole and he worked on shadow walking together. Cole was pleased to see that his old friend had retained what he had taught him so many years ago. But he pushed him harder than he had back then just to assure nothing went wrong on the night that Greygor just had to sneak into the camp.

On the third day the plan that Greygor had worked out with Charles went just as they had wanted. Both Cole and him met with their parents secretly to let them know what was going on and to tell them not to worry that all would be fine. They ate with their families before dusk and then went to their tents to ready their gear. After dark they would meet outside of camp and retrieve the horses and then wait for the informant to make his move.

Chapter 17

They had traveled most of the night and into the morning following the man at least two or three miles back. He was traveling Northwest on secondary roads most of the time but finally took to a major highway that he must have known the military was traveling. Cole was still in shock over which person it was that was informing the soldiers. They stayed to the woods along the side of the road tracking him along the way. It was easy since Cole had been this way checking out the military movement himself. The day went fast as they followed and at about four in the afternoon, noises ahead caused them to ride into the woods and up and around a steep hill. They left the horse up on top and cautiously made their way down through the trees and bushes. They watched with binoculars as the man was led to a large tent and went inside. An hour or so later they watched as General Snorpaly came out and began sending messengers out across the camp. From what they could hear a meeting was going to be held tonight after chow time. Greygor and Cole made their way back up to the horses to ready their gear for the night.

They both pulled out their old black outfits that which had gauntlets and special shoes that separated the big toe from the rest. They changed into them and then placed their weapons carefully in and on the clothing. Cole hung his shotgun holsters across his chest and then tied the shirt over them. Greygor had his long knives and stars hidden within his shirt. Their outfits had many hidden pockets and places to put certain weapons of choice. Greygor's Flying G as always was in the pouch at the small of his back. He tested his throwing knives strapped to his arm to make sure that they easily slid to his hand when needed. He checked all his weapons to assure none would hit together and give him away. This was a recon mission for information and they didn't want it to turn into a blood bath. Cole checked all his blades as well for easy access. As time flew by they watched as the camp below lit campfires and bonfires as night invaded the day. It was only a matter of time before they would head down and into the camp.

It was time and he concentrated on the darkness around him, it felt as if the shadows were engulfing him as he pushed his senses out from him and into the night. His breathing grew shallow and his body felt lighter. He felt his senses become enhanced.

He remembered the quote that Cole had taught him;

"The shadow walkers travel amongst the living in the dark of night. Seeing, hearing and feeling all things around them. Capturing secrets and knowing the thoughts of those who wish to harm the innocent. They show no mercy, no forgiveness to those of evil nature."

Over the ages this ability had been called by many names as well as used by many cultures. In Asia it was used by the best in martial arts. The assassins of medieval times in Europe used it to enhance their abilities. In the Middle East it was used by the thieves of Baghdad. Cole had been taught it in the Marines Special Forces years ago and had pushed himself in his training so hard he had become one of the best. He had taught his best friend this ability; it had come in handy many times.

Greygor could feel the darkness surrounding him like a cool breeze swirling around his body. He felt a slight buzz in his head as if he had just had a shot of liquor. He could see, hear, smell and feel everything around him. This was so different from the thing he called his Warrior sense. This was more peaceful and calm whereas the other was more wild serge of energy throughout the body.

He picked up a rush of air going pass him and heard Cole whisper. "Meet you near the main tent remember what I taught you and you better be very careful!"

He began to walk down the hill his movements seemed as if time stood still around him. Not a sound could be heard from his footsteps as he increased his speed dodging anything that got in his way. He reached the bottom of the hill and stopped behind a fallen tree. He listened carefully and scanned around him. It was at least one hundred yards of open ground to the first row of tents. A fire was burning in front of the tents and he could already smell the wood burning even that far away. He leaped over the tree and ran hard towards the camp not making even a whisper of a sound as he went. Greygor reached the edge of camp and jumped to the back of a tent quietly landing and rolling to its edge. He listened for anyone inside and decided that there wasn't any one so he slipped under the back of it.

Inside it was dark and he could smell the damp mildew that most tents got when they get wet. Walking to the opening he peered out and saw a few soldiers walking towards the main tent where Matthews would be speaking. He again used his senses to check the area outside for any possible threats. Not feeling any he slipped out and used the shadows of the tents to move to the center of Camp. He kept his mind on his objective and blocked everything else from his mind. It wasn't long till he was lying in the prone position next to the last of the tents shadows waiting to make a jump that would place him under one of the wagons where he would be hidden and able to listen to Matthews. His body tensed up for the leap and he started to move but stopped! Something wasn't right! He relaxed as two soldiers walked right pass his face. As they went by Greygor let his body leap up and over to the wagon mere inches from their backs! He rolled under the wagon and stopped. One of the soldiers looked back as he talked to the other one; he shrugged and continued on his way. The wagon was situated a few feet back from the mass of soldiers sitting on the ground awaiting the words of their leader. He slid over to the wagon wheel and looked out at the large tent in the center of the camp.

"That was a tad cocky if you ask me." Cole's whisper seemed right next to his ear. "Next time you need to wait till they walk a bit further."

He knew Cole was right but he just shrugged it off. He also knew not to try and look to see where Cole was he would never see him. He focused on the murmurs of the soldiers trying to pick up any useful information that he could. He scanned the camp for any signs of armored vehicles or anything that could hurt his people's chances of survival.

"I did a full recon of the camp before coming here I didn't see anything either." Cole whispered as if reading Greygor's mind. "They are keeping all the weapons and ammo in the ammunition tent over to the right of the main tent and its pretty much the same set up as I have seen each time they stop and camp."

The flap of the main tent opened and out walked General Snorpaly and Captain Frank. They walked up to the makeshift podium as the soldiers began to clap and cheer. Greygor smiled at the sight of Captain Frank with one less hand courtesy of Luck's crushing jaws.

"That's the guy who killed your dog?" The silent whisper came to him as a hand patted his back.

Greygor's knuckles turned white as he tightened his fist, he let himself calm down. The General raised his hand to silent the soldiers. They immediately became very quiet. He shuffled through some papers on the podium and then again looked out at the crowd.

"Tonight we have new information on the movement of the civilians who have committed treason against the United States of America!" General Snorpaly shouted. "Our Commander and Chief will now speak to you on the new findings and our mission! Please welcome President Jonathan Matthews!"

The crowd cheered and clapped again and stood to their feet as Mathews came out of his tent and approached the podium! They all sat back down and became very quiet as he raised his hands and smiled out at them. The man responsible for his new information stood right behind him. Greygor felt his anger growing within him! He wanted to rush out and take out all four men standing at the podium! He started to feel his warrior sense trying to over take the shadow walker senses!

"Easy friend his time will come" Cole whispered. "Relax and just listen."

"Tonight we welcome a hero amongst us!" Matthews's deep voice shouted out. "This man has risked his life to bring information pertaining to the civilians who are attempting to escape our grasp! These people have even gone so far as to form small fighting groups in an attempt to go against us in hopes of getting to some hidden location! Their leader is a man who has time and time again attacked us and killed our fellow soldiers! He even went as far to rip Captain Franks hand off and feed it to his dog! I am sickened by this killer! He will not be allowed to continue his murderous ways! I will personally make him kneel at my feet and repent and then I will take his life as he has done too many of our heroes!"

The soldiers began clapping and cheering their leaders words. He raised his hands to silent them once again smiling and waving at his men.

"This Greygor Josephs will die at my feet!" Matthews continued as he placed his arm around the informant and patted him on the chest. "This man here has come to us to let us know his plans! These people whom we shall destroy are willing to go against us at the border of North Carolina! They wish too attempt to hold us off while the larger mass of people try to sneak off like cowards to the west and escape us into Canada! All of you, my military will keep this from happening! Yes, we will meet them at the border in a few days and yes we will look down on them with pity and remorse! We will then remember that they are committing treason against our great country and rapidly take from them what they hold so sacred! Their lives will not be spared! We shall send them straight into hell and then we will hunt down their families who are running to the west and kill them as well! Perhaps we will just capture their murderous leader and hold him while we search out this hiding place of his and wipe out his family who are waiting for him there and let him watch the slaughter and then kill him as I said before!"

Greygor's eyes were fixed on the man who had betrayed everyone! He could feel his anger welling up again! How could he tell the military everything including the information about the Hidden Lair and his family there? What kind of sick human being was he to do this to his own? He had to be taken care off and he would be!

"Our friend here must head back now to learn more and to keep us posted on anything new that develops!" Matthews said and began to clap for him.

Again the soldiers gave him a standing ovation as he walked over to his horse and mounted up. He waved and saluted them as he kicked his horse into a run heading through the tents and into the darkness. The soldiers settled down and waited for their leader to speak once more.

These are trying times my friends!" He continued. "We must make decisions and do things that we may not like to do! We must keep military strong at all cost and rid ourselves of every weak link that we find!"

As he spoke Greygor and Cole both noticed Frank slipping slowly behind the General, they saw a flash of metal and watched as the Captain grab him from behind and slice his knife across Snorpaly's neck! The shocked gasping expression on his face caused Greygor to look away as he fell dead to the ground! Matthews looked down at him and then over at Frank and smiled!

"Unfortunately, our beloved General Snorpaly has become weak and must resign from his post! Matthews shouted to his men. "Today my new second in command General Frank will be taking over for him!"

Cheers went out as General Frank walked a few steps forward wiping the blood from his knife on his pants. He raised it up into the air smiling out at the crowd. Cole tapped Greygor on the shoulder letting him know that was their cue to get out of there. In seconds

Greygor knew he was already gone and then snuck out from under the wagon and headed off through the shadows of the camp. He made it to the bottom of the hill and looked back before heading up to meet his friend. He made himself a promise that he would see both Matthews and Frank dead before returning to the Hidden lair! The informant would get his as well!

He ran full speed up the hill trying to wash away his anger by pushing his body hard! He made it to the horses winded and his heart beating rapidly. Cole was already up on his horse and ready to go just shaking his head at his friend.

"Do you feel better now?" He asked.

"What are you talking about?" He answered trying to catch his breath.

"You can't fool me my friend." Cole leaned down towards him. "All that stuff Matthews said about taking out the people and your family just ripped you apart inside!"

"It did at first my friend." He mounted up and checked his gear. "I realize something now that I didn't expect would happen."

"What would that be?"

"Matthews is scared of us and he knows we may have a chance of getting over on him! I could see it in his dark eyes tonight and that is something we can take advantage of. With the information he has he isn't going to be ready for an all out attack by us! With that in mind we are going to catch him with his pants down!"

"I take it your canceling your plan C then?" Cole asked.

"Yes, I have better plans going through my head now!"

"What about our informant, any new plans for him?"

"No way, I really want to see his face once we take down Matthews and then have our little talk with him!" He smiled. "I want him to feel that fear that people always worry about feeling!"

"So you're going to put the fear of God in him?"

"Oh no my friend," Greygor replied with a slight growl in his voice, "I am putting the fear of me in him!"

"Are you getting cocky again?" Cole laughed.

"I just want him to know he put my friends and family in jeopardy and he will pay for it in a big way!"

With that they began riding down the other side of the hill and back towards camp. They decided to take the horses cross country and through the forest instead of using the same road as they did before. They rode hard and fast to make it back to the camp.

Chapter 18

Greygor was worn out and sat upon a small hill watching the men and women working out below. Cole and he had arrived back two days ago met with the leaders of the groups and made the necessary plans for the coming days. He wiped the sweat from his brow and focused on the workouts. He heard footsteps from behind and looked back.

"Hello Anna, how are you doing with the Rapid Riders?" He asked.

"I fell from my horse earlier and Kent wanted me to take a break." She answered softly.

"You didn't break anything I hope?" He said as she sat next to him.

"No just a bruised ego." She laughed. "How are you holding up?"

"I am fine, just want to get this all over with and get back to my wife."

"She must be very special to you." She replied, "It must have been tough leaving her for so long."

"It was but we both knew that I had to do it. Love is important but life must be protected to keep love alive."

She smiled and reached over and kissed him on the cheek. "You're a very special man Greygor Josephs. Thank you for everything!"

With that she got up and walked away. It made Greygor smile and hope even more that their plans would work out the way they wanted. Though optimistic he knew that even the best laid plans could go wrong! Lives were going to be lost in this battle and that scared him. He had dwelled on other possible ways that he could get all these people to safety without any losses. Unfortunately, their only chance was to meet the military head on and go from there.

He got up and stretched and began walking towards the place

where he was to have another meeting with the group leaders and the council. This would be the last one before all the fighters would head out towards the border in the morning. He was greeted by Uncle Jake and his father. Reverend Grant walked up to them and waited for them to finish talking.

"Greygor I would like a word with you if you will?" He said.

"What can I do for you?"

"I know you have your head set on fighting our way through but perhaps if we talk to the military we can get through this peacefully?"

"Reverend, we have been over this, if there was a way I would definitely love to do it. Matthews is out for blood and he means to take it out of us." Greygor tried to explain once more.

"Perhaps you are just misreading their intentions." He replied.

"Hearing Matthews tell his troops too slaughter all of our people and leave no one standing is pretty much to the point if you ask me."

"You may have been caught up in your emotions and just heard wrong."

"Well, Rev, I heard a lot more than G in the last few weeks and it sounds like he wants us all six feet under!" Cole said coming up from behind him. "I saw what they tried to do to some of my people in Ohio and it was not pretty!" Have you ever seen a man slit open from his chest down to his privates with a sword? It's not a pretty sight."

"I am sorry for what you may have seen or heard but I must say no I haven't."

"Lend me your sword Greygor I will show him first hand what it looks like and feels like." Cole replied.

"Chill out Cole." Greygor got between them. "He is just voicing his concerns."

"He is calling you a liar in his all so proper way." Cole stared at the reverend.

"I certainly was not." Reverend Grant said, "I just don't want lives to be lost."

"For your sake Reverend Grant I hope to God you weren't calling my son a liar!" Darla came walking up to the men. "So far it seems he has done everything in his power to keep all of us safe! He has even risked his own life to make sure that we have heard the truth about the military."

"I just feel that there can be a peaceful way to get through this." He said sternly.

"I will tell you what Reverend." Greygor placed his hand on his shoulder. "I actually was planning on trying to talk to Matthews under a flag of peace before anything happens. I will ask him to allow our people to go peacefully to our new home. How do you like that?"

"That is all I ask for Greygor." He smiled.

He began to walk over to the group leaders and stopped and turned to him once more. "Oh I forgot, since all my men are going to be busy at the time of this situation you will accompany me out to the border by my side and assist me in this peace talk. If lets say that the military decide to attack us then you can help me fight till the rest of the fighters can intercede!"

"Someone needs to be with the people for their religious well being I can't be off doing such things." Reverend Grant replied nervously.

"Excuse me Reverend; I don't believe that I was asking you!" Greygor said firmly. "You will be out there with me and you will be carrying a sword! Remember sir, we have God on our side!"

Greygor left him standing there and walked with Cole to the group leaders. Cole kept quiet till they reached the others. Greygor smiled as he started discussing the plans for the next few days. Everyone seemed ready for what was to come. Arthur, Kent and Cole would be leaving in the morning to set up their men where necessary. Cole would be getting his people ready as well as getting ready the night before the fight to infiltrate the camp and deal with the weapons and ammunition.

"Arthur, I plan on setting up their ammo tent for a big surprise.

Cole said. "Think you can get a couple fire arrows into it during the fight?"

"Sure, I think we can add a little spark to the situation." Arthur replied with a smile.

"You sure your thieves can get everything done over night?" Rider asked. "I mean there will be guards and there are a lot of rifles to get out of there."

"That's why I want flaming arrows my friend. He answered. "I plan on leaving a few things I have in my bag of tricks as well as emptying most of there ammo on to the ground for some nice fireworks."

"Sounds very good Cole. "Now, the Warrior and Barbarian groups will march up the incline here." Greygor said pointing at the map. "They will wait for the signal to attack as will the Rapid Riders who will be ready to ride in from the south, the east and from the west. The Sharpshooters will begin firing from the two mountains like hills. I will be riding up the incline first with a white flag and a few men to attempt to talk with Matthews before the battle begin."

"Are you serious?" Cole asked. "You got to be kidding!"

"I am serious!" He said. "Your people will be hidden close by and I will have at least six fighters around me if things get tough to fight until the other groups can arrive to assist me."

"What happens if they decide to attack before you get the chance to talk?" Rider asked.

"I guess we will have to turn our horses around and ride like hell back to our fighting forces and then turn and fight them up the hill while the Rapid Riders, Sharpshooters and Thieves attack the military from behind."

"What makes you think that Matthews will actually come out and talk to you?" Wayne asked.

"He wants to meet the man who has taken him on. He wants to look into my eyes and see what it is that drives me to do what I do. He wants to tempt me into using my abilities for his selfish gain. He is conceited to no end and so power drunk he will be foolish enough to ride out to meet with me."

"What exactly will you say to him G?" Arthur asked.

"I am going to ask him to let us pass peacefully." He smiled at everyone. "Then I am going to give fare warning of what is about to happen."

"And if he says no?" Rider asked.

"Then may God have mercy on his militaries souls!" He replied and then shouted. "Prepare your men horses and weapons! Tomorrow at dawn all fighting groups will meet two miles south and then we send off the three advance groups! The rest ride out at noon!"

With that he walked away and came face to face with Reverend Grant. They stood there looking at each other before either said a word.

"I just wanted to apologize to you Greygor. He spoke first. "I never meant to imply that you were a liar in anyway."

"We ride out at dawn Reverend." He said calmly. "I will find a suitable weapon for you and expect you next to me when we ride out."

"Don't you think I would serve the people better here in camp?" Reverend Grant replied. "I mean if we have to rush out of here they need their spiritual guidance."

"We need you're wisdom and faith out on that possible battlefield. If with your voice you can talk Matthews into letting us by peacefully then that will be wonderful. If he insists on fighting us I want you by my side praying and fighting that way we stand a better chance!"

"You would risk a man of Gods life just to prove me wrong?" He said angrily.

Greygor grabbed him by the collar and pulled him face to face to him letting him see the anger in his eyes.

"No Grant I won't risk your life to prove you wrong! Matter of fact I will let you stay back and cower in your tent! As for you being a man of God, that is a bunch of crap! You are more like Matthews than you know! You love using your power you get from the bible to try and control all things around you! When you can't control it you use your words to persecute those you have a problem with! I could easily destroy you right here and right now! But I also believe in God and his words and live and let live but I want you to understand something! I love you and all of these people with all of my heart if there was another way of doing this I would do it!"

He pushed him back and away, he stumbled backwards a few steps but caught his balance. Greygor turned to see Cole with a big smile on his face. He joined him and they walked off together leaving the reverend to think about what just happened.

"I love it when you get angry my friend!" Cole laughed slapping him on the back.

"Think it worked?" He asked.

"For now, but he will be on you for something else after he finds a dry pair of pants."

"What?"

"You didn't notice he pissed himself when you grabbed him?

"I just thought he hadn't washed in a while! Greygor laughed.

The word was put out that all training and preparation for the day was stopped. Everyone was to spend time with their family and friends for the rest of the day. That night bonfires were made, music played and people danced and sang. The camp was filled with happiness and joy. Thoughts of the coming days were put on hold as much as possible.

Every so often Greygor would see the man who betrayed the people and at one point even said hello and asked how he was doing. He seemed so very nervous. He had heard the real plans but had no way to get out of camp to warn the military; Charles was seeing to that with double duties of inner camp guard and doubling up the guards. At night once he did get to bed it seemed that either Cole or Greygor was up just walking around with the guards talking because they couldn't sleep. Of course Cole had set up his tent close to his and kept his eyes and ears open.

Greygor socialized with the family all night and finally went to his blankets at twelve midnight. He sat up looking up into the sky praying that God would keep everyone safe and help him in all the things that would be coming in the next few days. He hoped God would forgive him for any lives that he may have to take and then prayed for guidance on all things he may have to do. He even apologized for his harsh words to Reverend Grant. He went to bed and fell into a restful sleep.

After farewells to loved ones and friends the five fighting groups headed out to the rallying point. Greygor, Arthur and Wayne rode side by side in the front as they went. They were followed by Rider, Hogan, Kent and Cole. The groups stayed close behind. The leaders all chatted as they rode. Chad followed with some equipment he felt would be needed before they took off to the border. He drove his small wagon. They reached the area that they were to use to get ready. Everyone stopped and Chad pulled his wagon up to the front of the fighters.

As the men and women took time to water their horses and drink a few swallows themselves Chad pulled the tarp off his wagon exposing a sound system that he had created. The group leaders had helped him work on it and they looked to Greygor to speak to the fighters while they were all together. He did his best to get out of it but decided it should be done. He got up on the wagon and looked out at everyone. The group leaders went to the front of the wagon to listen to what he had to say. Chad handed him a make shift microphone and turned on the speakers.

"We are about to send off our advance groups, the Sharpshooters led by my brother Arthur, the Rapid Riders led by my good friend Kent and the Thieves led by another friend of mine, Cole!" The speakers sent his voice out loudly so all could hear. "The rest of us will follow later in the day led by Rider of the Warrior group and my brother Wayne of the Barbarian group! We will be heading to the border to meet the military who want to destroy us and destroy our families who we have just left! Together we must fight for not only our lives but for theirs as well!

Greygor stopped as the fighters shouted and clapped. He thought about his words and something within him pushed him to continue. Everyone grew silent and waited for him to go on.

"All we wish to do here is keep our loved ones safe and away from harm! To get them to the Hidden Lair and live a peaceful life in the aftermath of what Matthews turned our world into! We don't do this for riches, glory or power! We do it for the love we feel for the people around us!" He again stopped but all were silent. "We have learned a lot about ourselves as we trained and moved down to this place! All of you now know what you truly are! We all will protect those around us at all cost and your greatest weapons are your heart, souls and minds! We have our greatest asset, which is the need to survive and to keep your friends and family safe from harm! Your greatest strength comes from your love and compassion for your friends and family! Deep within you, you have special abilities to assist you in the protection of all around you! You all are brave, noble and live by the golden rule! Your ability to now unite together and protect those around you from evil not only makes you the heroes you already are! Today you have become Guardians of our people! All of you are the Guardians of the Hidden Lair!"

The fighters all cheered and clapped all of them standing. The leaders raised their fist and clapped as well. He looked out at all the fighters and smiled. He dropped the mike and jumped down off the wagon and was greeted by handshakes by his group leaders. They then began to get ready for the battle at the border.

Chapter 19

The military had arrived at the border right on time. They set up their tents and secured the area on the highway as they had planned. On the hills on each side of them scouts sent out by Cole were watching them carefully and sending messages back to the group leaders. Arthur's Sharpshooters were ready on the other side to move after dark to their areas they would be firing from. Kent had his Rapid Riders ready to move south and ready for their attack as well. Part of the Rapid Riders would be attacking from off the hill as well. The thief group was ready to move that night as well into the field in the center after night fall. Cole had chosen eighteen of his best shadow walkers for their after dark mission into the camp to sabotage the ammo tent as well as the militaries rifles and other weapons. They knew that some of the soldiers would still have loaded weapons but hoped the surprise they had in store for them would help with that as well as the Sharpshooters firing down on them. Greygor and the rest of the fighting groups had had set up their camp four miles from the hill they would be traveling up early the next morning to meet the military. They had found a large field to set up camp and get ready. Arthur and Greygor had set up signals for the next day to help in the fighters surprise attack. Cole had also talked to Kent and Arthur about a few secret signals to start the events of the next day.

Greygor met with Wayne and Rider to go over the move south that night. They would travel halfway up the hill and stop. Greygor would ride the rest of the way with Rider, Wayne, Dale and Toni with a white flag in hopes of having a meeting with Matthews and perhaps try a peaceful arrangement. They all knew that that wasn't going to resolve anything but as Greygor explained it would give everyone a few extra minutes to get ready for the battle and get into position. If Matthews decided to attack the smaller group they would make a mad dash back to the fighting groups and signal the attack as planned.

As the final meeting was ending Cole had begun moving his men through the darkness and towards the camp. They cautiously shadow walked into the camp. Two outer guards had been killed on the way in and their bodies hidden. They made it into camp and took out the guards within the ammunitions tent and began taking care of the weapons by removing firing pins, bolts and unloading the clips in the boxes within. Cole and a few others set up explosives to go off once the tent was hit by a fire arrow. The thieves chosen as watch outs silently worked on the tents entrances and the used the militaries own barbed wire to secure the bottom of the tent so if the soldiers attempted to crawl under they would be ripped to shreds. They didn't make a sound throughout their activities. The hours passed slowly as the sabotaged everything they could. Landon and Cole left them to their work and went around camp in the shadows booby trapping it with explosives and other unique traps that the military would never realize were there until it was too late. They made their escape around three in the morning and headed back to there group. Cole and Landon began silently moving the thief group out and into position for the next morning. After things were set Cole grabbed a horse and headed out towards the Warrior and Barbarian camp to let Greygor know all was ready on his end.

Up on the hillsides Arthur moved his men into position as well hiding amongst the trees and bushes above. Bows and rifles and their ammunition were set into place. Arthur had half of the Sharpshooters on one side of the camp and Will had the other half on the other side ready to go as the night slowly went on. Kent and the Rapid Riders arrived a few miles south of the military camp; two other groups slowly moved to the top of the hills and would ride down once the border battle begun. Everyone did their best to keep the horses and themselves quiet. Luckily the sounds of the horses in the military camp would help hide any accidental noises from the hills.

Cole arrived at camp around five in the morning and met up with Greygor who was getting his weapons ready in his long black leather coat. He had his rifles in their holders on both sides of Sampson hind quarters and his shield was tied to the saddle horn. The sword that he had carried from the very beginning of his journey he placed in its sheath on his back, the handle over his left shoulder. Cole quietly walked up to him smiling at how well armed he was.

"Going into a battle or something?" Cole laughed.

"What are you doing here?" Greygor asked. "Don't you have a group to lead?"

"That's why you had us choose second in commands" He replied. "In case the leaders were needed for other things."

"How did the infiltration and sabotage mission go?"

"Here you go my friend," Cole handed him a handful of firing pins. "We only had to kill four guards."

"You must be losing your touch my friend." Greygor smiled.

"You told me to keep the kills to a minimal tonight."

"Is everything getting set up there?" He asked.

"Yes Grey, all groups are setting up and ready for the attack!"

"Don't you think you should be getting back it's almost time for us to start moving out?"

"Landon can handle it." Cole replied. "I am riding with you for that meeting with the Military leaders."

"Didn't I ask you to stay with your men?" Greygor asked him.

"Actually, no you didn't!" Cole stated. "Someone needs to watch your back old friend and I'm the best man for the job!"

"I have to agree with you there my friend." He smiled. "I will be honored to have you fighting by my side again!"

They both mounted their horses and rode through the camp as the fighters began moving by horseback and on foot. Wayne joined them with his battle axe strapped to the side of his horse. He had a large knife strapped to his belt and a pistol on his other side. Toni rode up and hugged her brother almost falling from her horse. She carried two long staffs bladed at both ends. She had her blonde hair cut short in a spike style and wore a tan headband around her head. They were soon joined by Rider with both his swords belted to his sides. Last but not least Dale rode up carrying a large sledgehammer that he held up on his shoulder and two double edged axes tied to his horse's saddle horn. They rode together south as the fighters followed close behind. Cole's double barreled shot guns crisscrossed his chest and a belt of shells was belted around his waist. They hit the road and traveled south waiting for the first glimpse of the morning light.

Greygor carried with him a makeshift white flag to wave once they reached the military. He knew that the meeting was pointless and had told his men he at least had to try some peaceful talks. Deep down he knew that his real reason to try it was to get close to Matthews and his leaders and kill them off quickly! He reached to the small of his back and touched the flying G. He wanted so bad to see his weapon of choice take out Matthews as well as General Frank. He turned and looked back at all the fighters behind him and said a silent prayer that all of his fighters would make it out of this alive somehow. He asked God to keep them safe and those who did die in this fight be accepted into heaven's gate. He then asked God for his blessing and to forgive the military for the evils that they have done. He didn't realize he was praying out loud.

Cole reached over and patted him on the back and smiled. "Amen my friend, Amen!"

Chapter 20

As dawn broke the six riders broke the top of the hill and could see the military camp before them. Greygor had the white flag held up high as they rode closer. They stopped three hundred yards from the camp as soldiers who had been walking outside of the camp ran back into camp to let the leaders know about the visitors. After a few minutes three soldiers rode out from the camp towards them.

"That camp is coming alive G!" Cole said. "Hope they aren't heading for the weapons yet?"

"Relax friend it's going as planned." He said looking over at him then back at the advancing soldiers who also carried a white flag as well as rifles on their backs.

They stopped the horses at least twenty yards away and let the animals calm down. The soldiers kept their hands away from their weapons. The camp now looked like a beehive as soldiers were running too formation within the center of camp.

"You are entering a military operational area!" The center soldier yelled out. "All civilians are to give up their arms and follow us into camp!"

"We want to meet with your Commander and Chief to negotiate safe passage through this area!" Greygor stated loudly.

"Your safe passage will be taken care of once you are in camp!" The soldier replied angrily. "You will give us your weapons and follow us into camp!"

"I am Greygor Josephs' leader of a large mass of survivors!" He said rising up in his saddle. "You will ride back to your camp and let your leader know that I am requesting time to speak with him!"

He saw their eyes widen and they looked at each other with fear in their eyes. One of the soldiers slowly reached back for his rifle. The three soldiers froze all movement as Greygor and the rest drew their pistols and Cole had his shotguns pointed at their heads!

"Who wishes to die first?" Cole yelled. "The three of you will not stand a chance against all of us! Now do as Greygor Josephs has asked you! One of you will ride back to camp and tell your leader what we have asked!"

The center soldier slowly motioned to the man on his right. He backed his horse up and turned and rode towards camp. The other two placed their hands on their saddle horn and looked over the six riders in front of them. Not a word was spoken between them as the soldier rode into camp and went to tell his leader. Time seemed to tick by slowly. As they watched four soldiers appeared riding out towards them, Mathews and General Frank and two new ones. The two leaders talked as they slowly advanced with the two other soldiers right behind them. Once they reached the waiting men they stopped. Each group stared at each other for a few minutes before any words were exchanged. They sized each other up and looked over the weapons that each man and woman had.

"Good day to you!" Matthews said loudly. "It is an honor to finally meet you Greygor Josephs!"

"Good day to you President Matthews!" He replied and got straight to the point. "We are here to negotiate safe passage for our people! We wish to pass without incident!"

General Frank and the others soldiers smiled and laughed at Greygor's word. Matthews looked back at them with a scowl.

"I apologize for my men's behavior." He said smiling now at the riders before him. "Due to the dangers that now exist in our country. Your people would be better protected amongst the soldiers who have pledged their lives to protect this country! We will welcome your people with open arms and care and protect them with our lives!"

"I have seen what your military have done to survivors they have come upon in the last few months!" Greygor said.

"I would like to know what you have seen my soldiers do." Matthews acted shocked. "I will not put up with them taking matters into their own hands!"

"In actuality they are following your orders perfectly!" Greygor replied back. "Your General there lost his hand after raping a woman and her fourteen year old daughter! He then killed a man in cold blood!"

"These are very strong accusations!" President Matthews said. "I will investigate this as soon as we get your people into camp safe and sound."

"I apologize to you President if I didn't make myself clear!" Greygor said. "We are to be given safe passage through this area without any military assistance."

"My dear Greygor, you know we cannot allow these citizens of the United States to go off without Military protection!" Mathews shouted. "I am sorry to bring this up at this time but you are wanted at this time for treason against our nation as well as murder of American soldiers! Too allow you to lead these people away from here is putting these people in danger and led by a possible murderer!"

"I protected surviving civilians from your soldiers who were out to harm or kill them!" Greygor replied loudly. "My actions against your military were warranted!"

"That is to be seen Greygor! We will place you on trial and find out the truth in all of this!"

"The only truth there is here Matthews is that your military is bent on world domination and the destruction of all survivors whom you deem unfit!" Greygor shouted angrily. "I will ask you one last time! Will you allow these people safe passage or must we make our own passage through your military!"

"Are you willing to place the lives of all your loved ones at risk Greygor?" He replied. "Please could we talk man to man before this erupts into violence?"

"Let's do that Matthews." Greygor let Sampson take a few steps forward as Matthews did the same.

The two men walked their horses slowly to one another and stopped directly in the middle of the two groups. Both of them kept stern looks on their faces as they looked at each other.

"Now, Greygor." Matthews said quietly leaning towards him. "I do understand how you feel about the things that you have seen my soldiers do and honestly I do believe you."

"Then it should be very easy for you to let us pass then." He replied placing both hands on his horse's neck as he leaned forward.

"We both know sadly enough that is not possible." Matthews said back, "Even if these fighting groups decide to get aggressive and hold out for even a whole day. We will overwhelm them and chase down your people who are now traveling west in their attempt to escape us. Unfortunately we will catch them and slaughter them all for treason. Last but not least think about your wife and children in that, what you call the Hidden Lair. My military will find it and then we will be forced to kill them as well. We will show no mercy sir."

Greygor acted shocked at his words. He used his abilities to let his face go ashen as if he was afraid at what the militaries leader had just said. He shook his head sadly letting his chin drop a little. Matthews was eating it up and started grinning from ear to ear thinking he had hit the right nerves in his adversary. He lost his smile as Greygor raised his head high with a huge smile on his face and chuckled at him. He thought for a second that he may have perhaps gone a bit mad.

"Do you really believe that the information that your informant gave you was correct?" Greygor smiled. "Do you honestly believe that he was actually telling you the truth about everything going on as we traveled here? Have you even wondered why you haven't seen him since his visit to your camp a week ago?"

Matthews leaned back a bit in his saddle looking at Greygor a bit confused and somewhat bewildered.

"I hope you don't mind being quoted from a few nights ago, sir" Greygor leaned forward and repeated Matthews word for word. "Tonight we welcome a hero amongst us! This man has risked his life to bring information pertaining to the civilians who are attempting to escape our grasp!"

He went on reminding Matthews of the speech he had given to the soldiers that night. He remembered every word exactly. When he finished Mathews face showed shock and confusion.

"Truthfully though, you should have killed my man when you had the chance just like Frank killed Snorpaly that night!" Greygor smiled at him.

"You are a resourceful man Greygor Josephs." He replied respectfully. "To think you actually were able to make this man so convincing, he seemed to really hate you and your family! He seemed so intrigued by the treasures he would get for turning your people over to me. I am utterly impressed!"

"Unfortunately, he is also the man who will be firing the arrow into your heart once this battle begins." Greygor replied nonchalantly.

"Now Greygor you don't honestly think I am to believe that there is someone hidden around here ready to fire upon me? I know you have your fighting groups ready to attack behind you but please, I am not a fool."

"I would never place a man alone on a hillside ready to assassinate you sir." Greygor said letting his left hand rise up and pat his chest.

Arthur saw the signal that Greygor just gave. He pulled back on his bowstring and took aim! He let the arrow fly through the air and watched it make its descent! It hit right at the horse's feet that Matthews was on. The president and the soldiers behind him showed the shock on their faces as the arrow created a thud and vibrated seconds later. Matthews looked into Greygor's eyes.

"No Matthews!" He said. "I would not place one lone man up on these hills to attempt to take you out! I would line these hills with a large group of sharpshooters ready to fire down on your military when I give them the signal! I also would surround you with a large group of Rapid Riders ready to attack you from all sides and from behind! And yes Matthews before your military even make it a few feet from your camp my Warriors Thieves and Barbarians will reach this spot from behind me and destroy every last one of you! We will show no mercy!"

Matthews gulped a heavy gulp as he looked around at the hills that surrounded him. He thought he saw men on the hillsides but couldn't be sure. He could tell that Greygor was not bluffing. But he also knew his men had rifles and the ammunition to cause a lot of damage.

"You are certainly a top grade leader to have achieved all this if you really have what you say going on." Matthews replied as sweat beaded up on his forehead. "Would you consider perhaps joining my military? I could use a new second in command with your abilities. General Frank is resourceful but you are so much more Greygor Josephs! Please consider this a legitimate offer!"

"I am sorry Matthews but I must decline it!" He smiled.

"You don't trust me do you?" Matthews asked.

"I want you to understand something Matthews!" Greygor leaned forward, grabbed Matthews's horse's reigns and pulled him close and then whispered. "At this point of time all I have to do is signal my Sharpshooters and the shots you hear and the arrows that come will be aimed right at you! It doesn't matter at this point if my friends behind me or your soldiers behind you die or even if I get killed when this begins! You will fall right here on this spot! After that nothing else will matter! My people will be moving in the actual direction that they are to go and they will get to the actual Hidden Lair where ever it is! You sir will be lying dead in a puddle of blood, amongst everyone who dies here today!"

"You have me at a disadvantage Greygor." He said leaning back. "I will talk to my soldiers and work it out so that your people may move freely through this area as you have asked."

"That will be appreciated sir!" Greygor said reigning Sampson to the left and walking him back to his group as Matthews rode his horse back to his soldiers.

Greygor returned to the spot next too Cole as Matthews began whispering to his men. Explaining to them what he had just been told. The soldiers in camp were still moving around readying for orders to come. Frank's horses stepped to the right as if being gently nudged.

"He's trying to give cover to Matthews." Cole whispered to Greygor.

"I know everyone get ready!" Greygor silently said to the group. "Use your Firearms first then blades and steel."

Arthur sent another arrow into the sky flying back behind his brothers and others to signal the groups down the hill to begin moving up towards the camp. Cole waited for Greygor to let him know when to give the signal for the fire arrows to be launched into the camp ahead. The explosions would alert Kent to begin their assault on the soldiers as well. Matthews seemed to have finished his talk with his troops. He turned towards Greygor as General Frank moved his horse beside him on the right where the arrow had come from. Cole looked behind them and the groups less than a half mile away moving fast he knew that Matthews would see them coming soon. They all looked towards the camp and could see the darkness between the tents. The military was waiting for word from their leaders.

"I have discussed our negotiations Greygor with my soldiers your terms have been considered. We want the best for everyone here and feel that the decision that we have made are for the best interest of our great country" Matthews shouted over to him. "We have signaled our camp to prepare for your departure!"

Chapter 21

"It will be your departure straight to hell!" Matthews yelled and they turned their horses and began galloping towards the tents.

General Frank raised his sword high as they stopped a few yards from the camp and began yelling orders. The tents began to fall as the military began rushing out of the camp. They were armed and ready to follow their leaders into battle. They began advancing at a steady speed.

Cole drew his shotgun from his chest and fired it in the air as the others reached for their weapons. The fighting groups behind them moved up and over the hill. Greygor had his shield up and on his arm and a pistol in his left hand.

"Hold your ground!" He shouted as he turned his horse and looked back at his men. "Lair fighters get ready!"

Arrows began raining down from the hillside and into the mass of soldiers. Fire arrows flew into the camp where most of the military still were. The first explosion went off rocking the whole area and throwing soldiers and equipment everywhere! Matthews and General Frank reigned in their horses and looked back in disbelief as another explosion went off in the camp! Black smoke and fire rose up high into the sky as a third explosion laid waste to the camp!

Kent had seen and heard the explosions and led his Rapid Riders from the South up towards the devastated camp! They all readied their weapons as they rode hard towards the smoke filled camp. One of his men blew a horn loudly, signaling the rest of their group to begin their attack! From the wooded hillsides on each side of the military the Rapid Riders rode out with weapons ready!

"Rider and Wayne fall back now!" Greygor shouted. "Cole,

get ready!"

Both of them turned their horses and rode back to their groups as they advanced and took up positions in front of them and shouted orders! They all readied their weapons and began moving faster!

Soldiers dropped to their knees or to a prone position and began firing their rifles! They were stunned when all they heard was a click or their triggers just collapsed back. The General yelled for bayonets or swords to be drawn. He ordered them to attack!

Arrows and bullets flew from the Sharp shooters hitting soldiers left and right! The Rapid Riders rushed into the soldiers from both sides slicing and slashing them as the horses knocked men to the ground. Kent had arrived at the backside of the camp; they began attacking the soldiers who were trying to go forward into combat!

"Do it now Cole!" Greygor shouted!

He had both his sawed off shotguns out and pointed them towards the first row of soldiers and fired them both together! The shots knocked two soldiers backwards! Dale and Toni jumped from their horses and began running forward! Toni used her bladed staff to cut down the first of the soldiers she met as Dale swung his sledgehammer into an advancing man's head sending him flying! Greygor and Cole kicked their horses into a run as the groups behind them arrived. They both fired at the advancing soldiers till their guns were empty! Greygor holstered his pistols and drew his sword as he began to feel his Warrior sense kick into high gear! Time itself slowed around them and the battle was under way! The double signal Cole had given set his group into action. Out of nowhere the Thief group rose up and began attacking! Swords and knives were slashing and cutting the unsuspecting soldiers! The Warrior and Barbarian groups reached the main body of the military and crashed into them hard! The sounds of steel on steel, firing rifles, arrows flying and the yells and screams of those were falling in battle filled the air!

"Keep your shots going into the center of the military and don't waste any shots!" Arthur yelled to his men from his position up on the hill. "If you see any soldiers actually firing rifles take them down quickly!

The Sharpshooters kept firing steadily as the loaders ran across the hill bringing arrows and bullets around to them. Across the way on the opposite hill, Will and his men kept up the pace as well. They watched for the flash of any rifles that may not have been sabotaged and took down the soldier who could possibly kill one of their fighters. From their vantage points they could see Kent and his Rapid Riders attacking soldiers who were still within the camp! The smoke and fire had settled down and they were slowly making their way through the camp towards the main battle beyond the tents. The explosions had taken a large toll on the military. The sharpshooters had watched the soldiers rallying for battle earlier. They had to laugh as they attempted to get into the ammo tent. Some soldiers attempted going under and must have been caught up in the barbed wire that had been left by Cole's thieves. They finally got through it and as they handed out rifles and ammunition Arthur ordered the fire arrows to be let loose! Hundreds of soldiers surrounding the tent were vaporized by the blast! The next two explosions took out just as many. Only a couple hundred were able to escape to the field of battle to find out that their rifles didn't work!

President Matthews and General Frank both were shocked by the onslaught! They attempted to rally the other leaders and troops to attack and keep on fighting! They stayed close to the edge of what was left of the camp and yelled to their soldiers.

Cole fired his shotgun again and jumped from his horse with his sword in hand assisting one of his men. He lashed out at an advancing soldier running his blade through his stomach! He pulled it out just in time to slice it across another soldiers face!

Wayne had his axe flying to the left and right of his horse cleaving soldiers to the ground! Rider had jumped off his horse and was using his two swords rapidly too take down soldier after soldier! Hogan joined his brother and the two fought side by side!

Greygor left the back of Sampson as well blocking an attack from another soldier with his shield and then bringing his sword across the man's chest sending him reeling! He slammed his shield into another soldier knocking him to the ground and then plunged his sword into his neck!

Donny and Danny Trotter reached their brother Rich and Dutch and fought hard against the soldiers.

MickYonder knocked a soldier to the ground and ran him through! A soldier attacked him from behind slicing him across the back! Three soldiers advanced on him! From out of nowhere his brother Landon was standing over him! He took all three on as they attacked. The first soldier's sword clashed with his and he twirled and ran his sword across the man's stomach! He turned the other way ducked as the soldier swung at him. He pushed his sword through his chest and let him fall! The last one ran at him as he let his stuck sword fall with the man. Landon drew two knives from his side belt and threw them into the soldier's neck! He got his sword back and helped Mick up! A rider reached them and he helped his brother up on the back of the horse!

"Get him out of here!" Landon shouted as he turned and ran towards another soldier!

Kent finally led his Rapid Riders out of the camp and advanced on the back of the soldiers on the main field. One of his men came out of the smoke and headed straight for General Frank! He had his spear ready and rode hard! He went to hit the General but was shot from his horse by President Matthews! The two leaders rode their horses towards their soldiers as the Rapid Riders chased them. General Frank jumped from his horse and knocked his leader from his horse just as a spear flew by barely missing him. They hit the ground and rolled! They made their way through their troops trying to keep away from any more attacks.

Greygor spotted them and made his way towards them slowly fighting soldiers as he went! He caught a glimpse of both off them falling and then only saw Matthews get up and push his way through the soldiers trying to get to his horse. His shield once more slammed into a soldier as he let his sword slice through another advancing soldier! Warriors and Barbarians around him were doing there best to defeat their enemies! He was a few yards away from Matthews and then a few feet!

"It's over Matthews! He yelled. "Turn and fight me!"

He turned around and stared at Greygor holding his sword out. The two men readied to attack each other. Matthews's angry stare turned into shock!

He felt the sharp pain go through the back of his shoulder! He felt the cold blade plummet through his skin then muscle and he screamed in pain and fell to his knees! He couldn't breath as the pain increased as he looked to see the knife handle sticking out of his right shoulder!

Chapter 22

The laugh that came from behind him seemed far away as the shock and pain increased. He felt the warm sticky liquid running down his arm that could only be blood! A boot slammed into his stomach rolling him on the ground. He looked up to see the face of General Frank standing above him. He let his shield slip off his arm. He reached up with his left hand and pulled the knife from his shoulder. Matthews quickly got up on his horse and took off leaving the General to finish off his enemy! He raised his sword up and jumped at Greygor bringing his blade down at him! He was met by Greygor twisting around on the ground and sending his foot up into his groin! He crumpled over as Greygor sliced the bloodied knife across the Generals eyes. He screamed out in pain letting his sword fall to the ground as he placed his hands on his facial wound!

Greygor grabbed his sword and got up from the ground a bit wobbly but he advanced on the General who turned and began to run back towards the tent as fast as he could his hands still holding his injured face!

He dropped his sword and reached to the small of his back and pulled out the flying G! He threw it hard at him and watched as the blades snapped out! For some reason Frank stopped and turned to look back just as the blades slammed through his neck! His body crumpled to the ground as his head flew to the side with a shocked expression still on his face! The weapon boomeranged and came back for him to catch! He raised it high in the air as he looked around for Matthews! He had disappeared in the smoke from the camp! Soldiers were running towards him now at a mad dash. He hit a button on his weapon that opened the blades half way and he threw it again! It struck one soldier then another slicing them badly as it finally slammed into the last one and shot back to him! He caught it again and put it away as he reached down for his sword. He began fighting soldier after soldier!

The fighting groups were pushing the military back as the Sharpshooters began shooting down soldiers who were already attempting to run. Kent and his men were riding hard and slicing down soldiers in the main field now as were the Warriors, Barbarians and Thieves! Arthur had begun bringing his men down off the hill as did Will. Arthur ran out towards the fight firing his arrows at soldiers as he went! He shot one that was advancing on Cole's back! He saluted him and went on his way shooting down the enemy!

"Kent gets over here!" Greygor yelled slashing another soldier.

"I am on my way!" He yelled as he galloped over to him.

He rode up on him knocking another soldier away with his sword. He could see Greygor's wound and knew it was bad.

"I need a message sent to Charles!" He yelled to him as he parried a sword and stabbed another soldier. "Begin moving the people down here immediately victory is ours!"

"I am on my way G!" He said back to him reining his horse around and taking off.

He rode to one of his men and gave him the order and he took off to relay the message.

Kent ripped open another soldier with a downward stroke and rode over to Wayne. "Your brother is wounded bad he needs help!"

They both looked over as Greygor tripped and fell to the ground as two soldiers went after him! Arrows slammed one after another into both men's chest! Arthur ran up to Greygor and began firing at soldiers all around them! Ten arrows into ten men within ten seconds! Cole got over to him as well using his shotguns to blast his way through soldiers. They rolled him over and he gasped for air.

"Get the people to the Hidden Lair for me." He struggled to speak.

"You're going to be alright G!" Arthur said as he fired another arrow. "We need to get you out of here!"

One of their medics arrived and took a look at his wound. "He has lost a lot of blood; we have to stop the bleeding."

Cole fired another round into a soldier. "How can we do that?"

"Give me one of your shotgun shells!" He replied.

He cut the shell open and dumped some of the black powder on the wound. He lit a match and placed it against the wound. It flashed and smoked as the smell of burning flesh made them all flinch away. Greygor let out a yell from the pain and then blacked out. A Rapid Rider came up who had been sent by Kent. They lifted him up on the horse and made sure he was secured. They returned to the battle that was almost at its end!

As the last of the soldiers were finished off Cole gathered his men and chose a few to go with Landon to pick off any military that may be trying to escape into the hills or down the roads. The groups gathered together celebrating their victory over the military! Cheers echoed through the hills as they congratulated each other and checked over the wounded. The leaders of each group directed their men to find their dead and bury them first. They had won the battle but at the lost of many great fighters. The final count of their friends who had died was two hundred and forty three. After they took care of their fighters they buried the soldiers on the hillsides away from their friends. They gathered what ever supplies from the camp that they could. There really wasn't much due to the massive explosions that had crippled the strength of the military. They set up camp there and waited for the rest of the people to arrive.

Five days went by before word came that the people would be there by morning. Once everyone was reunited they celebrated the victory that night as well as mourned those who were lost. The next few days were used to get ready for the trip into North Carolina. Landon returned to report that a few soldiers had been hunted down and disposed of but there had been no signs of Matthews. Cole wanted to go track him down but wanted to keep his promise to Greygor who had still not woken up from his injuries and loss of blood. Marie had been looking after him with the help of her daughters. They were doing what they could for him but they didn't know if he was going to make it.

On the fourth day the people began going south into North Carolina. The trip to the Hidden Lair would take another ten to twelve days. They all were ready to finally see this place that they had only heard of so far and hoped that it would give safety from the world outside.

Chapter 23

He felt like he had been in the darkness forever. He finally could hear the sounds around him. They seemed distant but it was better than the complete darkness and quiet he had been in for so long. His right shoulder started to throb and he reached over to feel the cotton like bandage over his wound. He moaned as he let his arm fall to his side. He felt so weak and he just wanted to go back to the darkness.

"Honey, can you hear me?" Darla wiped his brow with a cold cloth.

It felt good and cooled him down. He felt his mothers hand in his now. He gently squeezed it still to weak to talk.

"Marie he is coming around!" She said. "His fever has broken as well."

His sister came over and checked his pulse and felt his forehead. She then checked his wound to see if the swelling had gone down. "I still can't believe they used gunpowder to close his wound! That alone could have killed him!"

"They were worried that he was bleeding internally." Darla replied.

"I know mom but that's why the infection got so bad." She said changing his bandages.

"Where am I?" He whispered feeling how dry his throat was.

"We are in North Carolina Grey." His mother said helping him sip some water. "How do you feel?"

He opened his eyes and let them get focused. He looked at his Mother and sister who was looking down at him smiling that he was finally awake.

"You have been out for a long time Grey." Marie said. "You need to drink some more water and try to eat something."

"Are my brothers alright? Where are Cole and Rider?" He asked feeling his strength coming back.

"Everyone is fine honey." Darla reassured him. "They have been checking on you everyday."

They helped him sit up and made him drink more water. After a few moments Marie spoon fed him some broth. It was salty and warm going down his parched throat. She fed the whole bowl to him. He sat against the side of the wagon. He looked out at the camp watching people go back and forth.

"Well son, I see you're up!" Robert said happily.

"Hi dad I am still a little weak but hanging in there."" He said groggily.

"I will let your brothers know you're awake." He said patting him on the arm and walking off.

He fell back to sleep and slept through the night. He awakened feeling the wagon moving the next morning. He ate throughout the day and drank water building his strength back up. His friends and family visited here and there as they traveled and camped. They had told him that they were about six days away from the Hidden Lair. The group leaders visited and told him about the battle and let him know the losses as well. He was a bit upset that Matthews had escaped but knew that his time would come someday.

Another day of travel went by and though his shoulder hurt he was now able to stand and walk on his own now. He was ready for some real food that night and couldn't wait to actually sit with his friends and family to have dinner. He had begun exercising that day to regain more of his strength. His wound had started healing now that Marie had helped get rid of the infection. Charles had stopped by to check on him. Greygor asked him to make sure certain friends were invited to the dinner table that night and to let Cole know that this was going to be the night that he had been asking about.

That night at dinner he enjoyed a filling meal of beef stew, home-made bread and canned green beans. Each bite was so delicious. He could feel his strength returning. He finished it all off with a drink of his coffee and sat back in his chair quite satisfied. He looked around the table at his parents, his three brothers and sister and their children. Cole and his wife and daughters were there as well. He had even invited Janice's father Carl. After dinner was done the young children ran off to play as the adults talked over more coffee. Darla and Robert bid their good nights and left.

"Well it looks like everything is looking up so far." Greygor said after another sip of the warm bitter liquid.

"I bet you're happy and excited about seeing your wife and boys soon." Wayne smiled over his pipe.

"Yes I am." He replied. Unfortunately there is a small matter that must be taken care of before we reach the Hidden Lair."

"What is that bro?" Arthur asked.

"During this trip I do appreciate everyone who gave their all and trusted me to lead them to this place." He said standing up. "Sadly though not all of us here are what they seem to be."

Everyone looked at him wondering what was going on. He looked down sadly and then over at the man who had betrayed them all. He could see the fear in Carl's face as sweat began to bead up on his forehead.

"I want to know why we were betrayed." Why would you put your family in danger? Why did you sell out to the military Carl?" He asked staring right at him.

Everyone looked over at him with shock and anger on their faces.

He looked around the table fearful. "I never would do that! I don't know what you're talking about!"

"Come on Carl." Cole said. "Greygor and I trailed you to the military camp and heard the information that you had given to them."

"I want to know why Carl?" He asked again.

"I did it for money! I did it because ever since your sister and

I broke up I have been treated like an outcast even by my own daughter!" He yelled at Greygor.

"Perhaps had you not abused her mentally and physically you may have been treated a little better! You're lucky none of us brothers ever got our hands on you!" Wayne growled at him slamming his fist on the table.

"You betrayed over a thousand people over your feelings and want for revenge?" Arthur added.

Greygor shook his head and looked at him once more. "You are a sick man Carl. I want you out of here and out of this camp tonight."

"You all can go to hell!" He said standing up from his chair.

Janice sat there with tears running down her face. "I can't believe you did this!"

"Watch your mouth girl I am still your father." He slapped her shoulder hard.

"Don't you ever touch my daughter again Carl!" Marie shouted walking around the table. "You're the one that needs to go to hell!"

"Shut up you stupid bitch!" He screamed in her face causing her to turn away. "You're worthless!"

She reached over to Cole who was getting up to get her away from him. She reached past his arm and pulled his sawed off shot gun from his holster and turned rapidly pointing it at Carl's face! He was shocked at first but then just smiled.

"For years you treated me like nothing, called me names punched and pushed me!" She cried as Greygor tried to slowly get close to her.

"Marie calm down." Greygor said as he reached out to her shoulder. "Just let him leave the camp. If he does go to the military they think he is a double agent. You don't want to do this."

"Put that damn gun down you stupid B!" Carl was about to say.

The blast from the shotgun knocked her back into Greygor's and Cole's arms as everyone watched Carl's face explode! His body crumpled to the ground in a heap! Cole retrieved his gun as Greygor hugged his sister. He hushed her sobbing as he looked down at the body. He consoled her for a few minutes as people began coming over to see what had happened.

"Janice honey I am sorry. " He whispered down to her placing a hand on her shoulder.

She got up and hugged her mother as May and Gary came over as well. They began to walk Marie to the wagon. Janice stopped and looked down at the lifeless body and spit on it.

"Don't apologize, Uncle Greygor." She looked back at him. "He sold us all out years ago, he deserved what he got."

They watched her walk away and join Gary and May in calming Marie down. Greygor could understand the anger she had felt. He had seen her bruises he had given her. He had heard him belittle her every chance he got. When one of the brothers wanted to confront him she always made them promise to not hurt her husband. At one time or another everyone at this table wanted a crack at him but for the love of their sister or mother they kept their promise to not lay a hand on him. Deep down he knew Carl had got what he deserved!

Greygor turned to Cole. "Want to help bury him?"

"I will take care of it." He replied. "You can't be doing any digging. Go get some rest."

He turned to the table and wished everyone a good night's sleep. He decided to take a walk alone to the outside of camp to calm down. He stood in the middle of a field staring up at the night sky praying that that was the last life that had to be taken. He prayed for the friends he had lost in the border battle and the lives lost throughout this journey he had taken. His mind drifted to the coming days and how he wanted to hold his wife in his arms and just melt once more in their love. He wanted to be home with his children and live a peaceful life. He felt his shoulder with his hand thinking about the scars he now had to remind him of this trip he had taken. There were wonderful scars as well. They were the fulfilling scars on his heart. He had found his family and had kept them safe from the evils of this world. The love for them was what got him through all of this and now he could actually say it as well as feel it! Greygor Josephs was going home!

Chapter 24

Greygor rode his horse Sampson once more. Along side Cole, Arthur Wayne Kent and Rider up the winding road they went together. They had gone ahead of the people that day up the back entrance to the Hidden Lair. For miles now they felt like they were being watched as they went along especially on this road. They were about to the top and rounded the last curve of the road. They stopped the horses and kept their hands in sight as they were greeted by seven horseman with rifles pointed right at them. Greygor didn't recognize any of them and waited for them to speak. He didn't want to cause any problems.

"What's your business here?" An older man of the group asked. "You're on dangerous ground here."

"I am Greygor Josephs!" He said calmly. "I am the son in law of Daniel Cause!"

The men looked at each other and the leader whispered to one of the men. He rode off behind them. He wasn't to long and returned with another rider. Greygor smiled at the sight of him. He told the men to put their weapons away and jumped down off his horse and walked over. Greygor jumped down off of Sampson and walked towards him as well. They hugged and then smiled at one another.

"I just got word you were riding in son!" Daniel said smiling. "I know someone who is going to be glad to see you back!"

"Believe me dad I have missed all of you too!" He said hugging him again.

"Well, from what I hear you got more than just these fellows." Daniel smiled and walked over to them shaking hands with them. "Let's see here I remember your Brother Arthur here and Wayne. Who are this other fine gentlemen?"

They all got off their horses and introduced themselves. As Greygor walked over and introduced himself to the guards who had greeted them. They tried to apologize for the greeting but Greygor told them he was glad to see them ready to protect the Hidden Lair.

"So Greygor from what I hear you found yourself a bunch of people." Daniel came up behind him. "We did pretty well ourselves. There are about seven hundred people here now!"

"Where are we going to put them all?" He wondered.

"There's plenty of room here son don't you go and worry yourself." He put his arm around his shoulder. "Anyway, we can stay up here and greet everyone. You should ride on into the Lair and say hello to your wife and boys."

"Shouldn't I wait too?" He asked.

"No way brother," Wayne said. "We got it from here, get down there and see your wife."

"I agree Greygor!" Cole smiled. "I promise to be nice to everyone!"

He didn't need much prompting on that issue. He jumped back up on Sampson and began riding away. They all began talking as they waited for the rest of the people. The excitement was building as he rode down into the Hidden Lair! He felt like a school boy as he tried to fix his hair and wiped his face as he went. Three fourths of the ways down two young men were waiting. He stopped his horse and stared at them.

"Are you two willing to challenge me or will you allow me safe passage by?" He asked firmly.

"Do you think you can take us both at the same time old man?" One of them smiled.

"That's more than likely boy!" He said getting down from his horse.

The two men rushed him and about toppled him over! He wrapped his arms around them and hugged them tight!

"It's great to see you too son's! He said as tears formed in his eyes.

"I can't believe your home!" Austin said.

"We missed you a lot!" Jacob smiled as well." Did you find anyone?"

"Oh yes boys I found many." He laughed. "My little brothers are up on top with your grandpa."

"You found Uncle Wayne and Uncle Arthur?" Jacob and Austin said together!

"Why don't you take Sampson up and greet them!" He hugged them once more.

They ran to the horse and jumped on his back and turned him back up the road. Greygor smiled at them and waved them off. He began walking the rest of the way into the Hidden Lair. He reached the road next to the lake and followed it around. He waved at people he knew and some that he didn't recognized but hoped to meet one day. He rounded the bend and stopped. On the porch of the hotel that his families were living in he saw a most beautiful sight! She was washing the windows on the bottom floor. He began walking towards the building. He saw Paula inside the door about to come out. He placed his finger against his lips so to surprise his wife. Paula smiled and stayed inside the door.

"Hey mom you have that clean water?" Pat yelled from the porch. "These windows are horribly dirty!"

He lightly walked up the steps and stood behind her. She rung out the water on her cloth and looked in the window that reflected him. She placed a hand against the wall and leaned forward.

"Oh great, now I am having visions of you even when I am awake!" She said as tears filled her eyes!

"It's not a dream baby." He whispered so not to startle her.

"God please stop this, now I am hearing his voice. "This is killing me."

He took another step towards her and lightly placed his hand upon her shoulder. "I am really here baby."

She brought her hand up and placed it on his and gently caressed it for a few seconds. She slowly turned keeping her eyes tightly shut. Her hand kept hold of his as she did. He placed his finger against her chin and gently brought her face up. He brushed his fingers across her cheek as she opened her eyes and looked deeply into his. Her sweet smile brightened her beautiful face as he smiled back at her.

"I am real my love and home for you." He whispered. "Our hearts are one together once more."

"We are intertwined forever." She couldn't help but begin to cry on the last word.

They kissed deeply as both their tears ran down their faces. As they did they pulled each other tight into each others arms. They could feel each others heart beat as one once more! Paula and Jessica came out on the porch crying happily for the two of them. They just watched and felt the happiness flooding the air! They stopped and let their faces gently brush cheek to cheek. Greygor let one hand run through her hair as the other ran up and down her back. All their focus was on each other for the longest time.

They turned to the other two women who immediately came over and hugged and kissed Greygor happy to have him home once more.

"Your wife has been very difficult to live with I hope you know!" Jessica laughed.

"No I haven't." She smiled at him.

"I am not saying a word baby." He laughed.

They talked for a few minutes and Pat led him into the house and up to their room grabbing him some clothes and some soap. They went out the back door to the warm springs out a few yards away from the house. She helped him undress and then took her clothes off as well. They both walked into the water that was very hot. She soaped up a rag and began washing him. She gently ran the soapy rag across his arms. She noticed the scar on his forearm.

He told her about the fight at the tunnel and how Luck had died saving his life. He then told her about reaching Xanadu Mountain and his trip into the military camp. The story went on to how he sent the first group of people to the meeting place and how he had found his friend Cole in Ohio. Another large mass of people were sent south as well. He told her of finding the family up near Pittsburgh and the finding of Wayne and his family. She listened intently as he told of how they traveled down into the Virginia's and met the other groups of people and how they had trained them to fight if need be! He explained to her about the traitor and how he died as well as the story of the Border Battle where he had received the shoulder wound. She felt his happiness at finding his family as well as the pain and sadness of having to take lives to keep them all safe.

After the washing was done she gently wrapped her body around his and they slowly made love in the water. They kissed so deeply and passionately! Their bodies became one once more as they loved each other deeply till they felt the ecstasy of there loves explode in rapture.

They again washed up and got out of the warm water and toweled each other off. They got dressed and walked hand in hand down to the road. He found the path that led up to look out mountain. They traveled up the path and reached the edge of the cliff. They held each other again kissing deeply. They stood there looking down as she placed her head against his chest.

Down below they watched as the people filled the road and came into the Hidden Lair. They were greeted by the people who came out of there homes to meet the new people. They watched the happiness below taking in all of it. It was a glorious day for all. The Lair was a huge place and Greygor thought how it wasn't going to be that hard to find everyone places to live. Pat rose up off his chest and kissed his cheek.

"You should be proud of yourself honey." She smiled at him. "You made this happen. They are all safe and sound now."

Greygor stood there silently waiting to see if the dream he had had was going to come true. He turned around and waited placing his hand on his sword.

"What's wrong baby?" She asked him. "Are you okay?"

All was quiet around them. He turned back to the cliff and smiled down at the people below.

"No baby, it wasn't just me it was all of us who made this happen. Every single one of us together made the Hidden Lair happen!" Greygor said with deep pride. "Together we became more than just people trying to survive. We used our love and compassion for each other to become Guardians of each other. Together we will keep each other safe from the evils of this new world! When the time comes now and in the future we will unite together to keep peace in our home here! All together we will be the Guardians of the Hidden Lair."

THE END!

CPSIA information can be obtained at www.ICGtesting.com
Printed in the USA
BVOW041219270812

298811BV00002B/6/P

9 781432 789725